BEYOND THE BLACK MIRROR

MATTHEW PONGRATZ

Beyond the Black Mirror *jumps right into the story, keeping the reader on high alert from the beginning. Though it offers a glimpse into another world, it also reflects our own in the way people can change when tempted by something wonderful yet deadly. Pongratz does a wonderful job transporting the reader back a few decades as well as to a place alien to us altogether.*

Cassidy Barker – author of *Spoon Licker*

Beyond the Black Mirror

Cactus Moon Publications, LLC
2407 W Nopal Ave; Mesa, AZ 85202
www.cactusmoonpublishing.com

ISBN 978-1-7347865-6-9

Acknowledgments

First and foremost, I would like to thank Lily Gianna Woodmansee and her crew at Cactus Moon Publications for taking a chance on me and bringing this book to fruition. She has been a pleasure to work with throughout the entire process, and her mentorship has been invaluable. Becoming a published author is a dream come true, and I cannot thank her and her staff enough.

I'd also like to thank my lawyer and longtime friend, Patrick Wall. One of the first people to check out some of my stuff back in college, he encouraged me to keep writing even when I questioned my own talent and chalked it all up to just a silly pipe dream. I'll never forget him telling me to keep going, and that one day I would "win the crowd." Cheers buddy. This one's for you.

I'd also like to thank you, the reader, for buying a ticket and taking the ride. I fell in love with horror films and paperbacks as a kid growing up in the eighties, and this book is a true homage to those great stories that molded me during such an incredible decade. I appreciate the support more than you know, and I hope you enjoyed reading it as much as I enjoyed writing it.

I: THE HOUSE ON HICKORY LEAF

CHAPTER 1

Anna gazed upon the flickering reflection of the candles along the cold steel as she carefully played with the razor blade. Meticulous as she did so, the tips of her skinny fingers traveled and studied its edges, its flat surface, and its firm, sharp points. She admired its immaculately crafted simplicity—so tiny and simple to the touch of her angular fingers, yet so horribly effective.

The rain plummeting the aging roof presented a pleasant background of white noise, entranced by the sound of the stormy night and the flickering dance of the candles placed about the bathroom. She took a deep breath, closing her eyes momentarily before carefully placing the razor blade down along the corner of the bathtub. Exhaling slowly, she leaned back into the warmth of the water, dragging her wet hands over her face as her corkscrew of thoughts circled back to the black mirror.

Staring at the wiry tendrils of blue wax trickling down the sides of the empty wine bottles, she could still picture those glistening, lavender tentacles squirming and slithering just beyond the murky darkness of an infinite oblivion. She could still feel the cold touch of the metal serpents beneath her fingers, magically swimming seamlessly in and out of the mirror's intricately designed steel frame. She could still see the darkness of the deepest midnight within that cold, liquid-like glass; as vast and consuming as the black of space.

That darkness possessed more power than she ever imagined. The things she witnessed existed well beyond the imagination of most men. It was something she could no longer manipulate or contain, even with the herbal concoctions that she mastered over the years of endless study.

She felt dazed, almost ill to her stomach, slowly processing the magnitude of what she had done. Releasing another defeated sigh as she leaned her head back against the tub's edge, she closed her eyes again, wondering how it had gone this far. *Dear God,* she thought, slowly shaking her head back and forth as her eyes welled with tears. *What have I done?*

Accidentally allowing herself to plummet into the dark depths of a rabbit hole that proved impossible to escape, she finally realized that there was no going back. This is it. This is the end. This isn't an Atari game, and there is no such thing as a "reset" button that will magically make this all disappear. And because her obsession to tear past the fabric of reality while searching for realms undiscovered by man is paramount, she uncovered something that should be left alone. Ignored and forgotten; sealed away forever and hidden from this world of their own.

And even now, no matter how desperately she fought to push the images of their world from her head, the vividness of her experiences on the other side were simply too powerful. The memories were as crisp as a winter morning as she closed her eyes at night, desperately trying to forget while praying for sleep to take her—those wet, slithering tentacles and that glistening, indigo skin. Those glorious angelic wings that spread as wide as the mast of a sailing ship, flapping like a cracking whip in the grip of a powerful gust of wind. She could still taste the fruit that hung from their magnificent trees, her teeth snapping and sinking through the shiny membrane of their violet skins. She could still feel that unearthly sweetness upon her tongue, the golden warmth that swam through her soul. She could still see the incredible range of mountains—so magnificent and blue—towering high above the vast golden seas that stretched toward a sky so clear, it was as though you could reach up and touch the universe above you.

But it is all gone now.

Paradise slipped through her fingers with the elusiveness of the wind, and there was nothing that she could do.

Anna began to sob, picking up the razor and holding it within the trembling grip of her thin, pale fingers. Staring at its gleaming metal through a blur of tears, she knew this was the only option. She had to do it. After tasting the fruits of utopia, the piper must be paid. It was time, and she accepted this.

Gasping while momentarily losing her breath, the pain came hot and quick. Sliding the razor along the length of the inside of her forearm, her skin split open like a piece of foam. She watched as her bone white flesh gave way to a flow of warm crimson, spilling like dark oil into the warm bath water. The clear tub gave way to liquid plumes of a cloudy pink as she found the strength to finish the other arm, feeling the blood pumping from her radial artery as she grew weaker by the second. The razor blade fell from her limp hand on the other side of the tub, hitting the tile floor with a soft tink as her body slid further into the water.

And then, as quickly as it had begun, it was over. Completely bled out, she lay there lifelessly, so peacefully placid in her morbid display. Like a dead fish, floating along the surface of a cold, murky lake. Her wide, dark eyes seemed to stare blankly at the brittle, cracked surface of the bathroom ceiling. Her entire body, so delicate and pale, almost glowing in contrast to the blood tainted water, as dark and vivid as red wine.

It is over.

She is free.

The flickering little flames along the tops of the drip candles sent bouncing shadows dancing along the surface of the dark walls, casting an eerie effect upon the place of her departure. A quick flash of lightning sent a strobe-like spasm of blue light across Anna's lifeless face; the pattering of raindrops against the window's glass outside, like the claws of a monster tapping to come inside.

CHAPTER 2

Billy Baxton sat behind the wheel of his car as he studied the house on the corner lot. The yellow Century 21 sign swung gently in the August breeze as he glanced down at the newspaper again, convinced entirely that the listing price was a misprint. It had to be. Even as a foreclosure, there was no way that the bank would put it on the market for that low. No way in hell. Surely it was too good to be true, especially when it came to his rotten-ass luck as of late. If anything, the universe was due to throw him a bone here sooner or later though, right? And hey, who knows? Maybe this was it.

It's a sign! Billy thought for a quick second, that flash of a moment where your mind raced to the conclusion that anything was possible. *A chance for me to actually jump forward in life and finally purchase a place of my own.*

He thought about it for a while too. Studying the market trends and comps in the area, talking with his brother and his old man who were both knowledgeable about home improvement stuff and the current housing market.

Meanwhile, he was reluctantly still living in their overpriced apartment complex and its hallways that perpetually reeked of curry and cat urine. *God-damn*, he would think to himself, sitting there watching TV late at night as he glanced around at his surroundings, wondering when something was going to finally change for once. *I've gotta get out of this place!*

Gripping the folded-up newspaper in his sweaty hand, he combed over the details of the listing again, sliding his thumb away from the ad, careful not to accidentally smudge the phone number to call if he was interested. And at this point, to say that his interest had been engaged was a huge understatement. He confirmed the price and the address for the hundredth time, completely perplexed by the amount that the bank wanted for it. Not to mention, the fact that no one had come along and scooped it up yet. Now that was the real shocker.

Taking a swig from a King Cobra tall boy that he picked up from the party store after work, he studied the house from the curb, taking in what details he could upon initial glance. It wasn't much to look at, sure as shit, but the house reeked of potential. And again, what the place lacked in curb appeal, the price and location made up for it. It was literally a steal. Especially for a single guy in his mid-twenties who was pretty handy with most home improvement projects. His brother Brent, a contractor by trade, had shown him enough stuff over the years that he'd be able to do most of the updates himself. And that alone would save him some serious bucks that he would normally have to burn on contracting out someone else to do it. Sure, it would take some time, but the end result would be well worth it.

Studying the state of the place from the outside, he could see that its once lime green paint looked almost white in the light of the summer sun, faded and peeling in long, large strips. The broken edges coiled inward like wooden shavings, time appearing to have pulled most of it free from the house's wooden exterior. The overgrown shrubbery sprawled wildly in every direction; bushes that looked as though never trimmed covered the front windows and blocked most of the walkway leading to the front porch. A dusty, brown film covered the surface of the windows, the glass within their shoddy frames, smokey and opaque with caked on grime. The frames were brittle and beaten looking, their once white paint chipping and falling off in huge sections. They looked like hell, their condition giving them the appearance of something from colonial times. Not to mention, the neglected front lawn that looked like you needed to aggressively go at it with a machete prior to pulling out the lawn mower to do a decent job.

So yeah, in its current condition, the place is a shithole; no denying that. But again, being that he was only twenty-five, Billy Baxton felt like he had all the time in the world to fix the place up. And considering that you couldn't beat the price and it was only ten minutes from work, that alone made it well worth looking into.

Killing what was left of his beer until there was nothing but warm swill along the bottom, Billy tossed the aluminum can aside as it fell to the floor of the car. Ric Ocasek suddenly stopped singing about his best friend's girl as the rumbling engine sputtered itself to a slow stop. Tossing the newspaper onto the passenger seat, he pulled his keys free from the ignition and opened the driver side door. What started as window shopping had now accelerated to the next level.

His curiosity piqued, it was time to jump out and see what this house was all about.

Getting out of the car, Billy Baxton slowly made his way up the driveway to get a better look at the place. Taking in the surrounding neighborhood as best he could, he caught a whiff of the pleasant yet fleeting smell of burgers sizzling away on someone's grill; momentarily tickling his nose before vanishing in the gentle breeze. He could hear the distant sound of children laughing; surely relishing their time outside during such a gorgeous summer day. Some old guy next door was busy washing his black corvette, a hose gun in one hand and what looked like a beer in the other. He nodded and smiled in Billy's direction; an unlit cigar wedged between his grinning teeth; decked out in an old wife beater, complete with a pair of faded looking Bermuda shorts pulled up well past where his belly button must sit.

Billy smiled, waving politely in the old man's direction as he strolled up the driveway. Walking past a wild growth of unruly shrubbery, Billy stepped onto the house's tiny porch covered by a rickety, green and white metal awning, its corners and edges decaying with orange rust. He slid his finger along the fading orange foreclosure sticker along the front window, confirming that the bank had in fact taken the property. Running his hand over a thin layer of grime as he leaned closer to the glass, he shielded his eyes from the sun so he could get a decent look at the inside of the place.

As he figured, the house was a mess.

The jumbled and scattered wake of someone losing their home lie in disarray and shambles on the other side of the window. Through the translucent film of dirt, he could see several stacks of newspapers, pots and pans, a filthy looking wok still sticky with old stir fry, a yellow plastic popcorn machine, a busted up Rubik's Cube, a couple of He-Man figures, a brown sleeping bag, several stacks of old *People* magazines and *National Geographics*, and even a smashed up Atari laying scattered across the hardwood floors. All of it, tossed, lost, and forgotten by the previous owners.

Doing a walk around the house, the rest of the outside of the single-story home was pretty much as expected. A fuzzy green moss covered most of the uneven layers of shingles along the roof, clearly the shitty job of someone who didn't know what the hell they were doing. The roof sagged along the middle of its apex, dipping slightly from the weight of time, gravity, and neglect. Cobwebs and dirt thrived along the corners of almost every window, their edges and surfaces screaming for a good power washing. Ancient looking patio furniture lay scattered about a decent looking brick patio, their once colorful plastic faded nearly white by the scorching sun. What looked like hundreds of weeds protruded through every crack and divide along the patio, the entire area in dire need of a thorough weed whacking.

But the real kicker for Billy was the fact that the place actually had a pool in the backyard. A God-damn swimming pool! Its surroundings looked somewhat like a lagoon upon initial glance, nestled into the overgrowth of an unruly world of restless and unmaintained vegetation. Not to mention, its untreated water had an emerald-green tint to it, looking like a slimy cauldron of algae and microscopic growth that had gathered over several years of neglect.

But none of it bothered Billy too much. After putting in some hard work, he could have a pretty rad place to entertain out back by the following summer. His eyes were on the prize, knowing that it would take some patience to get the place up to speed. And if there was one thing that Billy had, it was patience.

Eager to get a look at more of the inside, he leaned into the glass door-wall along the back patio while cupping his hands around his eyes. As anticipated, he saw more of the same inside the kitchen: trashed appliances, a pair of discarded flip flops, a random copy of *The Joy of Cooking*, old, wrinkled magazines, stacks of yellowing newspapers, and a bunch of unopened mail scattered across the floor; looking like a bomb had gone off inside of the place. The rest of the kitchen looked dated as hell, knowing that he would have to eventually gut the whole thing, replacing all the cabinets, counter tops, tile, and even the appliances.

Perusing the rest of the backyard and the other side of the house, he had seen enough, slowly strolling back to the car as a million questions bounced about his endorphin fueled brain. *Maybe this is it*, he thought, nervously biting at one of his fingernails as he opened the driver side door of his old Grand Prix. *Maybe this is meant to be . . . your chance to finally get out of that shitty apartment and start the next stage of your life with your own place . . .*

Plopping back behind the wheel of the Pontiac, he slid on a pair of cheap aviators that he just scored from the Shell Station down the street, letting out a deep breath before he started up the engine. He sat there for a second staring at the house, eventually grabbing the folded up real estate section from the passenger seat beside him, checking it one more time:

FOR MORE DETAILS ON THIS MUST-SEE FORECLOSURE, BE SURE TO CALL ALAN SPAULDING TODAY!!

Playfully smacking the newspaper with his free hand, he glanced back at the dilapidated ranch with a hopeful grin. It looked like Alan Spaulding was the man to call if he wanted to check the rest of the place out. And once he got back to his apartment and cracked open another beer, that's exactly what he was going to do.

CHAPTER 3

Having an open slot in his calendar that Saturday morning, the listing agent, Alan Spaulding, agreed to meet Billy at the foreclosure on Hickory Leaf for a walk through. Alan smiled and waved in Billy's direction as he got out of his car and came walking up the driveway, looking exactly as Billy pictured him after talking to him on the phone. His hair consisted of a meticulously crafted part, not a single strand of hair out of place. His overly enthusiastic smile looked far from genuine, his teeth overly whitened to the point of obnoxiousness. With his pink Lacoste golf shirt and his neatly pressed khakis, he looked like he was born to play his role as the smiling, ever-serving real estate agent. Hungry for that next offer and a signed name across the dotted line. Besides, Billy worked in sales. He knew the type.

After a brief exchange of chit chat and the usual getting-to-know-ya banter, Alan led Billy to the front door of the house where a lockbox hung from the rusty, weathered doorknob.

Entering the combination to retrieve the key, he opened the door and held it ajar as the two of them headed inside.

"Alright, here we are," he said, reminiscent of a game show host, extending his arm to give Billy the courtesy of being the first to enter the house. "After you, sir."

Stepping inside, Billy immediately noticed a prevalent funk in the air that was impossible to ignore. It wafted through the house heavily with the odd concoction of rotting Chinese food, dried cat piss, damp mildew, and old moth balls. The place smelled nasty, but then again, he never did expect a house like that to smell like lilacs.

Avoiding and tiptoeing past the abandoned debris that lay scattered across the floor as he looked around, he immediately began to envision the various projects he would be forced to take on, all while trying to take mental note of what he liked and didn't like about each and every room.

"As you can see, the place can use a little work," Alan said as he hovered a foot or two behind Billy, as though able to read his thoughts while stating the obvious. "But being that it's a foreclosure and the bank's looking to get rid of it, the price they want for it falls well below the neighborhood comps. I know it sounds cliche, but it's true. You really can't beat the price for this neighborhood and school district."

"You got that right," Billy replied with a smile, briefly glancing back at Alan as he continued strolling through the house.

"I mean, sure, you'll be knee-deep in home improvement projects for the next few years, but as you'll see, the house has got some really good bones."

"Yeah, I can see that. Which is fine, I don't mind at all. I'm pretty handy, so I'm picturing what I could do over time with the place."

"There ya go," Alan replied, clearly liking what he was hearing. Billy was fairly certain that the first impression of the home's condition had already scared away a good number of potential buyers. Especially the yuppies looking to move into that type of neighborhood. Their types were looking for something cosmetically pleasing to the eye and move in ready. This place definitely wasn't that, but for Billy, it was the perfect opportunity to become a first time homeowner in a desirable neighborhood.

Moving through the front room and into the kitchen, it was much the same: a cheap flooring composed of fake, plastic tile—brittle and cracking around the corners and edges. The countertops were a hideous shade of brown, their surface sticky and gummy with grease. Ancient dark-brown cabinets starkly stood out amongst the dirty white walls that appeared stained a weird yellow color. Not to mention, a pea green colored dishwasher that was so outdated, it looked like it belonged somewhere in the Smithsonian.

Yet still, none of it fazed Billy. He ran a hand through his dark feathered hair, staring out through the glass door-wall toward the swimming pool outside, daydreaming about the potentially epic barbecues and pool parties that he and Buddha could throw once they got the place fixed up a bit. Hell, for a couple of single guys like them, the possibilities were endless.

After poking around and inspecting the bedrooms, the closets, the bathroom, and the pool area out back for a second time, Alan and Billy eventually headed down a steep set of stairs to finally check out the basement.

Expecting the basement to be much of the same—a dingy, dark space utilized as nothing more than a place for extra storage, Billy's jaw nearly hit the floor as he reached the bottom of the stairs. Flabbergasted, he looked around to find a sprawling finished basement. The wall-to-wall carpet was beige in color, hard enough that you could bounce a tennis ball off it. Though it looked newer, it still had a few stains, but nothing horrible. The ceiling above was a nice drop ceiling; the lights throughout even set to a dimmer switch. An old refrigerator that looked like it could have sat in June Cleaver's kitchen stood along the far corner; an old bar-style pool table sitting along the opposite corner. However, it was what was sitting along the wall at the base of the stairs that really blew his mind—a full sized Pac-Man arcade machine.

Damn, he thought, as he walked over to check it out, amazed that the previous owners had actually left it there along with the pool table. *How much does one of these things even cost?*

If forced to bet on it, he guessed that the thing was broke. But hey, maybe he and his brother could tinker with it and see if they could get it to work.

Billy whistled, running his finger along a layer of dust covering the surface of a plastic Pabst Blue Ribbon sign hanging from one of the wood paneled walls. He had to admit, he was impressed by what he saw. Any doubts that he had about moving forward were quickly cast away. Surely the basement along with the pool out back would prove to be the main selling point of the place.

"Pool table over there, beer fridge over here . . . Pac-Man machine right over there. Man, not bad Alan. Not bad at all."

Alan smiled, glancing about the basement. "Yeah, you could actually say that the basement is the real heart of the place. It's a great room for entertaining. You could have some good times down here."

"Hell yeah," Billy replied, stepping over an old Clue board game sitting along the floor as he made his way back over to the Pac-Man machine. "Hey, do you know if this thing works?"

"Actually, yeah, I heard it does."

"Nice! How's the furnace?"

"Not too old, actually. You probably wouldn't need a new one for a good five or six years."

"Good to know. What about this water heater over here?" Billy slid his finger gently across the blue and green crust that accumulated along the top of its protruding pipes, noticing right away that the thing was no spring chicken.

"Well now, that thing's pretty much a dinosaur. You've probably only got a year, or two tops left in that."

"Yeah, that's what I figured."

Turning away from the water heater, Billy then guided his attention to a door along the opposite wall. Wood paneled on the surface, it blended right into the rest of the wall, completely flush as a little doorknob protruded from its hidden, rectangular shape. Trying to open it, Billy met with resistance while giving the knob a good yank. Twisting the knob a bit harder in his hand, he turned it again and gave it a tug, but the door simply wouldn't budge.

"What's in here? It looks like it's locked."

"Not sure, the owner never provided a key. A rep from the bank this week is supposed to come by to change the lock. I'm guessing it's a closet. Maybe a little work room or a wood shop?"

Billy nodded, knowing that he could always catch a peek at it later once Spaulding got the key.

"Alright," Billy said, spinning in Alan's direction as he clapped his hands together. "I'm not normally so spontaneous, but I'd hate for someone else to come along and scoop this place up while my dumb ass sits around thinking it over. Soooo, what I'm trying to say is, I think I'm interested in making an offer."

"Great," Alan replied, pushing a smile that appeared a bit forced across his face before it quickly faded. "Now Bill, as the listing agent of this property, there is something that I need to disclose to you."

"What's that?" Billy looked intrigued, not sure what Alan was getting at.

"Well, I need to be very upfront and very clear with you. See, the woman that owned this house went into a heavy depression that caused her to get behind on her mortgage notes. Ultimately, as tragic and unsettling as it is, she ended up taking her own life inside this very house. I know that something like that is a lot to take in, but as the listing agent assigned to the property, I'm legally required to disclose this information to you."

"Are you serious?"

"I'm afraid so. She did it in the bathtub. Slit her wrists and bled to death. The owner of the house had no family or legal will, so, the bank took ownership of the house, and here we are."

"Wow. . . damn."

Billy didn't know what to say. In fact, it was the last thing that he expected to hear. He took a few slow steps as he glanced about the basement, the gears inside his head churning as he tried to figure out where to go with all this. "That's pretty messed up. I'm not really sure what to make of all that."

"I know, I know, but as a potential buyer, you have the right to know. Now listen, I'll completely understand if this changes your mind about making an offer. Believe me, I understand more than you know. Most people would be extremely bothered by something like that, and I get it. However, if you're not, you might want to consider it. The place would be a great investment if you're able to overlook something like that."

Billy ran a hand over his mouth as he paced the room, sliding a finger along a thin film of dust covering the screen of the Pac-Man machine, glancing dazedly about the basement. Sure, it was creepy as hell, but then again, people died all the time, right? Even if the owner did take her own life inside the house, it wasn't like he believed that her ghost haunted the place or anything. Sure, some people believed in that stuff, but if ghosts were so real, then how come he'd never seen one? Besides, people die at hospitals every day, right? And it's not like those places were hunted. So, in the grand scheme of things, what was the worst that would happen? He'd scrub the shit out of the tub one more time with some water and some bleach and bam, problem solved!

And as sad as it was, it appeared that the previous owner's tragedy left him with this incredible opportunity to move forward in life. Like his old man always told him as a kid—sometimes the universe operates in strange ways. To squander the opportunity of snagging the property based on fear would prove to be stupid. He had to do it. The place was just too good to pass up. Suicide or no suicide, he had to make an offer.

"Screw it," he said, a queer smile creeping along the corner of his mouth as he turned toward Alan, his heart thumping a bit faster now as he did so. "Let's do it. Life's too short, right? I know that I'll be kicking myself in the ass if I walk away from this place. I want to make an offer."

"You don't say?" Billy watched as Alan's eyes lit up like a stripper spotting a twenty- dollar bill, not believing what he heard. "The suicide doesn't bother you?"

"Naw," he said, shaking his head confidently, looking around the basement one more time as it suddenly wasn't even a question in his mind. "Let's do it."

+-+

CHAPTER 4

"Dude, you bought a house?" Buddha's voice sounded strained, hard to understand. He was doing his best to hold in the smoke from a giant bong toke he just inhaled through a long, plastic tube.

"Well, not exactly. I made an *offer*. See, the bank still has to *accept* my offer, and if they do, then it's my house."

Buddha's eyes widened, exhaling as he blew a huge, fluttering cloud of gray smoke across the main room of their apartment. Billy looked disgusted, doing his best to wave away the smoke with his hands.

"Damn dude, can't you smoke that shit in your room or something?"

"Sorry dude," Buddha replied, putting his mouth back to the top of the bong as though nothing Billy just said registered at all.

"Anyway man, get this — the place has even got an in-ground pool out back. Once I get the thing fixed up, I'm thinking pimped out, Miami Vice style pool parties and shit. Can you believe that shit? It's going to take some work, but I'm gonna make it happen."

Buddha's eyes shot open as he looked up from his blue, plastic bong. "It's got a pool, dude?"

"Hell yeah it does! It's got a whole kick ass set up back there, brother. Brick paver patio, inground pool with a diving board and a little slide; the whole nine. It's even got a gas grill right there next to the patio. Imagine the badass pool parties that we're gonna have back there, man. I'm telling you, dude, this place is gonna be rad!"

"Nice. So, what's this we're? Are you saying it's cool if I room up there with you?"

"Hell yeah that's what I'm saying, dude. What do you think I'm gonna do, leave you stuck here to find a new roommate or something?"

"Well shit man, I don't know. For a minute there I thought I was going to have to ask Roger to move in or something."

Billy laughed, slapping his old buddy along the shoulder as if this was the funniest shit he'd ever heard. "Dude, fuck Roger! You're coming with me, man. Your half of the rent will help me out with the mortgage and some of the projects around the place. What do you say, man? Are you ready to set sail onto the next chapter of our lives here? The bachelor pad, baby, come on!"

Roger was this dude that Buddha and his buddies used to play Dungeons and Dragons with back in high school. Skinny and socially awkward, he wore his jet-black hair slicked back like a vampire and walked around wearing a black trench coat, even when it was hot as balls out. Their clique was a bit on the odd side to put it mildly, existing along the outer ring of the social solar system of the high school hierarchy, roaming the halls in their own little pack of three or four of them. Billy used to see them up at the mall in high school all the time – wandering around aimlessly like zombies, gawking at girls who would never date them, dressed head to toe in their weird, black clothing. You could find them sitting around the food court for hours smoking cigarettes, or down at the arcade dumping quarters into the Galaga and Donkey Kong machines. That, or buying cassettes of their shitty new wave music down at the Harmony House next to the Gap and the old Cinnabon that closed down months ago. Billy didn't really know why Buddha still hung out with the guy. But hey, who he chose to hang out with and see on his own time was his business. Billy just didn't want Buddha to think that he'd leave him high and dry like that.

Though Buddha didn't run around in the same click back in high school as Billy did—the football players, the jocks, the party guys—he had always been welcomed with open arms at any of their parties, known by most as the guy who supplied the grass. And considering that he sold dope to almost half the football team, he had a little more than his foot in the door with the upper level of the high school hierarchy. Not to mention, he was a good dude and about as loyal as they came. And being that Billy always vouched for Buddha like that, the guy would have tossed himself in front of a train for Billy. And being that they both needed a roommate around the same time shortly after college, fate had intervened in a funny way, placing this Oscar and Felix combo into a perfectly functioning coexistence that worked out well ever since they signed their lease. And from what Billy was hearing for his loyal confidant, it was looking like this roommate relationship wasn't ending anytime soon.

Buddha smiled, his Asian eyes nothing but red slits along his smiling face. His chin, a series of chubby rolls resembling a fat caterpillar, easing back into the couch as another plume of rippling smoke traveled into the air through his pursed lips. Far from a burning furnace of ambition, Buddha had always chosen to ski down the bunny slope of life. Even though the guy was obsessed with movies and even studied film in college, he chose to sell insurance for his old man's company rather than taking a gamble and blazing his own path in the field of his passion. The comfort of consistency and predictability always trumped that of the exciting unknown for the guy. But hey, that was Buddha for ya. As long as he had his weed, his music, and his movies, the guy was as content as a hog in shit. A simpleton. A go with the flow kind of guy, happily marching along while eager to please the rest of the herd.

"Well shit man, I didn't know," Buddha said between rips. "For all I knew you were having Diane move in with you or something. I never know with you two."

"Diane?" Billy quickly replied, a sour look along his face as though he just bit a chunk from a lime. "No. Fuck no. We're not moving in together man; this is the bachelor pad. The palace of possibility. Our new oasis. Our place of solace and brotherhood. I can't let her bring that down for us, my man. No way in hell, ain't gonna happen."

Diane was Billy's on-again, off-again girlfriend; an old friend of theirs from high school who they've both known for years. And gauging from the reaction when he brought up her name, Buddha guessed that they were currently somewhere in the "off-again" phase.

"Speaking of which, is she coming over tonight?"

Strolling over to the fridge in their tiny kitchen, Billy grabbed a beer and cracked it open.

He took a quick sip while shaking his head back and forth as if to dismiss that suggestion. "I don't think so. But then again, you never can tell with the queen of the unannounced visits."

And the undisputed queen of that, she was. At any given moment their door would fly open while Diane, the human tornado, would frantically come storming in as she went into a tirade about her day and whatever random thing happened to be pissing her off at the moment. Then, as if she lived there, she'd reach for something cold to drink from the fridge and make herself at home, launching into a wild venting session that was almost always all about her.

Sure, she was plenty nice to look at, but she could be nastier than an aggravated snake in the sun on a hot day if you caught her at the wrong moment. Yet on the flip side of that coin, she was like one of the guys on a good day; literally one of the coolest chicks one could ever meet. It was always a crap shoot with Diane. A pull of the one-armed bandit, hoping for the best but tossing fate to the wind. A case of Dr. Jekyll and Ms. Sajnecki. But like it or not, they were stuck with her. Whether she and Billy were dating or not, she was the rash that wouldn't go away. A third wheel that somehow made the perfect fit.

Overall, Buddha didn't really mind. In fact, he found her to be pretty damn entertaining most of the time. A true enigma who was fun to sit back and watch. Besides, it took a lot more than Diane's random drop-ins and her frantic ramblings to ruffle Buddha's feathers. His world was that of bliss and serenity; a happy place that refused to be easily rattled.

Taking another sip of his beer, Billy kicked off his shoes before plopping down into an old, brown leather Lazy Boy sitting along the corner of their apartment. "So, why do you ask if she's coming over? What do you have going on?"

Buddha grinned, sinking even further back into the ancient orange couch they scored at a garage sale years ago, kicking his feet up onto their old, shitty coffee table covered in gouges, scratches, and tiny clumps of dried candle wax.

"Tonight, my friend, we are going to be watching my VHS copy of *The Empire Strikes Back*. I figured maybe a little Chinese food, a little herb, and we, my man, are good to go."

Billy's eyes widened as he almost choked on his beer, leaning forward in the chair as Buddha seemed to have gotten his attention." "Dude, you've got Empire on tape? Damn, I didn't even know that the second one was even out yet."

"Yes sir! Finally picked me up a copy the other day. Figured I might play, 'may the bong be with you'."

"What's that?"

"Oh, it's a game I created where every time they mention the force, you gotta take a bong rip. Gets you really fucked up."

"Hmmmm," Billy replied, nearly draining the last of his beer. "I could get into something like that. It's Friday night, I got a twelve pack of High Life sitting in the fridge . . . shit man, sounds like a plan."

"Nice. I figured that you'd be down for a little Empire, buddy."

"Oh, hell yeah man. The *Empire Strikes Back* is the greatest! I'm in for sure. What are you thinking about for food? You mentioned something about some Chinese?"

"I'm thinking Imperial Garden. What do you think?"

"Delivery, or pick up?"

"Delivery."

"Nice. Maybe a little crab Rangoon? A little General Tsao's chicken?"

"For sure. And don't forget, we gotta mention that we want some extra spicy mustard. They don't toss any in the bag unless you mention it."

"Hell yeah, now you're talking."

As Billy slammed the rest of his beer and tossed his empty into an already overflowing grocery bag in the corner of the kitchen, he went to the fridge to fetch a fresh one.

"Oh, by the way dude, there is something that I've got to tell you about the house. I mean, I know it's not officially mine yet, but I figured that I should let you know."

"What's that, dude?"

His red, squinty eyes slid their attention from some Men at Work video on MTV back toward Billy.

"Check this out, you're not gonna believe this. So anyway, you know how this house is really cheap compared to most of the comps in the area? I mean like, *really* a lot cheaper?"

"Yeah."

"Well, I found out today why that is."

"It's a foreclosure?"

"Well, not only is the place a foreclosure, but get this—the realtor tells me that the woman that used to live there, the previous owner, well, I guess she committed suicide right inside the house."

Buddha's glassy red eyes beamed with intrigue, his round potato-like body now sitting upward as he leaned forward. "No way, dude! Are you serious?"

"Dead serious." There was a flicker deep within Billy's eyes as if all of this added some sense of intrigue or history to the house. "I guess she fell into a deep depression, got really behind on her mortgage. Ended up slitting her wrists in the bathtub. True story, dude. But like I said, if you're going to live there, I wanted you to know."

"Wow."

"Tell me about it."

"And you *still* made an offer on the house?"

Billy nodded with a smile as he brought the can of beer to his lips. It was as though the act of still going through with the offer made him some kind of badass. *What, some lady slit her wrists and bled to death in the bathtub? Big deal. In fact, a nice warm bath sounds pretty good right about now. Think I'll grab me a beer, put on a little Van Morrison, light some candles, and soak in the tub for a bit.* That was Billy's view on the whole thing. A bit of morbid history surrounding the place wasn't going to be enough to scare Billy Baxton away from such an opportunity so easily. Suicide or no suicide, he wanted that house.

"Whoa," Buddha replied with a childish grin, easing back into the recessed part of the couch formed by his weight over the years. "That's some pretty heavy shit, man. You sure that doesn't bother you at all?"

Billy shrugged, appearing nonchalant about the whole thing. He looked at the entire picture, the opportunity and the possibilities of the house vastly outweighing its creepy, morbid, dark little blemish. A blemish that currently added to his advantage.

In fact, he had more than made up his mind at that point. If Alan Spaulding called to confirm that the offer on Hickory Leaf was accepted, no question about it. He was pulling the trigger and moving full steam ahead with the deal. Besides, it wasn't like Billy Baxton was Donald Trump or something. He was a simple guy. A working man, doing what he needed to do to get by. What little savings he had he would be dumping into various projects around the house, which he knew he could make work. And if he didn't act now, he knew he wouldn't find a deal this good for years to come.

Sure, he'd sometimes sit in the dark alone, watching TV late at night, wondering what would have happened if he had actually applied himself across the span of his academic career and finished with a marketable degree. If only he "applied himself"—as his parents always used to say — the sky was the limit. Shit, for all he knew he could have been driving a 'vette by now like his buddy Kyle, an engineer over at Chrysler who was already running his own team. Then there was his other buddy, Trevor. The guy busted his ass in school, graduated early, and got a sweet supervisor job at a Tier 1 supplier making great money. He was doing so well; he already owned a little place up north on the water (and a jet ski to boot!). But still, stumble as he did while learning the lessons of life a bit later than most, he was doing alright now. It took a few years, but he planted his roots, finally establishing something of a career of his own.

After spending more time at the bar than he did in the classroom while slowly riding the pine on the school's baseball team, they tossed his ass out after his freshman year, putting an official end to his life at EMU. After that, he took a class here and there at the local community college, eventually falling into a sales job that he heard about through a friend of his. It was a company in Madison Heights that sold commercial reproduction and printing services. It wasn't the sexiest job by any means, but Billy soon found he had a knack for it, eventually cultivating enough accounts where he was finally making some decent money. After sucking it up for a year under his parents' roof, saving as much as he could along the way, he finally got his own apartment, taking Buddha on board as a reliable roommate to help out with the rent. Since then, the two opposites created quite the comfortable coexistence, riding out what would be the final months of their current lease.

So needless to say, buying a house over there in the Olive Park sub-division would be a big step forward for Billy Baxton. Moving on up, just like ole George Jefferson! He couldn't wait. He'd finally be out of that lousy apartment of theirs. No more lugging his laundry down into that dingy basement, pumping precious quarters into that old, beat-up yellow washer usually filled with someone else's abandoned clothes. No longer would he have to hunt for a parking spot after work, only to be greeted by a pungent smell of ethnic food as he entered the hallway from outside. But most of all, he wouldn't have to live beneath that asshole upstairs who blasted Van Halen's *Jump* every single morning while he was still sleeping.

"No," he finally said in a matter-of-fact way, answering Buddha's question as to whether it would bother him or not that someone committed suicide in the very house he was looking to buy. He wrinkled his bottom lip as he shook his head, shaking it off as though it were the absolute least of his problems. "No, I guess it doesn't really bother me at all. I mean, shit happens, right? And yeah, as creepy as it all is, it's not like it's going to affect my life in any way. What's done is done, and I'm looking to take advantage of the situation to better my life."

Buddha grinned, slowly nodding up and down. "Well shit man, if you're in, then I'm in."

"*Really?*"

"For real."

Billy was impressed, another relief and a box checked off along the quickly growing to- do list. For a minute there he thought Buddha might wuss out, too creeped out by the thought of some chick slitting her wrists in the bathroom to even think of moving in. But hey, that's how the guy was. Loyal as hell and go with the flow.

"Hell yeah," Billy shouted, raising his can of beer as if to say cheers. "That's what I'm talking about!"

As the roommates relished in the moment of their early celebration, they suddenly heard something from out in the hallway. It was the sound of the door leading outside opening and closing; the sharp, quick thumps of high heeled shoes against the floor, moving at rapid pace down the hall in the direction of their apartment.

"Ahh, shit," said Buddha, grinning deviously as he put his mouth back up to the bong for another hit. "Here she comes."

CHAPTER 5

As so precisely predicted by Buddha, Diane arrived for one of her impromptu social visits. As the echoing thump of the footsteps came to a rest, the door to their apartment eventually flew open as she came strolling in with the swagger of a runway model who was having a bad day. It was Diane Zajnecki, their regular guest, prancing into their apartment unannounced as she typically did, ready for a cold one and what Buddha and Billy sometimes referred to as her "therapy sessions".

Diane was cool, though. She hung out all the time. For as long as they could remember, it was always like that—the jock, the stoner, and the queen bee. Three opposites that jelled so well together, they ended up stuck with each other, like it or not. They had always been a bit of a trio, their little clique dating all the way back to junior year of high school, bumping into each other at all of the same parties, breaking down barriers that normally never crumbled within the walls of school.

Since then, they still hung out all the time, Diane usually stopping in two to three times per week. It was routine, eventually becoming like clockwork. Being that the office she worked at was right around the corner from Billy and Buddha's apartment, their place had become the convenient pit stop. A chance to kill some time at the end of the day while the rush hour traffic eventually dwindled. Her brief visits also allowed her to climb up onto her well used soap box, proudly and verbally venting about the myriad of annoyances experienced throughout her day. It was her own hour-long open mic session that allowed her to vent, preach, bitch, laugh, talk shit, and usually partake in a bit of gossip. But of course, during these visits she would usually lubricate herself via a cocktail or two, helping herself to whatever the boys had on hand (usually some frost covered bottle of cheap vodka stashed somewhere amongst the scattered contents of their freezer).

"Oh my *God*, these people on the road are the biggest *assholes*! I mean, where in the hell did these people learn to drive?" She tossed her purse—a big, bright blue monstrosity—onto the orange couch where Buddha sat nestled in his usual spot. She never skipped a beat as she went about her grand entrance, bitching about the perils of horrible drivers out on the road. Like a diva commanding the brightest of spotlights, she strolled across the room, walked into the kitchen, threw open the fridge, and began eyeing its sparse contents inside. She continued her griping as her narrow eyes darted back and forth."I mean, you would not believe what this lady just did as I was driving over here. I mean, this fucking-inconsiderate bitch who cuts me off has the nerve to actually give me the fing—hey, do you guys have any vodka?"

Billy sipped his beer, smiling as he looked over at Buddha as if to say, "*hey, watch this*".

"What do you think this place looks like, 7-11 or something?" Buddha started snickering a strange little laugh, almost choking and snorting at the same time as he tried not to lose it.

Diane arched an eyebrow as her green eyes shimmered with a quick yet intense glare of fury, her open hand quickly meeting the curve of her hip in a stance of a woman not to mess with.

"Dude, do you have any fucking vodka or not? Come on, Billy, I need a drink. It's been a shitty week. You have no idea."

"There's plenty of beer in there."

Again, she shot him that all too familiar glare. "Billy, how many years have you known me now? You know that I don't drink beer. You know that."

Billy exhaled slowly as he shook his head, easing back even further into the Lazy Boy with his cold one in hand. "Check the freezer. I'm sure there's something in there." She rolled her eyes, opening the freezer as she began to scan its contents. Moving some boxes around, her fingers quickly located a frost covered bottle of Jim Beam hidden behind a couple boxes of ice cream sandwiches and a Hungry Man frozen dinner.

Billy watched her from the corner of his eye, oddly entranced by her more so than usual. He couldn't help it, there was something going on with her at that moment. She looked good. *Really* good. She was sporting a colorful dress that exposed her neck and shoulders, browned nicely from the summer sun. She had on a pair of stylish new glasses that gave her the persona of a naughty librarian; yet to let her hair down and thrash it around as she shed her daytime disguise. A couple of chopsticks wedged their way through her hair that happened to be up in a funky little do, quite different from the way that she normally wore it. The lip gloss she wore looked unusually pink, her lips looking fuller and more puckered than they normally did. Even the smell of her perfume revved his engine a bit, a scent that had always driven him wild.

Every time she wore it, it instantly brought him back to the time they strolled off from a party and had sex inside one of the play structures in a park across the street. It was a birthday party for a friend of a friend, a decent sized gathering of mostly people they didn't know. After an hour or so of small talk with people they'd never see again while mixing drinks from a dwindling open bar, an opportunity to venture off and create a little fun of their own in the summer night suddenly presented itself.

"What do ya say?" Diane asked, standing along the driveway beyond the open garage while sipping a Bacardi and Coke from a plastic cup. Billy could see right away that there was a look of deviousness twinkling within her drunken eyes. "Wanna go get naughty in that playground over there?"

"You don't have to ask me twice," he said with a smile, putting his cup of beer down along one of the card tables inside the garage."

"Let's go."

It was the exact same perfume she was wearing that day—Calvin Klein's Obsession. Billy caught a quick whiff of it as she walked by, unaware of what her smell was doing to the animal- like instincts deep inside of him. Its mere scent took him back to that very moment, realizing once again that he always wanted what he didn't have.

The ice cubes clinked softly against her glass as she plopped down along the couch with her cocktail in hand, crossing her legs gracefully and throwing a playful smile Billy's way as if to say, *Ahh, now you see how it works here, William. I have the pussy; therefore, I have the power.* And she did, too. The limbo-like existence of their relationship as of late had been driving him crazy. As always, he wanted her more than ever now that they were no longer officially a couple. It was the old "the grass is greener on the other side" theory. And that Friday afternoon as she made herself comfortable on their couch, there was no question that the grass looked a whole lot greener on the other side of the fence.

But Billy was no novice in this game of handling Diane. Oh no, he knew her very well and he knew exactly what he was doing. And like most girls like her, the play-hard-to-get game always proved to be much more successful than the chase. And that right there was part of the problem. How do you play hard to get when the girl you want simply stops by your apartment anytime she pleases? The truth is it bothered Billy. And it was something that he would have to address here sooner than later.

"So," she said with a smile, sipping slowly from her glass of whiskey, her eyes locked on Billy's before sliding her attention over to Buddha's. "What's on your agenda for the evening, homos?"

"Well," Buddha began as he glanced in her direction with those squinty red eyes, kicking his feet back up on the coffee table. He reminded Diane of that caterpillar from *Alice in Wonderland*, perched lazily upon his mushroom while puffing away on some mysterious apparatus; his eyes sleepy and spaced out. "First, we're gonna puff some grass. Well, *I'm* gonna puff some grass while my buddy here knocks back some cold ones, and then we're gonna pop in *The Empire Strikes Back* and play a little drinking/smoking game called, May the Bong be with You."

Diane grinned but did not look amused. "You guys are gonna sit around here getting fucked up while watching *Star Wars*? Seriously? That's your Friday night plan?" She looked perplexed, clearly finding their plan a bit on the lame side.

"Not *Star Wars*," Billy corrected her. "*The Empire Strikes Back*. It's the second movie in the series."

Diane rolled her eyes, taking a sip of her drink with a wickedly judgmental glare in her eye. "Well, sounds like a thrilling Friday evening, boys. What's after that? A little Dungeon and Dragons before jerking each other off and going to bed?"

"Naw, Dungeons and Dragons is old hat," Buddha added quite matter of fact.

"Hey," Billy said with a smart-ass smirk, crossing his legs as he did so. "What do you say there, dragon lady? You wanna join us? We're gonna order some Chinese here in a little bit if you're interested?"

She squirmed slightly, hating when he did that, referring to her as the "dragon lady". "Gee, as much as that sounds like a kick-ass time, I think I'm heading out to Club Zero with Julie and Angela later on. If you guys get tired of your nerd fest, feel free to meet us up there."

"Yeah, we'll see," Billy said, staring straight ahead at the television as he casually sipped his beer, consciously playing it cool.

"Hey," Buddha quickly piped in, ignoring her invitation to join them at the bar later. "Did you hear the big news? Billy here bought himself a house."

"You bought a house?" Her head immediately swung in his direction, her green eyes now alive and wide with surprise and intrigue.

Billy waved his hands in the air as if to dismiss this new little tidbit of information. "No, no, I didn't *buy* a house. I made an *offer* on a house."

"No shit?" Diane replied, clearly a bit curious at this newly disclosed news. "Where about?"

"Street called Hickory Leaf. Between Twelve and Thirteen Mile right off Evergreen."

"Really? I didn't know that you were in the market."

He could tell by the look in her eye as she sipped from her glass of whiskey that his stock suddenly went up in her book. "Actually, I wasn't. But after stumbling across this place while flipping through the real estate section the other morning while having my coffee, I had to check it out."

"Not bad, Baxton. So, when do you find out if the offer is accepted?"

"The listing agent said that I should know by Monday."

"Well, well, look at you, stud. That's a big step there, Billy. I hope you get it." Her voice sounded genuine as she tilted her head back and polished off her cocktail, wincing slightly as she pulled the glass away.

"Fingers crossed." Billy smiled, showing two of his fingers crossed on his left hand.

"So, what happens if your offer is accepted? Are you bringing stoner boy here with you?"

"Of course. You think I'm gonna leave him here to fend for himself with some other roommate in this dumpy apartment? No way, man. We're tighter than that. We're like Crockett and Tubs."

"Like Poncho and Lefty," Buddha added.

"That's right. Only he's not gonna sell me out and leave me for dead in the desert for the vultures to nibble on."

Diane got up and grabbed her bright blue purse off the couch before flinging it over her shoulder then on the go again. "Well, hey, I gotta fly if I want to get ready and meet the girls later. But be sure to let me know what happens with the offer. Oh, and if you guys change your mind later, you know where we'll be."

"You got it," Billy replied, playing it cool as a cucumber, not a hint of desperation radiating off him in the slightest.

"See ya!"

And with that, she was gone. Making her presence known before blowing onward to bigger and better things. As the echo of the apartment door slamming sounded down the hallway outside, Buddha nonchalantly took another bong rip. Blowing it through an empty toilet paper roll filled with crinkled up fabric softener sheets this time to mask the smell, he looked over at Billy with an arched eyebrow. Billy knew what his lazy red eyes were saying before he even spoke.

"Chinese?" Buddha inquired with a creeping smile. "Calling right now, buddy."

CHAPTER 6

As hoped, Billy received a call from Alan Spaulding early Monday morning with the good news. Sipping his morning coffee as he was about to head off for work, the pea-green colored phone hanging along his kitchen wall rang to life with that loud, metallic rattle. Not used to getting calls so early in the morning, it startled him momentarily, the hot coffee sloshing around in his thermos as he eventually picked up. He knew who it was. It had to be, right? He was actually hit with a tiny cloud of butterflies in his gut, mostly expecting to hear bad news while nervously hoping for the best.

"Hello?"

"Good morning, is this Bill?"

"Yeah, this is Billy."

"Hey, it's Alan Spaulding, I've got some good news for you. Listen—the banks accepted your offer. The house on Hickory Leaf is all yours once you close. Congratulations."

Bam! Offer accepted. It was suddenly the most beautiful two words in the English language, music to his awaiting ears. It was exactly what he had been waiting to hear, alleviating a great weight of nervous anticipation sitting upon his shoulders. He was finally free of that apartment, now ready to enter the great and sometimes scary world of home ownership. Goodbye paper-thin walls and indoor hallways that reeked of ethnic food and cat piss, and hello bachelor pad complete with finished basement, pool table, Pac Man machine, and outdoor swimming pool. He couldn't wait! He'd be counting down the days until the closing with the excitement of a little kid waiting for Christmas morning, visions of what he could do with the place swirling about his imaginative mind that shot into overdrive.

And he'd be able to comfortably swing it, too. He crunched the numbers several times since checking the place out and everything looked feasible. Even with the city taxes and the utilities figured in, he'd still be paying about the same amount that he was paying now in rent for their menial two-bedroom apartment. Not to mention, Buddha's half of the rent would help immensely with the mortgage. And fortunately for Billy, Buddha was about as nonchalant about the whole suicide thing as he had been. Yes sir, it would take a whole lot more than some lady deciding to whack herself in the bathtub to deter ole Buddha from a spot in the bachelor pad. It was the mark of a new chapter in their lives. A time to celebrate.

And that's exactly what Billy did. On the very last Saturday before they moved out, Billy and Buddha decided to throw a party to put an exclamation point on their send off. It was their final hurrah at Sleepy Woods apartments, so why not go out with a bang? "Let's have the biggest and wildest party that we can squeeze into this place," Billy had said, Buddha smiling and going along with the plan. Besides, what was the worst that would happen? Either some drunken idiots were going to cause enough damage to cost them their security deposit, or one of their neighbors was going to call the police who would then have them kill the music or send the merry masses on their way. Either way, the bash guaranteed to be a kick-ass time. As long as Buddha had an ample supply of grass to burn and Billy had enough cold beer in the fridge, they were good to go.

And as expected, over the course of the days leading up to the party, word of their little fiesta spread like a bad rash. After a few days *everybody* was talking about it. By early evening that Saturday, a small sized mob of people began spilling into their apartment, beer cans popping and the stereo blasting as things got quickly under way.

Billy stepped out from his bedroom after an early round of tequila shots with a couple of chicks that he knew from work, stunned by the size of the growing horde of party goers as he gradually pushed his way through the growing swarm of people. The place smelled like body odor, spilled beer, and cigarettes. The air inside their apartment felt thick and muggy. Seemingly defying all laws of physics, he pondered how such an assemblage of people could squeeze into the confines of their two-bedroom apartment. It wasn't even nine o'clock yet, and the place already looked like the inside of some of the college parties he'd been to up at State. Even though they warned all their neighbors about the whole thing, he couldn't believe that the cops hadn't arrived yet. Needless to say, if they were looking to put an exclamation mark on their big send off, it was looking like they succeeded in doing so.

Roger and his group of weirdo buddies—pale and decked out head to toe in their strange, black clothing—stood around in the corner of the main room, sipping red wine and discussing the artistic progression of some shitty band that Billy never heard of. In the kitchen, Billy's buddy Larry was running the blender and mixing up a batch of his famous margaritas for a small clique of girls that looked like they were barely out of high school. He, of course, had on his self-proclaimed party shirt—an ugly-ass Hawaiian, short-sleeved number that looked like it should only leave the closet if heading out to a Jimmy Buffett concert or being used for a Magnum PI Halloween costume. Over by the window, a bunch of surfer-looking dudes with long blonde hair that Billy had never seen before were standing around in a cloud of hanging cigarette smoke, puffing on Marlboros, and whipping their hair around, playing air guitar while singing along to the Van Halen blasting from the speakers in the corner.

"Panama! Paaaanamahhaa!"

As Billy pushed and creatively eased his way through the plethora of party goers squeezed into the tight spacing of the main hallway, he finally spotted his trusty roommate easing through the crowd. Grinning ear to ear, he beamed as he spotted Billy and began making his way over.

"Dude!" Buddha yelled over the pulsating music, giving Billy a big sweaty hug as he left his arm draped over his shoulder for just a bit too long. "Fucking-epic party, brother. *Epic*! I knew this thing was going to be rad, but I had no idea how rad!" His eyes were glassy and pink, and his breath reeked of cheap rum. Looking like he just won the lottery; Billy couldn't recall the last time he saw Buddha so happy. As predicted, the party was exactly what the guy needed.

Hell, scratch that, it was exactly what they needed. A final hoorah to blow off as much steam as possible and scream *"fuck this place, we're out of here"* before sailing off into the next phase of their young lives.

"I told you, brother!" he said, playfully slapping Buddha along the back. "I told you. I mean, look at this shit. How did everyone get here so fast? I didn't think it was going to get this packed, this quick."

"I know! It's like the size of a college party. Say, have you seen Mickey around?"

Billy stood on the tips of his toes, scanning the crowd as he eventually spotted him hanging near Larry and the underage girls. "Actually, he's over there. In the kitchen over by Larry and those random chicks."

"Cool, let's swing over there. I promised him a little burn session earlier, but we got split up." Billy took a swig of his Miller Lite and smiled, trying to ignore the fact that he hadn't seen Diane and her crew of girls yet; a fact that was slightly bothering him.

"Cool man, let's do it."

Pushing their way against the resistance of sweaty bodies squeezed together, they eventually made it into the kitchen where Larry was pouring his batch of frozen margaritas into some red plastic cups.

"Hey!!" Larry yelled, spittle flying off his mouth as he spun around with the blender's pitcher still in his hand, his arms spread outward as he enthusiastically greeted his buddies. "Mi amigos! There they are! The very dudes that made this fiesta all possible! Bring it in, fellas. Bring it in!" He tossed his big meaty arms around their necks and pulled them both in, motioning to the two young girls while doing his best to introduce everyone through his slurred delivery. "Jenny, Rachel, I want you to meet some friends of mine. These two very disease free and very single gentlemen are Billy and Buddha, the guys that live here and threw this little fiesta together for us. Fellas, the lovely Jenny and Rachel. What do ya say, boys?"

The two girls smiled awkwardly, taking sips from their plastic cups of margaritas, wincing slightly as if they were a little too stiff for their liking (and if Billy knew Larry, the dude loaded that blender as high as he could with tequila).

"Hey there, like, cool party," one of the girls decked out like Madonna in her Like a Virgin video said. She was smacking away on a piece of gum and glancing around awkwardly, appearing as though this may have been the only party she'd ever been to.

"Yeah, cool party," said the other one dressed in an electric blue tank top and tight black pants, talking in the very same valley girl voice that gave away that fact that these two weren't exactly the sharpest knives in the drawer. Nervously sipping their drinks and playing with their Goomie bracelets, Larry roared with this raspy laugh he would get when he was drinking, draping his arms around them again as they awkwardly tried to move a bit away from him (though he was too drunk to notice). His overly white teeth stood out against the pink of his sunburned face, covered in a thin film of slick sweat. The guy was talking a mile a minute and doing that weird thing with his teeth again, looking like he already ducked off into the bathroom to snort back a couple lines. In fact, Billy thought that he even saw a small speck of something white along the bottom of his mustache as he yapped away about some guy he knew that let him borrow his Porsche 944 for the weekend.

"Nice to meet you, girls," Billy said as he smiled politely, opening the refrigerator door to grab a fresh Miller Lite. Trying not to appear too distracted as he pretended to be listening to Larry and his stories, Billy scanned the party again, surprised to see that Diane still hadn't shown up. *Where the hell is she?* Finding it perplexing as ever at how much he thought about her now that they weren't officially a couple anymore.

"Dude, we gotta get tickets! It's gonna be awesome, we gotta get tickets! What do you say, you girls wanna go?" Bringing his attention back to the conversation at hand, Larry was now yapping about some Huey Lewis concert that was coming at the end of the summer, but Billy was too distracted to even listen. Even though he was a free man and the host of his own party, the fact that everyone they knew was there while she still wasn't, was bothering the living shit out of him. He couldn't figure out why, but the girl, once again, found her way right inside of his head. And per usual, he was letting her win at his own little game while he was the one that should have been sitting back in the driver seat. *Shake it off, Billy,* he told himself, gripping the cold can of beer as he continued to scan the crowd. *Just shake it off and have a good time, buddy. Don't let that broad bother you and dictate your mood. This is your party, Billy. This is your time to shine.*

Cracking open his beer and sucking some foam from the top, he suddenly felt someone tap him on the arm.

"Hey man," Buddha said, standing there with Mickey Addleman who was sipping on some kind of cocktail with a lime in it. "Wanna go burn with us?"

Billy scanned the party again really quick, balancing his options for the night as he took another swig of beer. "Hmm, I don't know man. I don't wanna get all tired and shit. You know how that stuff makes me. You guys go ahead."

"Naw man, you'll be fine," Mickey piped in. "Just take a little hit or two to loosen ya up. As long as you don't smoke too much, you'll be fine."

"Yeah buddy, leave the overdoing it part up to us," Buddha laughed, exchanging a soft clink of glasses with Mickey.

Right then, Billy looked up to find Diane coming through the front door. She was carrying a paper bag (likely a bottle of Stoli) as Julie and Rachel strolled in behind her, followed by this dickhead, Gary who worked as a bartender up at Club Zero. *What the fuck is he doing with them?* Billy thought, perplexed by the fact that they were now hanging out with him, the Billy Idol wannabe who tried to sleep with anything that moved.

"You know what," Billy said, quickly turning his back to the front door so that she wouldn't see him, deciding that it was time to let her do some of the chasing. "Fuck it. You guys are right. A puff or two won't hurt. Besides, this is our big send off, right? Come on, let's go get high."

Billy plopped himself down in a big, brown leather beanbag sitting in the corner of Buddha's bedroom. He was mindlessly watching a bright green blob of ooze as it wiggled and swam its way to the top of a lava lamp sitting along Buddha's dresser. The lighting in his room was pleasantly dim, Steely Dan playing softly over his stereo as he broke up a nugget of herb on a small, silver tray. Once satisfied that it broke up nicely, Buddha packed some of the grass into a small metal pipe before handing it off to Billy along with a lighter.

"Fire it up, muchacho. The honor is all yours, my friend." Billy hunched his shoulders, reaching out for the pipe as he put it to his lips and brought the lighter's flame toward the tip of the bowl, sucking slowly as he did so. Getting a decent sized hit without launching himself into a painful bout of coughing, he passed the pipe on to Mickey, blowing out a hefty cloud of gray smoke as it went rippling through the air.

"There ya go, Baxton," Buddha said with a proud smile, looking like a dad who just watched his boy throw a perfect spiral for the first time. "Atta boy! See, no problemo!" Being that Billy only smoked once in a blue moon, it always made Buddha's day when he finally caved. The dude would twist his arm constantly, trying to get him to give in and join him in his favorite pastime, Billy usually passing in favor of a nice cold one. *Keeps me sharp*, he used to tell him, tapping the tip of his finger against the side of his temple. And what could he really say to the guy? Grass just wasn't his thing. Besides, it seemed like every time he gave in and smoked with the guy, he'd get all paranoid as a barrage of weird thoughts started swimming through his head. Meanwhile, Buddha would just sit back and laugh at him. And what fun was that?

"Man, I think that'll do me good," Billy said, easing himself back into the beanbag as he grabbed his beer from the dresser. He took a long swig, the cold soothing against the burn along the inside of his throat and momentarily easing the dry mouth that seemed to kick in instantly.

"Aww, you can take one more," Buddha assured him." "You'll be fine."

Billy waved his hands in front of him, assuring them that he was all set. "No way man, I'm good. One more hit of that shit, and I'll be a paranoid, antisocial zombie in no time."

"Hey, that's cool." Buddha smiled, exhaling after a rather large toke of his own as he passed the pipe over to their buddy, Mickey. "Say, where's Diane at? I don't think I've seen her all night."

"Naw, me neither," Mickey said, sitting on the corner of Buddha's bed, tinkering with a Rubik's Cube before tossing it aside to take the pipe. "I know that she and Rachel said that they were swinging by, but I haven't seen them."

Billy shook his head and quickly hunched his shoulders as if to say who knows, readjusting himself along the sloping beanbag. "Hey man, good question. You never know with those chicks."

"Tell me about it!" Buddha added with a quick laugh, tapping out the cashed bowl into a glass ashtray. "So, what is going on with you guys anyway? You two are more back and forth than a tennis match. I live with you, and I can't even keep up with what's going on."

"You're telling me. I have a hard time keeping up, myself. I guess you could say that we're currently in one of those limbo phases. A complicated state of affairs, I guess."

Buddha grinned like the cat that just ate the canary as he leaned in a bit, his silver tray back on his lap as he broke up some more weed. "So, are you guys still fucking or what?"

Billy crinkled his mouth, acting nonchalant about it. "Ehh, here and there," he said with a cool arrogance that Buddha admired, yet never possessed. "Like I said, the whole thing's about as complicated as a relationship can get. I mean, even when we're broken up and I need a little space, I can't even get it 'cause she's always popping in unannounced to shoot the shit or hang out. It's too much, man. It's too much."

"You gotta put a stop to that shit, bro," Mickey interjected, lighting up a Camel as he picked up the Rubik's Cube and started tinkering with it again.

"What, the sex?" Billy asked, a bit confused as to what he was getting at.

"No man, the unannounced drop-ins. Now that you've got this new house, it might be a good time to lay down the law. You keep letting her have it her way man, she's always gonna have the upper hand. You gotta let her know that it's all or nothing. You keep muddying the waters like that, and she ain't never gonna go away."

Billy's eyes lit up as though he just had an epiphany. He was right. What the hell was he doing? Though he was always in the driver's seat in the beginning, lately she had been playing him like a fiddle. Who was she to have her cake and eat it too when it was convenient for her? It was time to take the power back. It was time to let her know that it was all or nothing.

This house marked the beginning of a new chapter for Billy Baxton, and it was time to tell ole Diane Zajnecki that a major change was on the horizon. Like a wild stallion that roamed free, it was time to break this horse. And oh yes, break her he would.

At that very moment, right in the middle of his moment of clarity, there was a knock along Buddha's door—*boom, boom, boom, boom.*

"Hey, what are you guys doing in there?"

The three of them immediately knew that it was Lisa, recognizing that raspy voice that was just a touch deeper than most chicks, a product of smoking reds since she was fourteen. The three of them looked at each other as if to say, *speak of the devil*, completely sure of the fact that Diane herself was standing right outside the door as well.

"What's the password?" Buddha shouted over the Deacon Blues and the closed door.

"What?"

Buddha paused as he tried to be serious, struggling not to break out laughing at his own juvenile antics.

"What's the password?"

"Passport? Huh?"

"The password!" Buddha said with a bit more gusto this time. "What is the password?"

"Dude, open the fucking door you homos."

Billy looked at Buddha, stoned and acting like a chubby little troll as he chuckled merrily at his own shenanigans, eventually pulling himself up to his feet as he finally unlocked the door. Rachel, Julie, Lisa, and of course, the queen bee herself—Diane—invited their way inside the "VIP" confides of Buddha's cozy little den. It smelled like candles, weed, and patchouli oil; sweat socks and stale beer. The girls were laughing hysterically about something as they staggered into the bedroom with their cocktails in hand.

"What's up!" Diane snapped with a raised cup, a devilish grin on her mouth and a flicker in her eye that highlighted the fact that she was feeling pretty good. She started in on some story about Julie and her car, and how they were so drunk last night that they had to leave her car at the Red Lobster by the mall. Chomping on a piece of grape Hubba Bubba as she took quick yet sporadic sips from her cocktail, she then went into how they'd been pre-partying at Club Zero earlier in the night doing shots of Blue Zombies or some shit, and how there was some weirdo out on the dance floor dressed head to toe like Michael Jackson. Her energetically told stories were occasionally paused with a tiny little sniffle. Billy watched her from the comfort of his beanbag, noticing that the edges of her nose looked bright red. *Jesus Christ*, he thought, shaking his head in disgust. *Is she doing coke now, too?*

As Billy watched her, he promised himself that he'd play nice for now. Cool, slightly detached emotionally, but nice. But once the drunken escapades of the weekend were over and it was back to the start of the new work week, the unannounced visits would cease. Mickey was right.

She had been having her cake and eating it too for much too long now. And whether she liked it or not, it was time to put an end to it. He'd nicely explain to her that it was all or nothing and that would be that. Either this thing with Diane was going to work, or it wasn't. But the simple fact was he just couldn't have a girl that he had feelings for popping in all the time, being all buddy-buddy with him without the benefits of a physical relationship. What was the point of that? It was mental torture. He had plenty of friends that he could hang out and shoot the shit with without his cock being teased and tested all the time. As much as she would hate it, it was time to lay down the law. Draw a line in the sand and see what side of it Diane Zajnecki was gonna stand on.

After another fifteen minutes of sitting around bullshitting in Buddha's room, Billy decided it was time for a change of scenery. It was time to kick it up a notch, see how Diane might react to a little test of his. There was a bottle of Jose Cuervo sitting in a dresser drawer in his room, and that tequila wasn't about to drink itself. It was time to see if Diane was down for doing a shot.

Doing his best impersonation of Mickey Rourke in *9 1/2 Weeks*, he leaned in with that smooth, cool smirk and gently nudged Diane on the shoulder.

"Hey, I've got a bottle of tequila in my room," he whispered. "Wanna grab a quick shot?"

She shot him a playful, inquisitive grin. And to his surprise, she actually took him up on the offer. "Sure. Let's go."

"Hey, we'll be right back," they said, politely exiting Buddha's bedroom as the bowl began to circle the room again so the girls could get a hit. Stepping out into the hallway, they were immediately greeted by the body heat generated by the growing party; the roar of talking and laughing and the sound of Duran Duran blasting over the stereo system filling the air: *The reflex is an only child, he's waiting by the parrrrrk.*

Squeezing their way down the narrow hallway, he unlocked his bedroom as they ducked inside, the noise of the bash behind them suddenly muffled as Billy closed the door. Diane immediately moved to the bed, plopping herself down as she took a slow sip of her cocktail, her eyes looking directly into Billy's. He smiled, trying to appear as cool and confident as possible, pulling open the top drawer of his dresser as he withdrew a couple of clean shot glasses and the fifth of tequila.

"Whoa, look at you! You've even got some limes cut up and ready to go on a cutting board over there, huh?"

He smiled as if to say, *of course*, yet simply dismissed her observation. "So, how was Club Zero?" He asked, filling a shot glass for her as he politely passed it over. He then brought over the small wooden cutting board, offering a lime as she kindly obliged. Quickly thanking him, she barreled into a drawn-out rant, going on and on about this, that, and the other thing; none of it of very much interest to Billy as he politely smiled and nodded, pretending to be intently listening. *Goddamn, she's talking a lot*, he thought, watching her jaw just flap away as the words went in one ear and out the other. *Clearly, cocaine and Diane Zajnecki do not mix.*

"Well, on that note," Billy said with a smile as he raised his shot, finally spotting a moment to interject. "Cheers."

She smiled, spotting a twinkle in her eyes that he had seen many times as they clinked their tiny shot glasses together, holding them there for a moment. "Cheers, Billy."

He smiled back at her with a cocky grin that he hoped oozed with confidence *(no emotion. . . you're The Fonz, remember . . . you're fucking Mickey Rourke!).* Billy chased the shot with the rest of his beer as Diane chomped down on the lime wedge, making a funny face as she did so. Putting aside the glasses, they stared at each other for a moment, a silence falling over them that Billy found quite welcoming.

"So, what's the story, you girls gonna hang out for a bit?" He purposely said it in a way that didn't sound desperate, hoping to come off indifferent either way. He wasn't dumb, immediately getting the vibe that they weren't planning on sticking around his overly packed apartment party the moment they strolled into Buddha's bedroom. So why not casually toss it out there, right? He already knew the answer anyway. For her and her girlfriends it was just another convenient pop in. A chance to fill her glass, get a puff, and be social for a bit before taking off to the next social gathering.

Diane quickly ran a finger over the tip of her nose as she started in about possibly having to meet someone back at Club Zero before they headed back to the party. Her eyes darted around the room as her skinny fingers rifled through her purse, eventually pulling out an almost empty soft pack of Merits.

"No, no, come on," Billy said, a disgusted look twisting across his face as he watched her wedge an unlit cigarette between her lips. "Don't smoke that shit in here. I hate cigarettes, you know that. I don't want my room smelling like a god-damn bowling alley, Diane."

"Oh, it won't smell so bad, Billy! You'll barely be able to smell it as long as I smoke by the open window. Don't be a square, dude."

"Bullshit, that smell always sticks around. It reeks."

"Whatever. You guys aren't even going to be living here that much longer anyway. What's the big deal?" She snickered and looked at him like she owned the place, sliding the cig back into the flat, crinkled soft pack. "But hell, if you're going to bug out about it that much, I'll just smoke it later." Giving him a playful evil eye, she stuck out her tongue at him. "Jerk." She smiled, clearly just playing with him now as that natural flirtation exposed itself.

Billy got turned on. He loved that sass of hers. That attitude; always had. It was one of the things about her that turned him on the most. In his eyes, there was nothing sexy about a little mousey girl who just sat there politely and went along with everything. He liked the challenge. The fight, the attitude. He couldn't help it. That smart ass, queen-like air about her had a power over him that he couldn't quite explain. She was crazy as a shithouse rat at times, but there was always something about her attitude that drove him wild.

"Well, well, you are a sassy little thing, aren't you?" He smiled, acting as cocky as possible while knowing she would eat it right up.

"Yeah, I guess I am," she replied, the slightest of a smile curling along the corner of her lips.

"Is that right?" he said, moving in closer to her now as he gently took her by the arm and slid her against the wall as she stood up to toss her purse along the corner of the room. He said nothing as he stared into her glimmering green eyes as she stared back at him. He could feel her breathing. He gently pressed himself against her as he could feel himself getting excited. "You got a little mouth on you, don't you, you sassy little thing."

"Yeah," she moaned in a hushed whisper, "I guess I do." She dropped her head back a bit, closing her eyes slowly as he began sliding his hand against her breast along the outside of her shirt, kissing her softly now along her neck and ears. "Billy," she whispered, breathing deeper now as they began to gyrate slowly against each other, the kisses along her neck growing faster and more frequent as she closed her eyes. She slid her fingers through his feathered hair, her tongue, now fluttering in and out of his mouth as their lips finally met, beginning to kiss harder now as the passion flared.

She moaned now as he continued to press himself against her, squeezing her breasts with even more intensity now as her hand fumbled blindly at his belt buckle. Unsnapping it and eventually pulling open the fly of his jeans, she reached her hand into his underwear and began to massage him; all as he pushed up her shirt and bra, grabbing the underside of her bare breast as he began to suck along the surface of her nipples.

"Oh Billy," she murmured between deep breaths, continuing to kiss him as she stroked him faster now. "God, it's been too long."

"I know," he quickly replied, bringing his attention back to her breasts as his other hand began to reach down her pants. She was wet, moaning with pleasure as he began to slide his fingers further inside her underwear, her fingers grabbing harder now at his penis. God, it had been too long. He tried to hold out, though he felt like he could bust any minute, so turned on by this sudden frenzy of bottled sexual energy.

And right then, right as his plan was about to spring to life with amazing success, there was a quick pounding at his bedroom door.

"Who the fuck is that?" Billy said, his head shooting upward as he glared in the direction of the door.

"Diane?" Lisa's muffled voice sounded from the other side of the door. "Diane, come on, we gotta go!"

"Shit," Diane hissed while exhaling slowly, running her hand through her hair as she tossed her head back against the wall behind her.

"Are you fucking kidding me?" Billy said, his pants resting around his ankles as she hesitantly pulled away, fidgeting with her bra and her shirt. "*Now*? You guys just got here."

"Jesus, Billy, I'm so sorry. We promised Jenny that we'd meet her back at Club Zero before we head back this way. We're only going to be gone for an hour or so. I'll be back later, I promise!"

Billy took a deep breath and rolled his eyes, shaking his head while trying to hide his frustration (and sexual frustration) as he began pulling up his pants. "Whatever."

"Billy," she said, gently running her hands along the side of his face, leaning in as she gave him a slow kiss. "I am so sorry, but I promise that we'll be back a little later. I promise."

"To be continued?" He inquired, buttoning his pants and adjusting his belt. "'Cause you got me pretty worked up here."

She smiled. "You can bet on it."

She shot him a flirtatious wink as they finished adjusting their clothes, eventually opening the door as the roar of the raging party outside filled the room. Diane blew him a kiss as she quickly turned and joined her friends, disappearing into the thick of the drunken, sweaty crowd. Standing there as he watched her leave, left alone with his frustration and his blue balls, Billy picked up the bottle of tequila and took a nice, long pull.

"Alright," he said to himself, wiping the back of his hand across his mouth as he fought back the burn of the tequila's bite, knowing damn well they would never come back. "Time to get fucked up."

Locking up his bedroom, he began to work his way through the herd of sweaty, gyrating bodies, looking to head back into the heart of the party and find his buddies. The hallway reeked of body funk, the walls beginning to feel as though they were shrinking inward with the speed of spilled syrup. Struggling to shake it off as just a side effect of the weed, a wave of claustrophobia began to wash over him, noticing an increased heat rising throughout the apartment. Feeling fine just a second ago after the shot, Billy now felt queasy and jittery, bullets of sweat sliding along his face and neck, an expanding patch of moisture building along his chest. His heart thundered; his lungs lurching and falling rapidly. His legs were shaking horribly, feeling as though they could no longer sustain his own weight.

He needed to get out of there. He was going to be sick.

Turning and pushing his way back toward his bedroom, his head began to pulsate with a thumping pain that seemed to rattle through his skull as his balance began to teeter. He wondered if he was going to make it, doing his best to keep his body rigid and hold the nausea at bay. *Oh god*, he thought, putting his hand to his mouth in case he might spew all over someone. *Why in the hell did I smoke that weed?*

Managing to unlock his bedroom door, he ducked inside and ran into the bathroom, falling to his knees as he steadily held himself over the toilet. His arms were shaking, resting along its seat as his throbbing head hung limply. In doing so, the building nausea and its accompanying dizziness seemed to immediately subside, staring into the water below as it seemed to move reluctantly in a circular motion. Yet it wasn't water that he was now looking at, was it? It appeared vast and deep, almost infinite in scale to the bathroom all around him. The water began to take on a rippling texture as it darkened in color, its normally clear surface slowly growing murky and black like the deep spot of a lake. As his concentration on the rippling, circling water intensified, he thought that spotted something moving and squiggling beneath the water; something that looked almost . . . *alive?*

As the fluttering, fluid movements beneath the surface of the black toilet water seemed to float to the surface—looking like the wavering tentacle of an octopus—suddenly, he was filled with a sense of suffocating dread. An intense fear that held no origin, seizing upon him tighter and tighter with the strength of a massive vice, plaguing him with a sudden barrage of horrific visions that sent a siren of horrendous screams echoing through his head. Like a lucid dream, a world of grotesque images bloomed to life, sending waves of a violent trembling rattling throughout his entire body. And then, right as he didn't think that his body nor his brain could take any more, his stomach began to spasm and turn inward on himself, sending what reminded of the pizza that he ate earlier hurling upward and into the toilet water below. *Jesus*, he thought, taking long, slow breaths, running his palm slowly across his sweaty face. *What the hell was that?*

Sitting there in silence while slowly recovering from his body's involuntary seizure as a string of bile hung from his bottom lip, the fear, the nausea, the claustrophobia, the paranoia, the heat, the vast black water inside the toilet, and even the disturbing manifestations instantly dissipated like water wrung free from a saturated sponge.

Taking a deep breath, he rolled away from the toilet and sat himself up against the wall, running his fingers through his sweat-drenched hair as he heard his name being whispered from a distance: *Billyyyyy* . . . Slowly closing his eyes, he felt like he was floating, fading quickly as he teetered someplace between what was reality and what was a dream.

II: THE WALL

CHAPTER 7

Buddha had Juice Newton playing on the radio, a doobie hanging from his mouth, and his arm hanging out the window as he pulled up to the old, green ranch on the corner lot. Taking a final drag off the joint, he tapped it out and set it in the car's ashtray. In doing so, he took a good look at his new place of residence, proudly standing there in all of its battered glory. It wasn't the nicest house on the block, that is for sure. In fact, it was a bit of an eyesore amongst its pristine suburban landscape of predominantly brick colonials that were built during the late sixties.

However, considering the asking price, he could see why Billy jumped all over it. Compared to the old apartment, living here would be a breath of fresh air.

It was moving day, and Buddha decided to take advantage of the nice weather and get right to it. In reality, there really wasn't too much stuff for him to move. Fortunately, he didn't have any big, bulky pieces of furniture to worry about. His old man rented an economy van earlier that week, and they had already transported his bed, his dresser, and his desk, leaving just the rest of his random belongings that he figured he could get over in two to three carloads.

Shutting off the rattling engine as the music puttered out, he opened the driver side door of his car and got out. The usual sounds of a suburban Saturday in the summer filled the air: lawn mowers running, children laughing, the repetitive hissing of lawn sprinklers. People were chatting with neighbors, fetching their papers, and walking their dogs. Gawky teenage boys busy shooting hoops as dads took advantage of the gorgeous weather and washed their cars.

Damn, he thought, glancing around and taking it all in as he stood there by his car. *This is gonna be a nice change from the ole Sleepy Woods apartments. This is nice!*

The ancient, brown Toyota creaked as he shut the door, pushing his sunglasses up along the bridge of his nose as he began to head across the front yard. Though it resembled a jungle just a couple of days ago, it looked like Billy had finally gotten to the lawn sometime during the week. Big, damp clumps of dark, green grass clippings lay randomly scattered about the fresh yet carefully cut lanes, standing perfectly at a respectable length. It looked like he worked on some of the landscaping too, its curb-appeal already looking ten times better.

Reaching the driveway and heading up to the house, Buddha inspected the garage that anchored an old basketball hoop. Its metal rim was decaying with rust, the net barely hanging on in pathetic worn strands that swayed in the breeze like the drooping branches of a weeping willow. The garage door was shut, likely jam packed with boxes of Billy's stuff like it was earlier in the week. Tiny patches of orange and brown rust littered the surface of the garage door's flaking white paint that began to yellow with time, just one of the many projects that Billy would surely coax him into.

Knowing that the back door was open, Buddha decided to head inside and see what Billy was up to. Pulling on the handle to the patio door wall that leads to the kitchen, it resisted stubbornly with a squeaky whine. Buddha had to give it a good couple of yanks before he was finally able to muscle it open. Once inside, he wrestled the door along the track until it shut again, welcoming the contrast of the house's air conditioning to the muggy, August morning outside.

Thirsty and deciding to scan the contents of a very bare fridge—a bottle of French's mustard, a stack of Kraft cheese slices, and some cans of Budweiser—he noticed a sound coming from down the hall, something like sandpaper sliding back and forth along the surface of smooth wood.

"What up!" Buddha called out, slowly strutting down the hall.

"What's up, dude! I'm down in the bathroom. Come on in."

Buddha headed down the short hallway, pausing before the slightly open door. "What are you doing dude, taking a shit?"

"No man, I'm cleaning. Come on in."

Buddha pushed his way inside and started laughing, finding Billy on his hands and knees scrubbing the shit out of the bathtub. He wore yellow rubber gloves, his face red with exhaustion and slick with sweat in the dusty sunlight shining through the open window. A small patch of dark sweat had even formed along the chest area of his gray CMU Basketball tee, proof that he'd been really getting at the place with some serious elbow grease.

"Look at you, man. Making sure that there's not a single molecule of that woman's blood in the bathtub. Good man."

Billy laughed. "You bet your ass I am. You can never be too clean these days. I mean, who knows if that lady had AIDS or something. Shit, I don't know."

"Oh yeah, tell me about it."

"So, you got load number one packed up in the car?"

"Yeah man. I figure it won't take too long to unload it all and head back to the apartment for load number two. I'm just gonna get all my stuff moved for now and worry about unpacking it box by box tomorrow. It's supposed to rain, so it'll give me something to do."

"Good call."

"In fact, I should be done by early afternoon if you still need someone to help you paint outside? Figure I'll stop at the party store and grab a twelve pack after picking up the last load. A cold beer or two is gonna hit the spot on a hot day like this."

Billy looked proud as a dad who just watched his son hit a little league home run as he smiled at Buddha. "Sir, you are a man of first class all the way. Ya know what, fuck it. Make it a case. I'll go in halfway with ya. We'll need some extras for later tonight."

"No worries, I got it."

"Shit," Billy said as he extended his buddy a high five. "That's my man, right there!"

"What's going on later tonight?" Buddha inquired.

"Oh, you know . . . have some beers, watch a little Airwolf on the tube. Maybe even shoot down to the Blue Alligator for an hour or two and shoot a little stick."

"Sweet."

"Go on young man, get out of here. The sooner that we can get this all done, the sooner we can kick our feet up and enjoy this day."

"No doubt. Later."

After transporting the rest of his stuff over the next two hours, it was time to crack open a cold beer and start painting. While he was gone, Billy already taped the edges, set up a couple of ladders, and even laid down some tarp along the landscaping and the front porch.

Taking advantage of the shade as the late afternoon sun shifted, they painted, sipped some suds, and listened to some tunes on Billy's old boom box that he grabbed from the garage. They went at a good pace, talking sporadically but mostly focused on the chore at hand, hoping to get a first coat down as soon as they could.

And after a good couple of hours that seemed to quickly coast by, they managed to get it done, carefully cleaning up the brushes and putting all the tarps, buckets, and ladders away so they could finally enjoy their Saturday afternoon.

As Billy took the first shower, Buddha took a bong hit and popped in a Violent Femmes cassette as he began putzing about his new bedroom.

He used the small window of time to start organizing his boxes of Dungeons and Dragons stuff, his VHS tapes, a bunch of Stephen King hard-covers that he liked to collect, and most importantly, a wooden cigar box that lay home to his grass and his various smoking paraphernalia. Most of his belongings were still boxed up and standing in piles throughout the room, stuff that he'd get at tomorrow.

Once they were both cleaned up, they headed out to the Farmer Jack a mile down the road to pick up some stuff to grill. After grabbing some chips, hot dogs, burgers, condiments, and a package of buns, they swung back home, ready to do some serious grilling and celebrate their first night in the new house.

The cold beer was going down like water as their selection of meats sizzled across the hot grill. AC/DC roared from the boom box as Billy rolled the dogs back and forth with a long, metal spatula. Buddha sat comfortably within the confines of a foldout camping chair, glancing upward toward the sky as his eyes hid behind a pair of aviator sunglasses.

"So, dude, how'd the apartment look with all of our shit finally moved out?"

"Pretty bare, man. It was weird seeing it like that, especially the walls with all the posters taken down. I forgot all about that huge gaping hole right by the kitchen where Perry put his fist through the drywall that one time. That INXS poster that we used to cover it up had been there so long, I almost forgot about it."

"Oh yeah, that's right! I forgot about Terry and his explosion of sexual frustration after the bar that one night. That guy's a maniac. I don't know why Larry ever brought him around."

"Actually, his name is Perry."

"Wasn't it Terry?"

"No, it's Perry."

"Well, whatever his name is, the guy has some serious 'roid-rage issues. Whatever happened to that guy?"

"Who knows?" Buddha said, looking toward the sky as he took a slow sip of his beer, releasing a slow, tried sigh. "Say, what's even the status with you and Diane these days? I don't think I've seen her since our party the other night."

"Actually, on again if you can believe that." Billy replied, sipping his beer while poking around the hotdogs some more. "Gave her the ultimatum, dude. All or nothing, and she said all. I was kind of shocked to tell you the truth. I thought for sure she'd call my bluff, but she was all over it. Honestly, I think I was finally ready to move on if she still had her head in the clouds. I mean, I just can't go on the rest of my life letting that girl play with my head the way she did. If it doesn't work this time, I think I'm done. Life's too short to let some chick dictate it, man."

"Good stuff, brother. Good stuff. But hey, if you guys start getting really serious, just make sure to give me the heads up so that I can start looking for a new place."

"What are you talking about?"

"Well, you know, once you guys start getting really tight, you might want her to move in . . . go ring shopping . . . start thinking about getting married . . ."

"Dude, get the fuck outta here, bro! You must have fallen out of a tree and hit your head, boy. No way in hell that's happening any time soon!" The two of them burst out laughing as Billy killed off the rest of his beer, bringing his attention back to the grill as he playfully slapped Buddha along the shoulder. "Hey funny guy, get your ass up here and grab yourself a hotdog."

"Shit, I got the munchies like a mother fucker. You don't have to tell me twice!"

Like ravenous animals, they scarfed down a couple of hotdogs and a burger apiece, half a bag of Fritos and a small tub of French-onion dip, some store bought pasta salad, and not to mention, nearly an entire can of baked beans. Finally tapping out, the two of them leaned back into their lawn chairs, staring up at the dipping sun after a long day.

"Sure feels good to be out of that apartment, doesn't it?"

"Sure as shit does," Billy said with a slow nod of his head.

"Cheers, mi hermano," Buddha said, slowly lifting his beer.

"Cheers!"

After cleaning up their mess and spritzing themselves down with some Drakar Noir, they hopped into Buddha's Toyota and headed out to the Blue Alligator. The place was unusually dead for a Saturday. Except for a couple of regulars sitting at the bar and a pair of okay looking girls hovered over the jukebox, the place was a ghost town. Though initially geared up to go out and tie one on in honor of their first night in the new house, the long hours in the sun and the beers throughout the day caught up with them. After shooting two games of pool and barely finishing their first pitcher, they decided to head out, hit the Taco Bell drive-through on the way home, and call it a night.

Armed with their stash of late-night munchies, they mindlessly watched MTV while hunched over their Mexi-Melts and Mexican pizzas. Polishing off what was an impressive amount of shitty Mexican food, Buddha crinkled up the last of his wrappers and lazily tossed it onto the coffee table with the others. "Night dude," he said, lighting off a loud fart while easing himself off the couch with the speed of a two toed sloth, his eyes all glassy and barely open.

"Aw, come on, dude! That's disgusting."

"You love it."

"I'd love it if you did that shit in the bathroom. You're disgusting, buddy."

"I know. Goodnight, homo."

"Goodnight dick."

Gathering the accumulation of crumbled up balls of waxy paper along the coffee table and tossing them into the empty Taco Bell bag, Billy jumped, startled by the unexpectedly loud rattling ring of the phone along the kitchen wall. "Jesus," he whispered, slowly bringing his hand mockingly over the area of his heart. He let out a deep breath as he looked toward the kitchen. "Scared the shit out of me."

Pondering momentarily over the thought of a late-night visitor while dismissing the sound of Buddha's mockery in the background, he chose to ignore it. He let it continue to ring while collecting the rest of the discarded Taco Bell debris, deciding it was time to close up shop and call it a night.

Sure, a little sexy time between the sheets would've been nice, but he was still a bit pissed about getting blown off the other night at their party. Not to mention, he was completely exhausted. All that yardwork in the sun in conjunction with the twelve or so beers he sucked back drained him. Tomorrow was another day and he figured he'd let her squirm in her boots a bit, deciding to play a little hard to get while leaving her wanting him even more.

After brushing his teeth, washing his face, and shedding himself of his sweaty clothes, he free-fell onto his bed like a chopped down tree. Laying there a moment while too lazy to turn off his light, he studied a series of tiny cracks along the ceiling, branching outward in every which direction like the weavings of a spider web. Releasing an exhausted sigh, he pulled the sheets over his body, a bit chilled by the fan oscillating along the corner of his room. He was so tired. His cheeks burned against the cool breeze of his fan, realizing that a bit of a sunburn burrowed its way beneath the surface of his face. He momentarily thought about getting up to grab some aloe vera from the medicine cabinet, but the weight of his fatigue was too powerful. Within minutes, he was fast asleep.

After a few hours of solid slumber, Billy was abruptly awakened by the sound of the AC unit rattling to life outside his bedroom window. It wobbled and shook for a quick second with a series of metallic thumps, followed by that reluctant revving sound as its entire system finally kicked into gear. Doing his best to ignore it, he closed his eyes and rolled over, flipping his pillow to the cooler side as he hoped for sleep to take him over again quickly.

But try as he did, he just couldn't get comfortable, tossing and turning for the next twenty minutes or so. Eventually, he realized that it was no use. He was up. His mouth tasted like shit; sticky and dry. His bladder ached to the point that he could no longer ignore it, knowing that he had to get up and take a piss whether he liked it or not.

After relieving his bladder, he turned off the light behind him and made his way down the hallway into the kitchen. Fishing a plastic cup from the cupboard and filling it from the kitchen sink, he tilted his head back and chugged it down with the urgency of a man just rescued from the wild. His mouth and throat were parched, dehydrated from the beer and the salty hot dogs.

Even his temples throbbed softly with the early onset of an eventual hangover. Releasing a loud belch as he tossed the plastic cup into the garbage, it was time to head back to bed.

Yet, as he slowly turned on the heel of his foot to head back down the hallway, he began to hear something. He had no idea what it was, but it was a loud, deep, rumbling moan, sounding as though it were coming from the basement. As the sound rose and fell—coming in and out with the intervals of long, drawn out waves—it sounded like the noise was calling his name beneath a wet, gurgling vibration of mysterious sound: *Billyyyyyy . . . Billyyyyyy . . .*

"What the fuck?"

Completely perplexed by what the hell it could be, he walked to the top of the steps, standing there in his boxer shorts while peering down into the darkness. And then, as quickly as it started, it came to an abrupt halt. "What the hell was that?" He whispered, holding his breath a moment as he stood still as a statue, listening intently for a few seconds before he began to hear it again.

Only this time it sounded like a long and drawn-out release of steam, hissing like a serpent as it steadily rose and fell in volume, gently shaking the kitchen floor as it did so. Billy shuddered momentarily as he stood at the top of the stairs, quickly dismissing it as something explainable as he began to slowly head down into the basement.

Listening carefully with each and every calculated step, he tried desperately to focus on the point of its origin. *God-damnit*, he thought, a few of the basement stairs creaking beneath his feet as he slowly descended them. *I just bought this house . . . please don't tell me that something's already taking a shit on me down here!*

Reaching the bottom of the stairs, he slowly walked past the Pac-Man machine, the blueish-purple glow of its screen providing him some light as his fingers eventually located the light switch along the wall. He heard the sound again, coming from the cedar closet—the door cracked slightly open—then trailed off again right as he reached out and slowly wrapped his hand around the doorknob.

Moving with hesitation, he stepped slowly into the closet and was immediately greeted with an odd smell. It was vile and rank, hanging in the closet's space with the scent of rotting, moldy vegetation—a far cry from the closet's usual aroma of fresh cedar and mothballs. Even the air inside the closet felt wet, heavy with the thickness of a humidity that he never felt down there.

What the hell is going on? Scowling as he sniffed at the air. Not only was the basement usually cool, but the air conditioning was on as well. There was no way that it could be that humid down there. And what the hell was that smell?! God, it was putrid. Bad enough that he wanted to gag.

Covering his mouth and his nose with his t-shirt, Billy unknowingly began to gaze toward the brick wall at the end of the closet, mesmerized by it, beginning to forget about the mysterious sound that brought him down here in the first place. *What are you hiding behind there*, he found himself wondering, gradually stepping closer to it.

Walking slack jawed like a patient from *One Flew Over the Cuckoo's Nest* toward the end of the closet, he began to feel lost in every minuscule detail of the brick wall, slowly zoning in on it with a hyper-like focus: the chipped, uneven surface of that faded orangish-pink color. The imperfect overflow of dried cement that squeezed its way outward from the spacing between the bricks. The particles of dust and dirt clinging to its bumpy, uneven surface; cobwebs clinging to its jagged edges like puffs of snow perched along the branches of winter trees.

No doubt about it, there was something very peculiar about that wall at the end of the closet. It was just a brick wall, yet it seemed to call to him. Almost summoning him, reeling him closer as he began to feel a subtle sensation of heat coming off it like a warm fireplace. A *breathing* heat that came and went in waves, emulating from the very surface of its usually cool brick in a way that defied reality.

Exceedingly intrigued and completely entranced by it, Billy stepped even closer until he stood no more than just a few inches from the wall. Having forgotten about the mysterious noise while completely transfixed by it now, he gradually lifted his hand as if seized by the grip of some unearthly, hypnotic command. His eyes were distant and blank, his mouth hanging lazily open. He steadily brought his index finger closer to that unexplainable heat, his finger tingling with a pleasurable warmth the closer he brought it to the wall. Eventually touching the cool surface of its brick, a sensation like nothing he had ever known began to slither, creep, and wrap its way up the length of his finger before traveling the distance of his whole hand. Eventually scuttling its way through his entire arm and into what felt like every molecule in his entire body.

It was unreal. So very subtle, yet immensely powerful at the same time; unlike anything he had ever experienced, filling him with a sense of ease and contentment that he could never fathom within the world of his restless imagination. But whatever it was, it was simply incredible. And the mystery would only cease to exist if he broke through to the other side. There was no question about it now. He had to find out. There was *something* waiting for him on the other side of the wall.

CHAPTER 8

Over the next several days, Billy's intrigue with the brick wall at the end of the cedar closet, and what existed beyond it, began to snowball into a strange obsession. He couldn't explain why but trying to exert focus on anything else seemed nearly impossible. Whether he was showering, brushing his teeth, driving to work, sitting at his desk, working on the house, watching TV, hanging out with Buddha, spending time with Diane, or even taking a shit, his thoughts kept circling back to that mysterious brick wall down in the basement. And while most obsessions had degrees of reason or identifying desires behind them, Billy was at a loss as to why the wall consumed his thoughts as it did. It was as if something beyond his understanding was controlling him, denying his mind the ability to roam free and put it on the back burner of the never-ending project list.

"I'm thinking about getting a sledgehammer," Billy announced as he came walking in from work the following Friday, sliding his keys across the ugly yellow counter while placing a small pile of mail next to the microwave. Buddha—who usually cruised home from the office around four—was camped out on the couch, a joint burning in a glass ashtray along the coffee table while deeply immersed in a game of Burger Time on his ColecoVision.

"A sledgehammer? What for?"

"That brick wall at the end of the cedar closet down there. Think I wanna take it down and see what's behind it."

Buddha looked at him like he was crazy for a second. "Wow. You were really serious about that, huh?"

"Damn straight," he said without skipping a beat, fishing a cold one from the fridge before cracking it open and taking a nice sized swig.

"Thinking about heading up to the hardware store here in a bit, check out what they've got as far as sledgehammers and other materials for doing the job. I wanna get a head start on it this weekend while it's fresh on my mind."

Buddha was taken back by Billy's sudden burst of ambition surrounding this wall down in the basement. Sure, he talked about it non-stop all week, but did Buddha think he was actually going to go out, get the necessary tools to physically take the thing down and actually start chipping away at it on a Friday evening? No way. He figured all that shit about taking down that wall and possibly finding a big ole box of valuable coins or old baseball cards was nothing but talk. The usual late night bullshitting over some beers and doobies.

"So, what if there's nothing behind it?" Buddha asked, sneaking in a quick toke as his video game continued, a top section of the bun falling down onto the brown, video game hamburger patty. "I mean, couldn't that wall back into more . . . well . . . wall? Cement? I don't know man; it just seems like a whole lot of work to me. Too much work for my fat ass, that's for sure."

Billy shook his head, wiping his mouth with the back of his hand as he let loose a burp. "No way dude, there's something off about that wall down there. I can't explain it, but I've got this overwhelming feeling that it's blocking off something. It's got to be. Spatial-wise, it makes sense. I mean, shit, I checked out the floor plan of this house and everything. And hey, if I'm wrong then I'm wrong. I'll just have to patch it up the best that I can and make sure that it doesn't look like shit. But for now, I've got to see if there's something behind that bad boy. Hell, who knows? Maybe we'll find a collection of old watches or a box full of valuable comic books or something?"

"Doubt it."

Billy laughed, plopping down along the couch as he looked over at his chubby little stoner buddy. "Yeah, you're probably right. But shit, it's worth a shot, right?"

"I guess."

Billy shrugged, untucking his dress shirt as he headed down the hall to his bedroom to change. After tossing aside his work clothes and sliding into some jeans and a t-shirt, he ran out to the hardware store on the corner and grabbed both a five and a ten-pound sledgehammer, a flat mallet, a couple pairs of safety goggles, and even a small chisel and a plastic tarp to catch the debris and save the walk-in floor from damage.

Once he had everything all set up, Billy slid on some safety goggles and stepped onto a small wooden step stool that he grabbed from the garage to give him some height. Gripping his Dewalt power drill in his right hand, he carefully examined the top of the wall, sliding the fingers of his left hand along its surface. Diligently studying every bump and minuscule crack that blemished the front of it, he searched carefully for a good weak spot along the cement to start.

"Hellooo?" A familiar female voice called from the kitchen, soon followed by the quick thumping of footsteps coming down the basement stairs. Smacking away on a piece of gum while dramatically flipping a lock of hair from her forehead, Diane hit the bottom of the stairs and looked around, an unopened bottle of red wine still in its paper bag tucked beneath her arm. "Hey, what's going on dick lickers? Where you guys at?"

"In here, babe," Billy called from inside the closet, his focus directed at the task in hand. As she stood and watched, he placed the drill bit along a thin section of concrete that separated the top two rows of bricks, soon to be the first of a series of small holes. Once he loosened the cement around one of the bricks along the top, he'd have a much easier time hammering it loose, eventually providing him with a better look at what was sitting on the other side.

"What the hell are you guys doing?"

"He wants to take down that wall."

"Why?" Diane shot a perplexed glare at Buddha who just entered the basement.

Picking up a pool cue, he started taking some practice shots over at the pool table.

"'Cause it's pretty apparent to me that someone sealed off the rest of this room for some reason," Billy said, glancing momentarily over his shoulder before bringing his attention back to his work. "I say it's time to see what's on the other side of this bad boy."

"Are you fucking kidding me? I mean, it's a brick wall. It's not like you've never seen a brick wall before."

"Sure I have, Diane. Just not at the end of a cedar closet like this. Something just feels off, I'm telling you guys."

"Whatever." She hunched her shoulders while sliding her purse off her shoulder, tossing it down on the pool table where Buddha was in the middle of lining up a shot. "Say, you got any weed we could smoke while we wait for Bob Vela over here?"

"Do I have any weed we could smoke?" Buddha laughed, leaning the stick back against the wall. "Do dogs like to sniff other dogs' asses? Of course, I do. Come on, let's go get high."

While his girl and roommate disappeared upstairs to smoke some grass, Billy made sure that his drill bit was secure before placing its tip along his chosen spot between the bricks. He was ready to start drilling. Slowly squeezing on the pressure sensitive trigger, his electric drill revved to life, its narrow point burrowing its way slowly into the resisting cement. It sputtered and spun into the wall, tiny chunks of cement and dust hitting the surface of his goggles, the drill whirling like a tornado within its tiny, cylinder-shaped space. Keeping the drill gun steady as he applied pressure with his other hand from behind, he eventually pushed the drill bit through to the other side; the bit spinning faster now within its burrowed cavity as it finally busted past the concrete's steady resistance.

Giving the yellow rubber trigger a good couple squeezes to free up the drill from the narrow gap, he slid it free as he held it upward in his hand like an old-time gunslinger, the drill bit whirling in place before dying to an eventual stop. Leaning in toward the hole, he pursed his lips and gave the area a good blow, a tiny cloud of dust lifting to the air. Pleased at how easily he drilled through the spacing between the brick, he picked a spot a few inches down and repeated the process.

After ten to fifteen minutes of straight drilling, he burrowed a good number of small holes around the cement perimeter of the first brick. Eager to see if he could knock it loose, he put down his power drill and grabbed a chisel. As expected, the concrete resisted, but not too much. Pounding away on the chisel from behind with a small mallet, he began to make noticeable progress as the concrete cracked and popped free, large chunks of it falling to the tarp below. After deciding that he had tinkered with it long enough, Billy decided to bust out the ten- pound sledgehammer and give it a shot. A gleam flashed across his eyes, welcoming the weight of it in his resting hands. It felt good. It felt ready. After swinging it back and slamming the head of the hammer against the loosened brick a good couple of times, it finally broke free. The inertia along with its weight eventually pulled it over the edge, falling out of sight as it made a solid *thunk* sound while landing on the other side of the wall.

Billy stood a moment catching his breath, staring toward the black rectangular gap that now sat along the top of the wall. He smiled, hit with a brief flutter of riveting triumph. He'd been right. Even if it proved to be no more than even a foot or two behind the brick, there was definitely some blocked off space behind the wall. If not, the brick would have fallen forward or rested loosely within its freed space.

Looks like I was right, he thought, sliding the clear plastic goggles up along his forehead as he wiped the forming sweat forming on his brow. *Now, time to see what's on the other side of it!*

Anxious to get to it, he bounded up the basement stairs in search of a flashlight, not sure if he unpacked it already or not. It was a good one, too: a heavy-duty Eveready Masterlight. He could picture clear as day where he used to keep it at the old apartment—right there along the top shelf next to his old Wilson tennis racquet and that Chia Pet (still in the box) that his Aunt Carol had gotten him for Christmas years ago.

Heading through the kitchen and ducking into the main room, he walked past Buddha and Diane camped out on the couch smoking weed. Some Howard Jones video was playing on MTV in the background as Buddha listened politely to Diane bitching about some bar and how they no longer play new wave music.

"I mean, seriously, we walked in there the other night and they're playing *Debbie Gibson*. Fucking *Debbie Gibson*! I mean, can you believe that shit? No Talking Heads, no Tears for Fears, no Depeche Mode, not even Siouxsie and the Banshees. Just a bunch of bougee-ass bubble gum pop shit that my kid sister listens to."

Buddha just smiled and nodded, an agreeable perma-grin spread across his face, his eyes nothing but a couple of red slits sitting horizontally across his tanned, moon shaped face.

Billy shook his head as he swung open the closet door and began searching for his flashlight. After rummaging past a couple broken Atari cartridges, an old pair of Jordans, a VHS tape of *Ghostbusters*, a Trivial Pursuit box, an old Nerf football that looked like a dog took a bite out of it, and an old shoebox filled with a bunch of *Shogun Warriors* and *Micronauts* comic books, he finally found it.

"Bingo," he whispered, grabbing the flashlight, and clicking down on the rubber button along its metal shaft to ensure that the batteries still worked.

Heading back downstairs and clearing his tools safely out of the way, he slid his footstool into position and stepped on up. Maneuvering the flashlight, he steadily aimed its cone shaped beam through the rectangular gap where he smashed out the brick, doing his best to get a decent look behind it. *Holy shit, I was right*, he thought, moving the angle of the light across what looked like a whole other room on the other side, bits of dust and dirt dancing within the center of its spherical beam.

"Guys! Quick, get down here!" he yelled over his shoulder, quickly bringing his attention back to his discovery. "You won't believe what I found down here!"

III: THE BLACK MIRROR

Buddha and Diane stood a few feet back from the plastic tarp. Billy had it stretched across the floor and covered with scattered, discarded bricks. Like a small group of gawkers standing before the aftermath of some horrific accident, the two of them stood still and transfixed, amazed by Billy's focus. He was on a mission. A man with a purpose. His t-shirt was sticking to his skin in large, sweaty patches. His hair hung over his forehead in wet, stringy strands as he continuously swung away with that sledgehammer of his. His skin looked pink with exhaustion, shining with a sheen of sweat that completely covered him. Though he looked like he'd be ready to keel over, his eyes were ablaze with a gleam of unfiltered elation, something that Buddha had never seen in his old buddy.

But, as much as they had their doubts, Diane and Buddha had to give it to the guy. He was right all along. There actually *is* something behind that wall.

"Shit Billy, you weren't kidding about that wall, man," Buddha said. "I can't believe there's an entire room behind there!"

"Dude, what did I yell ya?" he replied, an arrogant grin that said, "*I told you so*" creeping across his mouth. "Here—" he said, putting the sledgehammer down for a second as he stepped back onto the stepstool, "—hand me that flashlight if you could. Now that I've got some of those bricks knocked outta the way, I can lean in a bit and get a better look back there."

Like a PA handing off a surgical instrument to the head surgeon of the operating room, Buddha plopped the flashlight down into Billy's waiting palm. Eager to get a better look now that he had a hole big enough to squeeze his upper body through, he flicked on the flashlight, eased through to about his waist, and sent the narrow beam of light traveling through the darkness. He could see that it was square or rectangular in shape, not too big from the look of it. The light's beam exposed a bunch of dirty and dusty corners, a cement floor littered with tiny stones, cigarette buts, and random bottle caps. But oddly enough, along all four of its gray brick walls were a bunch of symbols and shapes that looked as though drawn in chalk. There were circles intersected with straight lines, triangles overlapping other triangles pointed in the opposite direction, and even some drawings that resembled some kind of ancient hieroglyphics along the far wall.

What the hell? Billy thought, steadying the beam along the drawings so that he could get a better look. In doing so, he spotted something else along the far wall. Something his flashlight missed upon initial inspection.

It was long, thin, and metallic. Its multi-textured surface was shiny and gunmetal in color, rippling and dancing as the light slowly traveled over it. An intricate design and craftsmanship covered the length of its surface, resembling several snakes and mythological looking serpents along with interloping vines and leaves. They twisted and interweaved through each other as they ran along the edge of a large, dark, rectangular shaped surface that ran vertically along the same brick wall. As Billy meticulously cast the light's beam over the surface of the rest of the object, he eventually registered that he was looking at a large mirror showcased within an elaborately detailed frame, hanging vertically along the far brick wall.

Yet there was something strange about the mirror that just didn't make sense.

It's flat surface—normally composed of reflective glass—was black as night beneath the light of the flashlight's beam. Not even the slightest flicker of a reflection cast back at him as the beam moved over it. It was as if someone painted over the glass with a thick layer of black paint. Its grandiose looking steel frame of slithering, hissing serpents and long, twisting vines seemed to dance beneath the flashlight's beam. Yet the mirror's center was nothing but a big, rectangular black hole of gaping space.

Between Diane's bachelor's in psychology, Billy's associates in business, and Buddha actually being able to graduate high school despite all of the days he missed, the three of them were clueless. They stood on their tiptoes behind him, dumbfounded and wondering what the hell they were looking at.

"Here, step back," Billy said, grabbing one of the sledgehammers leaning against the closet wall. "I want to knock a few more out of the way so that we can climb in there and poke around."

After a good couple of swings that freed up the area even more, they finally had enough room to step over and onto the other side. "Weird," Billy whispered, brushing the dust from his shirt, the first to climb over. He slowly walked about dazedly, continuing to slowly move the flashlight's beam about the newly discovered room. It was so strange that this was closed off, his head buzzing with endless questions that he didn't hold answers to.

"Wow, that's kind of creepy," Diane said as she took a steady sip from her glass of wine. "I mean, what's with these freaky markings along the walls? Am I the only one that finds this all a bit strange?"

As slack jawed and wide eyed as a young kid who just laid eyes on his first Playboy magazine, Billy carefully guided the light along the strange markings and symbols along the walls. With the flashlight in one hand, Billy reached out with the other, the tip of his extended pointer finger gently sliding along one of the chalky, white lines. Slowly pulling his hand away, he rubbed the tips of his fingers together, the white substance dry yet gritty against his skin.

"Hey nice work finding this place, Indiana Jones. What do you think the previous owners used this room for, anyway? Sacrificing babies to Satan or something?"

While Diane playfully smacked Buddha on the arm—the wine sloshing about her mammoth goblet of a glass as the two of them started laughing—Billy continued to study the room while blocking out their childish banter. He was focused. Intrigued. Not in the mood for all this joking and bullshit. He was anxious to start peeling away the perplexing layers to this mysterious onion and find out what this was all about.

Moving closer to the mirror now as he guided the narrow spotlight along the pristine detail of its carefully executed craftsmanship, he marveled at its incredible detail, staring into it as though seized by some anomalous, hypnotic quality.

"Look at this thing," he whispered, allowing his hand to gently travel along the silver serpents composing its solid, steel frame. It's. . . it's *beautiful*." The tip of his curious finger then went to the center of the mirror, softy sliding it along that smooth black glass, receiving an odd yet subtle sensation of heat coming off it. So strange, Billy thought, pulling away and rubbing the tips of his fingers together as he studied them, wondering if the warmth it emulated had been his imagination. *That's the same warmth I felt coming from the wall the other night. . . weird.*

"Yeah, well, I'm not so bad on the eyes myself, cowboy. Besides, you said you wanted to go out tonight. Are we gonna sit around here fucking around with this old, sealed off room all night, or are we gonna hit up The Bullfrog for some drinks?"

"Naw," Billy replied, never peeling his eyes from the black mirror as he continued to study it. "Go ahead without me. I want to get a lamp down here with an extension cord so that I can get a better look at all this."

"Unbelievable," she said, rolling her eyes and she kicked back the remaining wine. "Well then, I'm calling Lisa and we're going to the bar. You guys have fun dicking around with your secret little room here. Where's your phone at down here?"

"You gotta use the one on the kitchen wall upstairs," Billy replied, his thoughts a million miles away from her petty concerns at the moment as she headed upstairs to call her friends. "Say, Buddha, you still got that old, green lamp up in your room? That big, tall one?"

Squinting against the light, Buddha moved out of the way and nodded. He knew the one that Billy was talking about. It was an artifact that traveled with him since the days of college (along with his lava lamp and his plastic bong). "Yeah, I still got it. Works just fine, too. You want me to go grab it."

Billy nodded really slow as he continued to stare about the hidden room. "Yeah, why don't you go do that. I want to get a better look at this room down here. Especially this interesting looking mirror along the far wall."

CHAPTER 10

The glass along the face of the mirror was black. But not just black, it was beyond black. Blacker than the waters in the deepest region of the ocean. Darker than the clearest of country skies at night, void of the moon. Its darkness was infinite and encompassing, hypnotizing in all of its vastness. Almost pulsating gently with a life of its own if you stared into it for too long. It was a darkness that felt like it could consume you. A darkness that was titanic, almost magical in nature. A darkness, clearly, that was not of this world.

Billy felt like it had only been minutes that he stood there swooned by the hypnotic quality of the mirror's cold, black surface. So lost in its infinite darkness, he barely remembered Diane saying goodbye right before Lisa swung by and picked her up. In fact, he was glad she went out, giving him the opportunity to further check out this mysterious room in the basement that had been sealed off from the rest of the house for reasons still unknown.

Leaving Billy down there to do his thing, Buddha decided to head upstairs and jump in the shower. After quickly toweling off and sliding into a pair of jeans and an old, faded Black Flag t-shirt, he banged out a quick game of Pac-Man before popping in to see how Billy was doing. Leaning against what very little remained of the busted brick wall, he licked the length of a jay and slid it behind his ear.

"Hey man, *Miami Vice* is gonna be on in a little bit. Why don't we head upstairs and chill out for a while? We've got all day tomorrow to get back at this." Ignoring him initially, Billy continued to poke about the room. He'd slide his hand gently along the cryptic symbols drawn upon the walls, pushing against the bricks with his fingers as though some hidden, secret passage would miraculously expose itself. After pausing and gazing blankly at the wall for a second, he finally turned toward Buddha, nodding slowly as a smile finally found its way across the somber expression along his face.

"Yeah, you're right," he said, crinkling his bottom lip as he glanced about the room one last time. "We've got time. Let's call it a night and get back to it tomorrow morning."

As Crocket and Tubbs rolled around undercover in their white Ferrari, Billy and Buddha sat in silence, sipping lazily from a couple cans of Miller Lite. Billy's eyes gazed blankly at the television, looking transfixed on the story though his thoughts were elsewhere. Even though Philip Michael Thomas and Don Johnson were quickly closing in on the drug running criminals that appeared as legitimate businessmen, his mind kept traveling back to that strange room downstairs.

What the hell was that room used for? Black magic, or some kind of witchcraft? And not only that, but why was it closed off from the rest of the house like that? It's just all so weird —the strange markings along the walls, the mirror, and that odd black glass. What the hell does it all mean?

As the two of them sat there in a state of comfortably lazy silence, Billy wondered if Buddha had also seen what he did within the vast darkness of that unearthly, black glass. It was subtle and hard to discern, yet when he stared into the mirror's center for too long, there almost appeared to be an indistinct movement fluttering about somewhere within its cold darkness.

Something so faint and evanescent, he questioned if it was merely the weavings of his wandering imagination.

Letting out a loud belch as he leaned back into the couch, Buddha finally broke the silence. "So, what exactly did the realtor tell you about the chick that used to own the house? I mean, besides the fact that she killed herself in her own bathtub. Like, was he able to give you the rundown on any specifics about her?"

Billy shook his head, getting up from the couch to fetch himself another beer. Cracking it open as he began rubbing his chin with his free hand, Buddha thought that he resembled one of the detectives from *Miami Vice*, trying desperately to put the pieces of a perplexing puzzle together.

"Nope, nothing. Well, legally he did have to disclose the whole suicide thing, but that's about all that he actually disclosed. I'm telling you; this house is as much of a mystery to me as it is to you, my friend. But I think that it's time that we dig a bit deeper into its history. I've always had a pretty good gut, and my gut is telling me that there was a whole lot more at play here than we can possibly imagine."

"So, umm, what should we do?"

Billy wasn't the least bit surprised by the question. It was typical Buddha. Waiting patiently for the other guy to lead while sitting back comfortably as the situation unfolded, always allowing the course of action to be plotted out by the leader in his small pack. It was the Buddha way as long as Billy knew him: why drive anywhere in life when someone else can drive you? His lack of motivation suddenly frustrated the shit out of Billy as he paced the room. With this new-found discovery festering right below their very feet, he expected a little more intrigue and some outside the box thinking from his perpetually stoned confidant.

"What the fuck do you *think* I'm gonna do, dude? I'm gonna hit up the public library this weekend and do a little research. If the realtor can't disclose the type of information that I'm looking for, then I'm going to find it myself."

Buddha laughed, almost choking on his beer as he quickly sat back up. "*You*? The *library*?"

Billy took a long swig of his beer and released an impressively loud belch, slamming the can down along the coffee table with some authority as he stared at him with a look that meant business.

"You're God-damn right, buddy. I mean, shit, I know that I didn't spend too much time there in college, but a man's gotta do what a man's gotta do."

"Yeah man, you're right. Say, is it cool if I go too? I'd like to poke through a copy of the *Yellow Pages* and jot down any numbers for psychics, clairvoyants, numerologists; people in the area that might know a bit more about those strange symbols on the wall and what they might actually mean."

Billy smiled, nodding proudly at his loyal protege who jumped in and took some initiative for once. "See? Now that's what I'm talking about! If we do the leg work and dig a bit deeper into this shit, who knows what we'll find out?"

"Right on, man. Right on. So, what's the story? When do you want to go?"

"Let's do it on Sunday. It's supposed to rain all day anyway, so it'll be a good day to dive into this stuff."

"Cool. So, what's on the agenda for tomorrow?"

Billy smiled, playfully raising an eyebrow as he did so. "Yard work."

"Yard work, huh?" Billy watched as Buddha rolled his eyes. "Quite the ambitious Saturday that you've got planned there."

Billy winked before hitting Buddha along the shoulder. "I'll buy you a dime bag if you help me out? Won't take much longer than a couple hours."

Buddha frowned, looking like he was pondering the offer. "How 'bout an eighth?"

Billy nibbled at his bottom lip as he considered the counteroffer. "Sure, you got it. Believe me, I know. Yard work sucks. And the last thing I want to do is take advantage of your labor there, pal."

"Hey man, you know I ain't gonna say no to some free grass. Well, free enough, right?" Billy smiled, patting his old friend along the back with a playful slap.

"My man."

Deciding to knock out some games of Q*bert on the ColecoVision, Billy let Buddha go first as the front door swung wide open, laughter and loud voices suddenly filling the main room. *Oh great*, Billy thought, rolling his eyes as a handful of their friends came trudging in from the bar, looking to continue the party at his place. *The drunks have arrived.* Though he wasn't in the mood for some big post-bar after party tonight, Billy forgot that he told Larry it was cool if they wanted to swing by later. An offer he was immediately regretting.

"Heyyyyyy, buddyyyy!!" Larry shouted, stomping into the main room as though shot out of a cannon, drinking from an open bottle of Asti Spumante, wildly waving it around as random suds spilled all over Billy's carpet. Decked out in his signature Hawaiian shirt and a pair of yellow tinted aviator sunglasses, he wrapped his ape sized arms around Billy in a playful bear hug, lifting him straight off the couch while spilling even more of his cheap champagne all over the furniture in the process. The little orange Q*bert character went flying off the edge of the pyramid of three-dimensional cubes on the screen as Larry—clearly *plastered*—slammed Billy down sideways into the couch cushions.

"Dude, what the *fuck*? You just killed my last guy!"

"Come on man, don't be a homo. Turn off the fucking video games, it's time to party!"

"Alright, alright man. Jesus Christ, get off me!"

Pushing himself off the couch and straightening his shirt, Billy noticed that Larry had some cute little Asian girl in tow that couldn't have been any older than eighteen or nineteen years old. *What the fuck do these girls see in this neanderthal?* She was clearly well out of his league. Not to mention, being that Larry was now twenty-six and owned his own plumbing business, where did he even meet these girls that looked like they were fresh out of high school?

A few seconds later, Stephanie and Karen come strolling in with a full bottle of Bacardi and a two liter of Pepsi, yapping away about some weirdo at the bar that kept going out on the dance floor and doing the worm. Though clearly a bit sluggish from all the weed he'd smoked earlier, Billy couldn't help but notice Buddha suddenly perk up the moment he saw Karen. He had always carried a bit of a thing for Karen. Yet at the same time, he knew that he didn't really have a shot with someone of her caliber. While he was hanging out at the arcade with a bunch of geeks dressed in black trench coats, she had a fake ID and was already hanging out with college guys. He had to give it to Buddha, though. The guy gave it the ole college try a few times, accepting it quite well each and every time she shot him down.

Yet oddly enough, as their usual crew of friends piled into his house to continue their Friday night celebration, Diane, once again, was nowhere to be seen.

Reluctantly shutting off the ColecoVision and joining the small soiree forming around the kitchen, Billy grabbed another cold one and lazily cracked it open. Commanding the room as he often did, Larry began into some story of drunken debauchery where the night ended with some girl puking all over him while they were having sex.

Rolling his eyes as the rest of the kitchen roared with laughter, Billy ducked down the hallway to go take a leak. His eyes felt tired and stingy, his body just not feeling up to it. Though it was one of his favorite things in the world, the last thing Billy wanted at that moment was another beer. After zipping himself up and flushing the toilet, he washed his hands, wondering how much longer he could live like this.

Sure, he loved to have a good time as much as the next guy, but it was all starting to become a bit too much. The party life, night in and night out, was beginning to wear him down. Yeah, Billy Baxton could still suck down a good six pack or more each night and function just fine the next day if he got enough sleep, but it had become tiresome and routine. All of it. Every weekend it was the same thing: everybody would come over and pre-drink before they all headed off to the bar. After the bar, they would all head back for after hours. Saturday morning, he and Buddha would stroll out of bed somewhere close to noon, order some carry out, watch a movie, take a nap, get up, shower, and get ready to do it all over again. So yes, the whole thing—as fun as it was for a few years there—became incredibly exhausting.

Sure, the apartment days were a blast, but this was his house now. His property. His investment. He was a homeowner, for God-sakes. He didn't want to have to tip toe over passed out overnight guests, knocked over ashtrays, and crushed beer cans on Sunday mornings anymore. He wanted to relax, have a cup of coffee, maybe read the morning paper before embarking on a day of productivity. This was his place now. His escape. His serenity. Yet since he moved in and tried fixing up the place, their circle of friends conspired to make it their new party spot while trashing and disrespecting the place each and every weekend. A plan that was starting to *get really* old, *really* quick.

Deciding to nip it in the bud before karma caught up with him in the morning, he fished a bottle of aspirin from the cluttered medicine cabinet, tapping a couple into the palm of his hand before washing them down with some warm water. Letting out a deep breath, he carefully examined himself in the mirror. He looked tired. Drained. His eyes were bloodshot. His face, pale and older than it normally looked. Though there was a room full of friends out there all revved up and ready to go, he just wasn't feeling it. He'd let the party rage on for now, but he didn't want any part of it. It was time to call it a night. Time to sneak off to his bedroom, watch a bit of TV, and drift into dreamland. Tomorrow was another day, and the secret room and the mystery behind it awaited him.

Walking from the bathroom to his bedroom, he could hear Larry from the kitchen doing his best Mr. T impression followed by a bunch of giggling laughter. "I pity the foo who don't do a shot with me!"

Billy rolled his eyes as he gently shut his bedroom door, slightly bothered once again that Diane was still out and about doing who knows what while most of their friends were there. Shit, they were *dating* now. She was technically his *girlfriend*. So, the question remained: what the hell was going on with her and why was she so distant all of a sudden? Whatever it was, he kept telling himself that she was skating on thin ice, knowing that if this thing didn't work out this time, it was on her.

After setting a glass of water down that he filled in the bathroom, he allowed his tired body to free fall onto the bed like a cut down tree. As his bouncing mattress came to a rest, he fluffed up the pillow beneath his head to make himself comfortable. Snatching the brick sized remote off his nightstand, he flicked on the cable and found some story on 20/20 about a Satanic cult down in Ohio that murdered an entire family in some small, rural farming town. The story was pretty wild, but he could feel himself fading fast, his eyelids growing heavier by the second. Within minutes of turning the TV on, Billy Baxton was fast asleep.

Hours later, he woke up to find himself laying on top of his bed while still in his clothes.

A soft blue light from the television filled the room. The muffled sound of laughter and conversation beyond his bedroom door vanished. The house, finally, was nice and quiet. Though his head was okay from the aspirin, his mouth was sticky with thirst. He took a drink from the glass of water still sitting along the nightstand and slowly got up.

Shuffling slowly down the length of the dark hallway with the speed of a slug, he could hear that the television in the main room was on. He turned the corner to find Diane sipping a glass of wine while watching MTV, her foot nervously tapping up and down upon the floor. She sniffled as she shot her head in his direction, quick and attentive with the sharp movements of a nervous bird.

"Hey babe, what's up," she asked, chewing nervously at her bottom lip.

"Not much," Billy answered as he yawned, rubbing at his tired eyes. "Didn't know that you were here. I'm just gonna make sure that everything's locked up for the night."

"Cool. Sorry that I missed you tonight. By the time we left the bar and got back here, you were already in bed. I'm just watching a little TV before I call it a night. I'll see you in there in a little bit."

Billy hunched his shoulders as if to show that he was seriously indifferent to it all. "Cool."

After making sure that the front door was locked, he checked the door wall along the kitchen and locked up the back door as well. Empty bottles, beer cans, Taco Bell wrappers, Big Gulp cups, Mountain Dew bottles filled with dip spit, and discarded cigarette packs littered every visible inch of the kitchen table and counters. Letting out a tired sigh as he strolled past the cluttered mess, he noticed from the top of the stairs that there were lights still on in the basement.

After trudging slowly step by step down the creaking stairs, he turned off the Pac-Man machine, killed the basement lights from the dimmer switches, and headed into the walk-in closet to turn off the lamp that was still on in the newly discovered room. Stepping over small piles of scattered bricks and random chunks of broken up cement, he walked over to Buddha's lamp as it sat there buzzing softly in the corner. Reaching down to click off the circular shaped knob along the lamp's shaft, he caught a quick flicker of movement from the corner of his eye.

What the hell? It came from the black mirror, yet how is that possible? He turned to find it hanging there elegantly in its beautiful silver frame along the far brick wall, nothing moved or out of place.

Yet once he stepped closer, he saw it again; subtle and lightning quick, like a tiny wave rippling its way across the mirror's glass surface as though it were composed of liquid. *What the hell was that?* Billy rubbed at his drunken, tired eyes, stepping in closer while convinced that it must have been a flicker of light reflecting off the glass. That, or he seriously needed to lay off the bottle for a while and dry his head out.

But right then, while standing there and questioning whether he had seen anything at all, he saw it again—a quick, fluid movement that was undeniable. Only this time, it wasn't a trick caused by the lighting or some strange reflection. Something definitely moved within the black glass of that mirror. It was as though something was swimming amongst its darkness right beneath its surface. Like a fish, thrashing about beneath the dark waters of a murky lake. But how? he wondered. How is that even possible? Stepping even closer now as he gradually reached his hand out, he half expected to touch the wetness of a liquid surface as his fingers got within inches of that strange, black glass.

But it wasn't at all. It was hard and solid, just as it should be. Billy slowly ran his fingers along its smooth surface, staring into its heavy blackness as he waited for its texture and consistency to change again. But it never did. Yet as the tips of his fingers continued to gradually travel the surface of the black glass, he began to feel that unusual heat coming off it. It was much like he experienced with the wall— soothingly warm, magically trickling its way through his fingertips and into his hands.

Scared and a bit surprised, Billy slowly pulled away, rubbing his fingers softly together as he could still feel that warmth continuing though his arm. *What the hell is this thing? Where the fuck did it come from?*

A little spooked by the strangeness of it all and wondering if he lost his marbles, he finally turned off the lights, shut the closet door behind him, and headed off to bed. As he laid there, teetering on the edge of a half sleep and a hard slumber, he began to dream. Like the fluid-like movements he had seen within the darkness of the black mirror, strange textures and images began to slither and slide their way into the world of his subconscious, wandering mind. He could see flesh; wet, glistening, and pink as it curled and squirmed into a series of strange, rolling waves. Rows of tiny teeth began to move in unison as thousands of small tentacles swam and swayed amongst a dark, purple liquid that was coming from everywhere. As his mind fell faster into a heavy sleep, he drifted further toward something not of this world. Something fantastic. Something grotesque. Yet, at the same time, something so very, very beautiful.

CHAPTER 11

"Dude, how long have you been going at that for?" Buddha was leaning against the kitchen counter, munching away on a piece of cold pizza as he caught Billy at the top of the basement stairs with a bucket full of bricks. Billy smiled as he put the orange plastic paint bucket down for a second, wiping the sweat from his brow with the back of his forearm.

"Ehh, about a good hour or so now. I woke up around 8:30 and couldn't sleep. Figured I'd get started on cleaning up that room down there."

8:30? Buddha arched his eyebrows and nodded, impressed with his buddy's sudden burst of ambition so early on a Saturday morning.

"Shit," he said, taking a swing from a carton of orange juice sitting along the counter. "You're making me feel like a lazy ass. You need any help?"

Billy's face twisted in disgust, watching Buddha's lips curled around the unfolded top of the orange juice carton. "Dude, don't drink straight from the carton, you filthy animal. I drink out of that too, ya know."

"Shit, sorry man." Buddha smiled nervously, wiping his mouth with the back of his hand like a little kid. "So, what do ya say, you need a hand? There's still gotta be a shit load of bricks down there."

"Naw man, thanks, but I think I'm good. I've only got about another bucket or two left and then I'm gonna sweep the floor really quick. Save your energy for all that yard work that you and I are gonna tackle later."

About to step out the back door to drop off another load, Billy paused in the doorway, sticking his head back inside as his eyebrows crinkled inward. "Say, where's Diane at? Did she take off or is she still sleeping?"

"Naw, she's still crashed out. I don't think that she'll be up any time before noon. Noticed that she and Lisa were playing hockey pretty hard last night."

"Hockey?"

"Yeah man, you know? Snorting some blow? Doing some toot? The two of them were in and out of the bathroom all night after you went to bed. They were trying to be all sly about it, but it was pretty obvious what they were up to."

"Jesus Christ," Billy replied, shaking his head in disgust. "That shit is bougee, dude. It'll rot your brain, you know that?"

Buddha smiled, putting his hands up in defense as he arched his eyebrows. "Hey man, you don't need to tell me. I won't touch that shit. If it grows in the ground, then you know I'm down. But snort some snow up my nose? Fuck that! I'm pulling a Nancy Reagan on that shit and just saying no."

Billy cocked his head to the side with the rise of an eyebrow as if to say, really? "Dude, I'm pretty sure she meant marijuana too when she said that."

"Really? Oh, well fuck her then."

Billy laughed as he finally pushed open the back door with the bucket in tow. "You need some serious help, you know that?"

"You're right about that."

"Well, at least you're aware. Listen, I'll grab you when I'm ready, cool?"

Buddha gave him the thumbs up as Billy headed outside. "You got it."

Later, as the young men took to the yard to tackle the overgrown foliage that had overtaken the landscaping, the Indian summer heat beat down on them from a vibrant sky of cascade blue. At just a little past noon, their shirts were already wet with patches of sweet, the sun's rays feeling more like that of a late August day than the final days of September. After popping in a Huey Lewis and the News cassette tape into Billy's old boom-box, they went to work immediately. Buddha was on his hands and knees in the dirt pulling out weeds as Billy started trimming the hedges and bushes that stood about as tall as corn stalks along the front of the house.

About twenty minutes in, Diane came strolling outside with an unusually lackadaisical speed. A big pair of black Ray-Ban Wayfarers covered her eyes, looking like a Hollywood starlet strolling out into the sun. Yet far from some glamorous celebrity, she looked miserable. Clearly paying the painful price of her partying antics the night before—hangover 1, Diane 0.

Billy wiped his sweaty brow, smiling as he saw her walking down the driveway with the enthusiasm of a death row inmate being walked to the electric chair. "Morning, sunshine! Or should I say, good afternoon! How're we feeling today?"

She paused, sliding her shades down the length of her nose just a tad, casting a glare in his direction, not amused. "I feel like my head is going to fucking explode. Thanks."

"Sorry I fell asleep before you came over, babe. Sounds like you guys went hard last night, huh?"

"Umm, yeah," she replied with a sarcastic stab. She slowly shuffled her way towards her Honda Accord parked along the front curb, her overstuffed purse flung over her shoulder swinging lazily in rhythm with her zombie-like walk.

"Well, get some rest and give me a call later. I'm still down for getting some sushi tonight if you're up for it, cool?" Billy looked over at Buddha with a devious smirk while she wasn't looking, knowing damn well that he was pressing her buttons. *Shit*, he thought, watching her in all of her glorious misery, dealing with the after-effects of the prior night's festivities. *Serves her right for messing with that shit. Maybe she'll finally learn her lesson.*

"Yeah, well, the thought of sushi right now makes me want to puke."

"Hey, if you're not up for dinner later, maybe we could just do some apps and some drinks. Maybe some sake bombs or something."

Diane stopped dead in her tracks as she was about to get in her car, looking back at him with a disgusted look on her face. "Sake bombs? Seriously Billy, gag me with a spoon. Listen, I need to get home and lay down, alright. I'll give you a call later."

"Don't worry about it. Get some rest and I'll talk to you later."

"Later guys." With that, she moaned and groaned as she slid herself behind the wheel of her car before starting it up and taking off. Buddha started laughing, tossing a handful of weeds into a lawn bag as Billy just laughed and shook his head.

"What did I tell ya, dude. Devil's dandruff. That shit is bad news, brother. Bad news."

Over the next two hours, Buddha and Billy began to make some serious progress in the front yard. Dirty and dripping with sweat, they filled a good number of lawn bags with pulled weeds, old leaves, and all the fallen sticks and pieces of trimmed branches from the overgrown bushes along the front. As Billy carried the last of the overstuffed lawn bags to the curb for the Monday pickup, Leo—the old Italian guy who lived next door—came casually strolling down his driveway while trying to get their attention.

"How's it going, boys?" he asked with a smile, his signature stogie wedged between his teeth that looked tinted by years of coffee and cigar smoke. He was wearing an off-white golf shirt and checkered Bermuda shorts, his feet slid into a pair of leather slip-ons.

Billy watched as Leo waddled in his direction with the speed and dexterity of a penguin, smiling as he gave the old man a polite nod. "Hey, how's it going there, Leo?"

"Well, the joy stick's still working and the ole ticker ain't gone out yet, so I guess I'd say I'm doing okay!"

Billy laughed, dropping the bag of yard waste to the side of the curb, wiping the trickling beads of sweat from his face with the back of his arm. "Hey, it could be a hell of a lot worse, right?"

"You got that right, pal." Scratching at his protruding belly as he chomped softly along his cigar, he looked around at the work they did so far. "Wow, you guys are really getting this place whipped into shape."

Billy nodded, glancing at the progress that they made while fairly pleased with the results so far. "Well, we're trying to do what we can. Already got a fresh coat of paint on the exterior, now we're just trying to clean up the landscaping a bit." He rested his hands on his hips as he looked over at the old man and smiled. "A little bit at a time, ya know? Just trying to cross some things off the never-ending list."

He laughed with a joyful, raspy sounding chuckle, playing with the cigar as he chewed on it gently. "Well, I gotta say, you boys are doing a real hell of a job. The place looks great. Say, I hate to bug you when you guys are so busy, but would you fellas be able to give me a hand for just a few minutes? My son's coming over in a little bit to help me stain the back deck and I need some help getting the patio furniture moved."

"Sure, not a problem. Let me grab my roommate here and we'll get that taken care of for ya."

"Thanks pal, I appreciate that. I know that it'll only take a few minutes, but I got a cold one with your name on it once you boys are done."

"Hey, now you're speaking my language."

Furnished nicely with a beautiful wrought iron patio table and matching chairs, a newer looking umbrella, and a matching bench that ran along the far railing, the old guy had a pretty decent set-up in his backyard. And like he said, it hadn't taken much more than a few minutes for Billy and Buddha to move the outdoor furniture off the deck and onto the grass. A smaller radio sitting along the top railing blasted some classic rock tunes a few feet away from a can of Thompson's Water Seal and a couple of clean paint brushes. A gentle breeze came through as a set of wooden wind chimes hanging from the corner of the overhang played softly in the wind.

Taking a quick breather, Billy and Buddha took a seat along the deck's bottom step as the old man went to fetch some cold ones.

"Stay here a second, boys. I'll be right back." After disappearing inside through the screen door, Leo reappeared a minute later with a few cans of Strohs, still attached to the thin, plastic rings that once held together a full six pack. "Here ya go, boys. Grab a brew and relax for a second."

"Hey, a man after my own heart," Billy said as he caught the cold and slippery can that Leo tossed underhand his way. "Thanks Leo."

"Don't mention it, kid."

The three of them took a seat along the patio chairs now stationed about in a small circle along the lawn, each of them letting out tired sighs as they sat down. The cold beer tasted good, a much-needed break from the hours of sweaty yard work beneath the heat of the blistering sun. Billy scanned the perfectly blue sky overhead, taking a long pull of the beer as Leo leaned forward in his chair.

"So, how're you boys liking the new neighborhood? It looks like you guys have made some serious progress with that house. That yard was looking like the jungles of Vietnam before you fellas went to work on it."

"Shit, tell me about it. I don't need to tell you, but the place was in rough shape when I bought it. Just trying to do what we can to get the place looking up to par again." Billy let out a deep breath as he glanced next door at his house, happy with the progress so far, but knowing that they still had a long way to go.

Leo let out that raspy, rolling chuckle of his as he leaned back in his chair, his protruding belly shaking slightly as he laughed. "Well, it already looks ten times better than it ever did the entire time that kook job lived there. I mean, I know I shouldn't really say that with everything that happened to her, but that lady must have been allergic to yard work or something. In fact, I can't recall a single time I saw her out there working in the yard the entire time she lived there. Occasionally some sketchy looking guy driving an old truck would come by and cut the grass for her, but that was about it. I mean, she was an odd duck, that broad. A real odd duck."

Billy and Buddha looked over at each other at the same time, their eyes lighting up as they did so. They were suddenly intrigued, leaning forward and looking to find out more about this mysterious lady who used to own the house.

"An odd duck, huh? How so, Leo? What was her story?"

"Wow, that's a great question, kid. I didn't really know her, to tell you the truth. Like I said, she was an odd one to say the least. Pretty much kept to herself most of the time. Hell, I could probably count on one hand the number of times I actually talked to her. Not sure what drove her to take her own life like that, but I'm glad to see that a responsible guy like yourself came along and bought the place with everything that happened. I was starting to worry that the place was going to sit there abandoned for God knows how long."

"So, based on the few times that you met her, what was she like?"

"Well, she was just one of those people that gives off an odd vibe, you know? I mean, she was a real artsy-fartsy broad, always dressed head to toe in black, had really short, spiky black hair and what not. She even drove this real old, rusted out hippie looking bus that was falling apart. Everything about her was just a little different, ya know? Eccentric, I guess."

"Sounds like quite the interesting character," Billy added, taking a quick swig of his beer, intrigued by what he was hearing.

Leo chuckled again, easing back into his chair as he rubbed at the short gray stubble along the point of his chin. "Yeah, you could say that, Billy! She was about as weird as you get. I think her name was Ann or Anna, something like that. Like I said, she really kept to herself, didn't talk much with the other neighbors at all. Oh, and get this," he said, leaning in even closer now as the bit of a smirk formed on the corner of his mouth. "I even caught her and a couple other people one night butt-naked out in the backyard right over there. I came out to have a cigar and thought that I was seeing things. At first, I thought she was just having a small bonfire in the backyard with a couple of friends. But when I stepped down off my deck and got a better look, I noticed that none of them were wearing any clothes. There were about three or four of them and they were all standing around the fire with their arms all raised up to the sky and what not, doing who knows what. It was one of the strangest damn things, I tell ya. I have never seen anything like it. But besides that one time, I don't think I ever saw her outside. Except for that, the place was usually really quiet."

"*Really?*" Billy's face suddenly twisted into a look of fascinated curiosity. He and Buddha looked over at each other a second before bringing their attention back to their new neighbor, clearly thinking the same thing. "So, wait, wait, let me get this all straight—they were all *naked* around a fire in the backyard over here?" He motioned with the beer in his hand toward his backyard on the other side of the fence as the three of them glanced over in the general direction that Leo was talking about.

"That's right, kid. Naked as a bunch of damn hippies at Woodstock. Don't ask me what the hell they were doing, though. Made me start thinking that she might be into some kind of witchcraft or something. Kind of made me think of that old Eagles song, *Witchy Woman.* I thought that maybe my imagination was running wild on me for a minute there, but nope, they were naked alright. I'm telling you boys, it was weird. One of the strangest things I've ever seen."

The gears inside of Billy's head started twisting and turning into overdrive. It was all starting to make sense. The hidden room closed off behind the brick wall. The strange markings and symbols drawn along the walls. And even that mysterious black mirror that hung along the far wall—all of it—pointing to the fact that the previous owner was dabbling into the world of the occult. Whether it was something Pagan, Wiccan, Satanic; who knew? But from what they were hearing, she was definitely into some form of witchcraft or black magic.

"Wow, that's really weird," Billy said, playing around with the metal tab along the top of his beer can, not really sure what to say.

"Tell me about it. I guess I could have called the cops considering it was technically public indecency, but then again, I don't want to go causing trouble for nobody. Ain't my business what folks want to do on their own time. It was just weird, that's all. It's not every day that you look outside to find a bunch of naked people standing around a bonfire in their backyard."

Billy laughed. "No, I guess not!" He stared off into space a moment, eventually bringing his attention back to Leo as he killed off what was left of his beer.

"So, that was the only time you ever saw anything like that next door?"

"Yeah, that was it. She was pretty quiet and private except for that. Unfortunately, that's probably the only good story I got for ya."

"And no idea why she went and killed herself, huh?"

Leo frowned, hunching his shoulders as if to throw out a guess or a stab in the dark. "Depression? Mental illness? Who knows? I heard from Clark Davis over there across the street that the police were there one night when I was gone, but that's all I really know. Shortly after the people from the bank came and slapped the paperwork on the door, I heard from Janet on the other side of me that she had gone and killed herself. I guess her sister hadn't heard back from her in days and found her when she came over to check on her. Couldn't believe it. But besides all that, it's a real quiet neighborhood. Been here for about thirty years and that's the first thing that's ever happened around here like that. For the most part, it's a great place to start a family, raise your kids; the whole nine yards."

Billy glanced back at his new house, his thoughts branching off into a million different directions. It was then that he heard a sound off to his left, turning to find Leo's son sliding open the screen door and stepping out onto the back deck.

"Hey, there he is!" Leo barked with a beaming smile, turning to face his son as he walked down to greet his old man. "Ready to help me slap down some stain on this dinosaur of a deck back here?"

"Hey, ready when you are, pop. I see that you've already cracked open some beers." Coming over and giving his dad a hug with a playful slap on the back, he turned to make his introduction to Billy and Buddha.

"Hey Tony, I want you to meet Billy, my new neighbor that just bought the house next door. Billy, this is my son, Tony."

"Hey, Billy, nice to meet you."

"Nice to meet you too, Tony." The two smiled and shook hands as Leo directed his attention toward Buddha.

"And this here is Billy's roommate . . . umm . . . oh shoot, I'm sorry pal, I forgot your name again."

"Buddha."

"Oh yeah, that's right. Buddha. How could I forget a screwy name like that? What are you, a Buddhist or something?"

"Naw, nothing like that. It's just a nickname that stuck. Long story, I'll tell you some other time."

"Well, you'll have to fill me in on that. Listen, it was nice chatting with ya fellas and thanks for the help. Oh, and keep up the good work on that house. The place is looking great!"

"Hey, not a problem," Billy said, stepping out of their way so that they could get to it. "Thanks again for the beer, Leo. We'll see ya around."

"Hey, don't mention it fellas," he said with a nonchalant wave of his hand. "Just get back to work and make sure that jungle doesn't spring back to life on ya, alright."

Billy and Buddha laughed and said their goodbyes as they made their way back to the house.

"Did you hear that?" Buddha whispered, leaning close to Billy to ensure that he wasn't being too loud. "This thing is even weirder than we thought! Sounds like our hunch was right about the previous owner. I'd bet my stash of grass and my VHS collection that the woman was knees deep into some sort of voodoo or black magic or some shit. I mean, it's the only explanation there could be for all this shit, right?"

"Exactly! I mean, what else could it be? It's all starting to make sense now."

Chapter 11

"When we hit up the library tomorrow, I bet we're bound to find out something more about this house or that weird lady that used to live here."

"Oh yeah," Billy replied, nodding confidently. "We're gonna find out more about this house, alright. We're gonna find out a *whole* lot more!"

CHAPTER 12

As the Indian summer temperatures from yesterday gave way to a bunch of cold and rain, Billy Baxton found himself holed up in the Southfield Library's microfilm room. Shifting through articles, documents, and public records, flashing past the rectangular screen like the illuminated windows of a speeding subway train, he decided to take a break. Leaning back into his chair, he rubbed at his tired eyes while taking a sip from a Styrofoam cup of coffee; his brain rattling restlessly.

Having scanned through pages upon countless pages of information—most of it useless—Billy felt like he was running in circles. Rubbing his temples gently with the pads of his fingertips while listening to the gentle hum of the fluorescent lights overhead and the pattering of raindrops against the window, he felt defeated. No closer to solving the mystery than he had been on day one. He felt like one of those gerbils on a plastic wheel, spinning feverishly with that ambitious exertion while getting nowhere fast.

Shit, he thought, leaning back even further in his chair as he crossed his legs and rested his hands behind his head, gazing at the dull white ceiling as though it contained some kind of answer to this crazy puzzle. *Maybe Buddha is right. Maybe we need to look into hiring some kind of paranormal experts that might know more about those cryptic symbols scribbled on the wall along with the strange black mirror. At this rate, it seems to be the best option.*

Heading home from hours of a wasted search, his windshield wipers barely kept up with the torrential downpour as the afternoon grew darker and drearier. Some band called Soft Cell was singing about a tainted love over the car's speakers. It was a terrible recording, coming in all scratchy as it whirled about in the car's old tape deck. It was a mixtape that Diane made him, more of that shitty new wave stuff that her and her friends always listened to. She loved that stuff, and Buddha did, too. Hell, he couldn't get enough of it. He absolutely swore by that shit.

But for some reason, Billy just couldn't get into it. He preferred to rock out to bands like Rush, Motley Crüe, Van Halen, or AC/DC any day over those gay-ass, synthesizer pop bands.

Distracted by the music as he tried to think, he turned off the radio and began racking his brain on who they could even call to look into such a thing. *A psychic? A medium? A paranormal researcher? Someone who's an expert on ancient symbols that works over at the local community college?* It was a shot in the dark as to who would be their best option, not to mention, how much hiring a professional like that would even cost. He and Buddha weren't exactly the Rockefellers, and some kind of a budget on all of this would definitely have to be figured out.

Parking his car in the driveway and heading inside the house, he found Buddha in the main room smoking a joint and watching MTV. Though normally cool as a cucumber, slumped into the couch as though he planted roots into the thing, he appeared nervous and rattled.

Billy thought he spotted trepidation in his eyes, sitting there along the edge of the couch, his foot rapidly tapping up and down all fidgety. Billy tossed his keys to the coffee table and took a seat, Buddha immediately spinning in his direction, wild eyed and frantic looking.

"Whoa man, what's going on with you?"

"Dude, we've gotta get rid of that thing. We've gotta get rid of the mirror, man. It's evil, man, it's some kind of a port—"

"Whoa, whoa, slow down buddy," Billy interjected as he put up his hands, doing his best to calm the guy down, clearly shaken up over something. "What's going on, man? What happened?"

Buddha tapped the ash from the tip of the joint into the glass ashtray as he took a deep breath. He stared at Billy with a look of absolute panic in his eyes. Billy could tell that whatever it was, it was nothing to scoff at. If there was one thing that he knew about Buddha, the guy sure didn't scare easily. This was the same guy who was watching old 70's slasher movies back in middle school when most kids were watching *Smokey and the Bandit* or *Blazing Saddles*. While other guys in high school were meeting up at the Burger King parking lot on Friday and Saturday night, hoping to find out where the party was at, Buddha and his circle of buddies were breaking into old abandoned mental hospitals, daring each other to wander their dark, desolate corridors armed only with a flashlight. So yeah, if he knew his old buddy Buddha, something significant had *definitely* happened to rattle his cage like this. And if Billy were to guess, it had something to do with the black mirror.

"I saw something, Billy. I swear man, I saw something inside that mirror's glass down there. I saw it move! It was fluid and quick, like a snake slithering right beneath the surface of some dark lake. Dude, I know it sounds crazy, but the glass *moved*. There's something supernatural about that thing, dude. It ain't right, man. It's fucking dark-sided, brother . . . it's evil!"

After talking his buddy down off the ledge, calmly assuring him that he too had seen things within the darkness of that strange black glass, he sat down beside him on the couch, placing a comforting hand along his shoulder as he looked him straight in the eye.

"Buddha, listen. Listen man, this is what's going on and this is what we're gonna do. Now, yes, there's definitely something strange and supernatural about that black mirror down there. We know this. We've seen it. So, what I'm going to do is hire a professional paranormal investigator to come in and take a look at that thing. Take a look at that whole room—"

But before Billy could finish, Buddha started vigorously shaking his head back and forth as he raised his hands up in defense. "No, no, no, no, we need to get rid of that thing, dude. We need to get rid of it immediately. That room was blocked off for a reason. It's evil, man, it's gotta go!"

"*Buddha!*" he snapped, firmly planting the palms of his hands on his roommate's shoulders. It was time to assure him as he always did that ole Billy Baxton had this thing under control. "Dude, it's going to be alright. Just listen to me for a minute. I know this is gonna sound crazy, but just listen."

Baxton took a deep breath before he started in again, keeping his delivery calm and calculated. "I saw them, Buddha. I saw them, too. I mean, I know it's crazy, but I've witnessed things in that mirror that I can't explain, either. Sometimes when I stare into its black surface, I don't just see things floating and swimming around in there, but I can sometimes actually see another world beyond our own. Now, if this thing is as magical and supernatural as you and I both think it is, then who knows what we're sitting on here. We may have discovered something huge here, buddy. Something historical, something *monumental*. And to find out, we need to get some expert opinions here. We need to hire a psychic . . . possibly a ghost chaser or some kind of paranormal researcher . . ."

"You mean like the Ghostbusters, dude?" Billy almost broke out laughing, but quickly held it together upon spotting the serious expression along Buddha's face. He had to snap his buddy out of it and do it quickly. Getting him on board with hiring a professional to give them some insight into what exactly they stumbled upon here was now priority number one. Otherwise, Buddha might get rid of the mirror behind his back. And Billy couldn't allow that to happen. The mirror clearly possessed some kind of magic; something beyond the grasp of their understanding. And until they consulted with an outside expert opinion on what this thing could be, simply getting rid of it just wasn't an option. It was his house after all. And from here on out, he'd be the one who calls the shots.

After bringing Buddha's boil of anxiety down to a controlled simmer, Billy got up, grabbed a *Yellow Pages* from one of the drawers in the kitchen, and dropped it down on the coffee table in front of Buddha.

"What do you say, buddy? Before we jump to conclusions, let's let our fingers do the walking. We need to find out what the hell we're dealing with here. If we can't find out anything about it, then fuck it, we'll get rid of the thing. We'll trash it. Smash it. Shit, we can even drive all the way up north and bury it in the woods if we have to. But for right now, where we're at with this thing, let's do this. Let's get a professional that knows a hell of a lot more about this witchy woman, dancing naked in the moonlight shit then we do. Let's find out what those markings on the walls down there mean, and let's find out what the hell this black mirror thing is, okay? What do you say, buddy? Are you with me?"

Buddha leaned forward, staring at the *Yellow Pages* as he bit nervously at his bottom lip. Resting his elbows along his knees, they bounced up and down in rhythm with his nervous energy. "Yeah man, sure." he replied, a shaky quiver of reluctance in his voice, nodding confidently though there was still fear in his eyes. "Let's do it."

CHAPTER 13

After sitting down with a notebook and a big, fat copy of the *Yellow Pages*, Billy and Buddha pounded out a good-sized list of names and numbers for psychic cleansers, clairvoyants, mediums, religious investigators, ghost hunters, and even a few field parapsychologists. Now the question remained—what type of professional should they call first? And not only that, but how much was all of this going to cost?

Billy leaned back in his office chair at work the next day, tapping his pencil against a pad of paper as he studied the list. He let out a long yawn as he caught a string of drool almost falling from the corner of his mouth, fighting off a late afternoon fatigue that hit him like a wall. He slid off the headphones from his Sony Walkman as he took another swig of lukewarm coffee from his orange Garfield mug. It was his third cup of the day, and it was barely doing the trick. He was dragging, wishing more than anything that he was back in bed.

Sleep the night before was sporadic at best, those familiar images within the black mirror swirling and dancing about his dreams with a vivid relentlessness that wouldn't let go. They were haunting. Grotesque and terrifying. Yet at the same time, absolutely fantastic.

Snapping himself out of drifting into yet another daydream, he slugged back his coffee, slid his earphones back on, and buckled down for the last few hours of the day. Managing to make his way through a pointless sales meeting, a scheduled customer-call on some upcoming projects, and a drawn out conversation with Tammy from accounting—who had a horrible habit of reeling you into the longest, most meaningless stories—5:00 finally arrived and Billy flew out the door like David Lee Roth leaping across the stage.

Chapter 13

Glancing at the notebook as it sat along the passenger seat beside him, he was anxious to get home and start getting some quotes. He tried to cross a few of them off the list during his lunch break, speaking as softly as he could to avoid the ever-curious eavesdroppers within the office's connecting cube farm. But try as he did, it was a bit tough giving the details of their newly acquired haunted heirloom that they found in that secret room in the basement without sounding like he completely lost his marbles.

As he pulled into the driveway, he could see that Buddha's car wasn't there. Though he normally came home a little after five to find the guy already camped out on the couch watching TV, it looked like he was actually out doing something after work. Billy figured that he was out somewhere with Roger, Joel, or one of those other weirdos that he still hung out with from time to time. They were likely playing video games down at the mall's arcade or chain-smoking cigarettes at the local Denny's, talking about Star Wars and their Depeche Mode tapes. Either way, it allowed for a quiet house, giving him the opportunity to zero in, focus and knock out some of these calls.

As he parked his car and walked up to the door, an orange cat came slinking slowly out of the bushes, rubbing itself along the bottom of his legs while Billy tried to get his key into the door. "Hey, get out of here!" Billy hissed, kicking his foot softly in the cat's direction, doing his best to scare away the roaming feline that had been lurking around his house as of late. "Go on, now. Get!" The cat slinked away from him, eventually darting off across the driveway and into Leo's bushes next door.

"Stupid cat," he whispered beneath his breath, shutting the door behind him as he tossed his keys along the kitchen table. Grabbing a beer from the fridge and cracking it open, he tossed the notebook with his list of contacts on the kitchen table; grabbed the *Yellow Pages* bookmarked with a bunch of multi-colored sticky notes and sat down to make some calls.

In doing so, he quickly noticed that the low, revving, vibration sound was back. It was once again coming from somewhere below his feet. It started with a low humming sound; a bass- filled rumble barely audible at first, eventually causing everything in the kitchen to start buzzing and vibrating to life. Billy froze, listening intently as he watched the basement stairs.

What the hell was that, Billy thought, feeling his hands instinctively grabbing for the edges of the table. After a few seconds the vibrations increased substantially with an even greater intensity, eventually building until it was literally shaking Billy's can of beer across the table in front of him.

"What the fuck?"

Clearly coming from somewhere down in the basement, he got up and grabbed one of his old baseball bats from the closet and hesitantly started heading down the basement stairs. *Jesus*, he thought, wondering why the hell he was heading into the basement instead of running out the front door. *Just what the hell are you going to do with a baseball bat Billy-boy if this thing really is possessed by some dark, powerful force not of this world? Treat it like a well-placed fast ball and swing for the fences? Damn, you really do need to have your head examined.*

Refusing to listen to the inner monologue of his head, he reluctantly crept down the stairs slow and steady, one careful step at a time. The baseball bat felt slippery and loose within his sweaty grip. His heart was thumping faster now as a queasy flutter of unease whirled about the pit of his stomach. As the growing fear as to what he might find within the darkness of the mirror's surface began to build, so did the compulsion to investigate; that low and steady rumble in the belly of the basement commanding and luring him forward with each and every step of the way.

Reaching the bottom of the stairs, that low, rumbling hum seemed to increase in both volume and force before falling again into a low and steady rumble. Its intensity kept peaking and plunging like a wave, steadily stepping closer to the closet door with a fear-infused hesitation. He could feel the vibrations traveling through the floor, so strong that they were oscillating upward into his feet and the bottom half of his legs. While gripping the slippery wood of the baseball bat in his right hand, he slowly reached for the closet door with his left, hesitantly turning its knob within the feeble grasp of his trembling fingers. Finally locating a decent grip along the smooth knob, he slowly pulled the door open. Meekly stepping inside, he began to travel past the threshold of the closet door and eventually into the secret, hidden room.

Stepping carefully into the cold darkness of the room, his eyes remained glued on the mysterious black mirror, sitting there in its usual spot along the far wall. Like something possessing a life of its own, the black glass within the border of its elaborately decorated frame steadily rose and fell as if it were breathing, sending a trickling chill dancing along Billy's skin.

Momentarily hypnotized by its movement, the rumble of the vibrations began to rise and fall in succession with the steady "breathing" within the mirror's darkness, continuing to defy the rules of space and time. Billy watched with an inquisitive gaze as its color began to change from black to dark purple. It then faded to several lighter shades of purple, then to blue, green, orange, and finally red; eventually fading back to black as it continued to pulsate invariably through the various colors of the spectrum.

His free will and his mind no longer his own, the power of the mirror somehow seduced him into slowly lowering his arms. The baseball bat fell from his slippery grip, its weight sending it clanging against the cement floor below. As the colors continued to pulsate and morph into different shades, a warmth began to emulate once again from the center of the mirror as it had the other night. A warmth that bled a comfort beyond that of anything known to man.

Whatever it was, Billy was immediately deemed powerless against it, victim to the sedative state that its hypnotic grip bestowed upon him. Standing just a few feet from the mirror—that golden blanket of majestic pleasure now tingling and running like an electrical current throughout his entire body—he slowly reached forward, the tips of his fingers now only inches away from the ever-changing colors of fantastic light. In doing so, Billy watched in astonishment as the very molecules of his fingers seemed to slowly disengage from his hand, dancing and swirling about in the air like miniature bees buzzing in a synchronized pattern. He marveled at the thousands of tiny flesh-colored orbs that once made up his hand as they began to swim and spiral through the air in a corkscrew-like pattern. He watched helplessly as it defied the laws of physics, an indescribable tingling of heat now traveling up the length of his arm, into his shoulder, all while eventually engulfing the rest of his body.

And as he continued to gaze deep into the mirror's center, he was granted a glimpse of something so glorious, so stunning, his imagination would cripple in its feeble attempt to conjure anything comparable. It was a glimpse of something utopian—a whole new world beyond their own, existing somewhere between the cracks in frequencies of the universe. It was dazzling. Astonishing. Like nothing he had ever fathomed. It felt like he was blindly punched in the chest, his breath escaping him in a sudden gasp, like the air rushing from the bladder of a saturated balloon. It was—simply put—the most beautiful thing that he had ever seen.

CHAPTER 14

After checking out the new Indiana Jones flick straight after work with Roger and their friend Stacy, Buddha came home to find that Billy wasn't home. Though his Grand Prix sat parked in the driveway, the house was completely dark, and the back door was left unlocked.

Thinking nothing of it, Buddha let himself in and found an opened *Yellow Pages* sprawled across the kitchen table next to a notebook where Billy had begun a list of paranormal investigators to call. The encyclopedia sized *Yellow Pages* was carefully book marked in multiple places with different colored sticky notes. Next to this makeshift work area, an open can of Budweiser sat along the table. Running his finger gently along the scribbled-out list of names and numbers of clairvoyants and paranormal researchers, he lifted the beer can and shook it lightly to find that it was nearly full. He frowned, placing the can of beer back on the table as he glanced about the room. *Well, that's weird*, Buddha thought, gently running his fingers along his chin, wondering what would have caused him to leave in such a hurry that he left a full beer. *Something feels off. . . something's not right . . .*

But for every bizarre situation there was always a reasonable explanation behind it all, right? Technically, it was quite possible that Diane came by after work, and they spontaneously headed out somewhere. A movie? A bite to eat? A bar to grab a drink? Bowling? But even if she had, why did he leave a full beer like that? Billy, of all people, was never one to waste a beer. Not to mention, even if he had popped it open right before she got there to pick him up, he was never one to shy away from grabbing a roadie to go. There could have been a million reasons why the door was left open—by accident, or, maybe on purpose if they were planning on coming right back; especially if they left right around the same time Buddha normally came home from work while knowing full well that he'd be there any minute. But the full beer thing? Now *that* didn't make any sense.

Deciding that his mind was wandering to ridiculous conclusions when everything was probably just fine, he plopped down into his concave spot along the old couch, picked up the clunky remote sitting along the cushion beside him, and turned on the ole boob tube. Leaning forward for his wooden cigar box sitting along the coffee table so that he could commence with his daily ritual, the front door suddenly flew open as it smacked against the wall behind it, scaring the living shit out of him in the process.

"Yo, what's up homos?" Diane Zajnecki shouted, bounding into the front room with a bottle of red in hand, dropping her purse along the couch as she strutted her way into the kitchen.

Sliding her keys across the counter, she started rifling through the kitchen cupboards, looking for a bottle opener or a wine glass. She looked back toward Buddha with her head tilted sideways, chomping on a piece of bright green gum with a confused look on her face. "Like, where do you guys keep your wine glasses again? I forgot. Oh, and I'll need a corkscrew, too."

Buddha paused for a moment, sitting there with his mouth slightly open, his brow flexed as though in the midst of a deep thought that struggled to find its way to the surface. "Hey, uhhh, is . . . is Billy with you?"

"Does he *look* like he's with me? No dude, I thought he was here. That's why I came over. Why, is he not home?"

"Uhhhh, no. No, he's not here. I just got back from the movies a little while ago, and he wasn't home. I assumed he was with you. The house was dark, the back door was unlocked, but I have no idea where he's at. He didn't leave a note or anything like that."

"Are you serious? We were supposed to watch a movie tonight. He told me to meet him here around nine and then we were gonna head out to Blockbuster to rent something. Are you sure he didn't leave a note or anything?"

Buddha got up and scanned the counter again, wondering if he missed one somewhere in the midst of all the clutter. He even looked around the kitchen floor, wondering if a small post-it note might have fallen from the counter and fluttered its way to the floor accidentally.

"Nope. Nothing. For a second, I thought that maybe his parents stopped by to take him out to eat or something, but that wouldn't make sense if he already had plans with you. Not to mention, his parents are up north right now, so that's definitely out of the question."

"Hmmm," she said, leaning into the counter with a perplexed look on her face. "That is kind of weird. Especially since his car is here and he knew that I'd be coming over. Maybe he walked up to the corner store to grab some beer or something?"

"Possibly. There's a 7-11 that's literally a quarter mile down the road, we walk down there all the time."

"Holy shit," She shrieked, instinctively grabbing the kitchen counter with both hands as the kitchen once again began to vibrate to life. *What the hell is that? Construction nearby? An earthquake? Thunder?* Her brain riffled through any reasonable explanation she could conjure, the flesh along her knuckles turning white with exertion as she stared across the kitchen at Buddha. "What the hell is that?"

Bracing himself against the doorway as his eyes started darting frantically about the room, he yelled back at her, "Fuck if I know!"

There was a deep, roaring rumble like an engine churning to life, joined by waves of powerful vibrations seemingly from somewhere downstairs. They watched as what felt like a ferocious earthquake began to rattle and jostle the contents of items along the kitchen counters.

Empty beer cans, dirty plates, and scattered junk mail fluttered and danced along the counter's surface, some of which toppled and fell to the floor below.

And then, just as quickly as it started, it abruptly ceased. "*What* in the living hell was *that*?"

Buddha stared at Diane as though he just saw a ghost manifest itself before him. His usually olive-colored, Asian skin was suddenly white as a sheet, a sheen of sweat forming across his forehead. "I don't know."

And right then, it started happening again. Only this time, the vibrations were much more reserved while that low, deep rumbling hum began to sound again; coming and going in ample waves as the windows began to shake within their old, rickety frames.

"Whatever the hell that is, it's coming from the basement!" Dianne shouted, looking toward Buddha as if he would know what to do.

But the truth was, he didn't. He never did. He always left that up to Billy, looking to him to grab the reins and take the lead during times of mounting pressure. But the truth was, Billy wasn't there, and it was time to buck up. Glancing frantically about the kitchen, he looked back at Diane, deciding that they might as well go down there and check it out.

"Well, there's only one way to find out. Come on. Let's go see what the hell is going on."

As they raced down the basement stairs—Buddha reluctantly taking the lead—the tremors that seemed to originate from the base of the home continued to come and go now in short, reverberating waves.

"It's coming from over there," she said, pointing toward the cedar closet leading toward the newly discovered room; a room that Buddha wished Billy never discovered in the first place. The two of them slowly approached the closet door as a soft, green light spilled forth from beyond its open gap in a subtle wave of steady pulsations. Hesitantly turning the corner and pushing the door open even further, they gradually peered inside.

They could see the black mirror along the far wall, its black glass pulsating up and down as though coming to life; taking on a dark green color as it rose, eventually fading back to black as it seemed to ease back into its normal, flat surface.

"What the *fuck?*" Diane slowly looked over at Buddha, her eyes looking like they might pop right out of her skull. Taking a few steps further into the room, they stood frozen before the mirror, eyes wide with wonder and disbelief, struggling to understand what exactly it was that they were witnessing. Though any sense of logic and reason should have told them to turn and run, they couldn't move. They stood transfixed, compelled and mesmerized by what they were witnessing as the "breathing" within the mirror's darkness began to increase in frequency, the green light within its black center becoming brighter as the growling hum grew progressively louder.

And then, quite unexpectedly, there was a brilliant flash of light. The brilliance of its intensity was so great against the dark backdrop of the dingy basement room, they instinctively shielded their eyes. They began to back away from the mirror as a powerful gust of wind came blowing forth from the center of its surface. It was gleaming now with a brilliant green light that was so intense, it almost looked white. As its color quickly faded again back to a dark green, the magical wind that gusted forth suddenly ceased as though it never existed.

It was then that they heard a loud suction-sounding noise. It was a slurping, wet gurgle that sounded like it was coming from the mirror. As its cold, black surface regained its natural color of absolute midnight, something began to magically ooze forth from its flat surface with the consistency of wet tar.

Diane reeled back in horror, her hands jetting upward through her hair as her mouth dropped wide open. "Holy shit, what is that?!" Stupefied, the two of them watched in a state of amazed repulsion as something large, wet, sticky, and slimy spilled forth from the mirror in the shape of a large ball. It fell steadily onto the cement floor in a heaping, slimy mess as the humming and the wind and the pulsating lights immediately ceased in succession.

Then . . . *it moved.*

Limbs pushed and fumbled about the slimy wet mess, like a newborn spilling forth from the womb into the world, ripping and tearing and pulling at a suffocating film of strange, gelatinous afterbirth.

"It's Billy!" Buddha yelled, racing over to the slime covered figure fumbling clumsily along the dirty basement floor. Diane nervously clamped her hands over her mouth, her eyes misting with tears as she watched Buddha struggling to help him up. Mucilaginous looking goop, the color of NyQuil, covered Billy from head to toe. As Buddha grabbed Billy's arm and helped gently pull him upward, Billy began to moan softly. He slowly moved his right arm toward his face, doing his best to wipe away the sticky looking rosin dripping off him.

Completely covered in the syrupy muck, Billy began spitting and coughing violently, tossing aside big, heaping handfuls of the dark green mess, doing his best to clear the breathing passages around his mouth and nose. Sucking in the open air like a drowning victim being pulled from the ocean, Billy began choking, hacking, and gasping desperately for oxygen.

"Jesus Christ! Billy! Billy, are you okay?" Diane ran over to him as he grumbled incoherently, struggling to get to his feet as though his legs had been robbed of their muscular function. He took no more than a step or two as his wobbling knees buckled beneath him, toppling to the basement floor as Buddha unsuccessfully tried to catch him. "Diane, give me a hand!"

She looked dizzy with fear, standing there petrified with her hands to her mouth as she stood over him. Buddha shouted at her again, hoping to snap her out of it so that they could get him as far away from the black mirror as possible before something happened again.

"Diane! Come on, we need to get him out of here. Let's go!"

Finally snapping to it, she jumped in to help, tears streaming down her face now as she grabbed his other arm and helped Buddha lift him to his feet. His dead weight worked against them, determined to pull them back down to the floor as they fought against it. Grunting and moaning with everything they had, they managed to drag him across the caliginous room that lay home to the mysterious black mirror that miraculously puked him out like someone's stomach getting rid of a bad burrito.

"Get him through the door!" Buddha shouted, still barking orders at Diane while controlling the situation; the mixture of his adrenaline and fear catapulting him to lead them through this. Grunting and moaning against the resistance of his weight, they managed to drag him all the way to the basement's main room, leaving a trail of the sludgy, slimy green gel in their wake like that of a slithering snail.

"Quick, shut the door and lock it."

Without a second of hesitation, Diane sprang into action, letting go of Billy's right arm as she swung the closet door shut. She then grabbed the small key hanging along the hook on the wall beside it, frantically locking it behind them.

Grabbing the knob in her trembling grasp, she gave it a good shake to ensure the door was locked. She then rushed to Billy's side, helping him wipe away the green gunk clinging to him like an oozy membrane as Buddha slowly eased him into a sitting position along the wall.

"Billy!" she shouted hysterically, trembling and crying as Buddha could tell that she was on the verge of losing it. "Billy, sweetie, are you okay? Billy, please say something!"

Vigorously hacking and coughing as the sound of phlegm and whatever else he inhaled broke free from his chest, he looked up at the two of them, his eyes glazed over with a look of utter confusion and dizzying fear. Finally, he spoke, his voice raspy and weak as the words barely spilled forth: "Where . . . where am I?"

IV: THE POD

CHAPTER 15

Running back downstairs with a handful of towels that he grabbed from the hallway closet, Buddha tossed one to Diane as they immediately began helping Billy wipe away all that nasty, green gunk clinging stubbornly to his skin like some otherworldly, alien afterbirth. Giving it enough elbow grease, it eventually slid free from the surface of his skin fairly easily; its consistency like that of jelly, although a little more wet and not quite as sticky.

Tossing the saturated towels aside as they got most of it off, they slowly eased Billy up and eventually to his feet, his feeble legs trembling beneath him as they began to slowly move him across the basement. Taking one tiny step at a time, they gradually eased him down into one of the metal folding chairs sitting near the corner of the basement just a few feet from the pool table. Looking a bit stupefied as he gazed despondently about the basement, they assured him that everything was okay; that he was home and that he was safe.

Eventually displaying signs that he was coherent and aware of his surroundings, Billy slowly began to seem like himself again. Focusing in on Diane and Buddha, they watched as the usual sparkle of life that normally danced behind Billy's eyes slowly drifted back home.

Diane gently rubbed Billy's back as Buddha let out a long sigh, crouching down to a knee next to him. Convinced that he was dreaming—cleaning some mysterious green slime off his roommate after watching him literally slide right out of the mirror's black surface (as impossible as that might seem)—Buddha gathered himself for a minute, looking Billy straight in the eye as he finally asked him, "Billy, where did you go? What the hell happened?"

"Another world," he replied in a hoarse whisper, his lips quivering as a hint of a smile crept along the corner of his mouth. His eyes gazed somewhere over their heads as he continued to speak, appearing as though he had just had the most amazing experience of his life. "This. . . this *place* was . . . it's just so . . . *so beautiful*. It was like nothing I have ever seen."

"Where?" Buddha longed to know. "Where is this world, Billy? What happened? Tell us everything."

For the next several minutes Billy rambled on and on about "the world beyond the black mirror." He spoke with a fiery passion about the ranges of magnificent blue mountains, so tall and majestic that their snow-capped apexes eventually vanished into the whirling fragments of misty, pink clouds above. He talked endlessly about the trees that were as tall and wide as skyscrapers, their violet-colored leaves bursting with a vibrance of color that would eclipse anything seen here on earth. He even spoke of the oceans and their magnificent golden waves, and how the fire-red sun that hung across the sky above them was unlike anything visible from earth.

"It's amazing," he continued, appearing as though drugged, smiling like a child that laid eyes upon something gloriously fascinating for the very first time. "Absolutely amazing."

Buddha and Diane glanced at each other with astonished looks of perplexed disbelief. If they hadn't witnessed the mirror come to life firsthand before Billy came spilling out of its surface all covered in that greenish-black slime, they would have thought the guy lost his fucking marbles.

Truth is . . .they believed him. Something happened. Something that defied science. Something supernatural. Something they didn't have answers for.

Desperate to wash himself clean of whatever it was that he brought back with him, Billy wasted no time jumping in the shower. He scrubbed himself feverishly, ensuring that he washed off all that gummy, green stuff still clinging to his skin and his hair in tiny little globs. He watched as the soapy water slid what remained free from his skin, swimming along the shower floor in a circular motion before eventually vanishing down the drain.

As he finished up, he noticed two very tiny red dots along the inside of his forearm, surrounded by an off-yellow colored bruise that was barely noticeable. "What the hell is this?" he whispered, gently running his fingers over a slightly raised bump beneath it, looking like it might be a spider bite. It didn't hurt, but the area surrounding it already began to itch as he softly ran his fingers over it, doing his best to ignore the urge to scratch it.

What happened to me, he wondered endlessly. *What the hell was that place?* Struggling to understand the magnitude of the black mirror's power, dumbfounded as to where in the hell it transported him. But there was no denying it—it had definitely taken him somewhere. *Another world? Another dimension? Some kind of parallel universe? Hell, maybe another planet if that were even possible.* But if it wasn't for Buddha and Diane being there to confirm that they watched him physically spill forth from the mirror's glass surface before tumbling onto the basement floor, he would have clearly questioned his own sanity. That, or assume that he had fallen and smacked his head against the cement floor, dreaming the entire thing as he lay there in an unconscious state.

But as incredible as it all was, it was far from a dream. It was real. It actually happened. He went somewhere fantastic and strange, some- where he never envisioned nor imagined in his wildest dreams. Frighten- ing and intimidating, the mirror was the very doorway into that anomalous, yet fantastical world. A place that has left him more fascinated and intrigued than he had ever been about anything.

Quickly toweling himself off before throwing on a pair of jeans and an old Detroit Tigers t-shirt, Billy could hear the muffled sound of their voices from down the hall, yapping away about what they witnessed down in the basement while trying to make sense of it all.

"It's that lady, man! I'm telling you. The one that used to own this house," he could hear Buddha saying as he made his way from the hall to the front room. "She must have been knee deep into all that black magic and shit, somehow opening up a portal into another world!"

"Right!" Diane interjected excitedly. "And that's why she decided to seal that room off from the rest of the house down there. Her experimentation and her descent into this world of black magic had snowballed way out of her control. I mean, why else would she have built a wall around that mirror down there! Whatever it is, it's haunted . . . it's cursed!"

"Dude, you guys have no idea," Billy interjected as he entered the room and plopped himself down on the couch. "The things that I saw and experienced there . . . it's just . . . it's like . . I mean, the sensations that you feel there . . . you don't—"

"What, Billy?" Buddha begged to know, eagerly leaning forward along the couch. "What the hell is that thing? That strange black mirror in that once sealed off room down there with all that creepy looking shit scribbled all over the walls. What does it all mean? What do we do!?"

Billy could hear the desperation in Buddha's voice, a look of pure panic flaring within his eyes. What initially began as a morbid fascination went much too far for him. And if he knew the way those gears were grinding and turning inside of Buddha's head, it was without question that Buddha, more than ever now, would want to get rid of the black mirror.

But the truth of the matter was simple—they weren't getting rid of the black mirror anytime soon. Not now. No way. Not after he felt the universe's most powerful orgasm before falling into the most serene sense of peace one could ever imagine. Not after he visited their world of harmonious paradise; a place that was void of any rape, or slavery, or injustice, or discrimination, or famine, or war. Just like the Doors used to say, he had broken on through to the other side. And as ole Jim Morrison also used to say, Billy Baxton was about to test the bounds of reality.

Besides, even if he wanted to, getting rid of the mirror would prove impossible. It had chosen him. Sought him out. Realizing that after thousands of years, the doorway had been located. And the key—the missing piece in opening the door to this paradise—right behind him. *All in due time Billy*, the soft, raspy voice right inside of his ear kept telling him in that cold, seductive tone. *All in due time . . .*

"See guys, the thing is this," Billy began as looked at the two of them. "This mirror, this . . . portal into—"

But before he could finish the rest of his thought, it was back—quite suddenly. Loud, like a roaring turbine engine as an unseen force sent a massive wave of vibrations rippling throughout the home's bones. The power felt like it could decimate the entire house, toppling it to the ground like a tottering house of cards.

"The portal! It's opening!" Billy shouted, leaping up from the couch and racing toward the basement. "Come on, we need to get down there!"

"Billy, wait!" Diane shouted after him.

But it was too late. Hitting the top of the stairs, he swung the door open and disappeared into the basement below, the thumping of his rapid footsteps echoing up through the stairway.

Diane and Buddha quickly looked at each other as they reluctantly jumped up from the couch and followed after him, terrified of what might happen next.

Hitting the bottom of the stairs, they saw that Billy had already opened the door to the basement closet and stepped inside. And as he did—crossing the length of the walk-in closet and passing the threshold of the black mirror's lair—the lights in the basement began to slowly fade in unison with the engine-like hum that was once again coming from the mirror inside the closet.

And as they rounded the corner of the door and stepped inside, they could see that once again, the black mirror—impossible as it was—came to life. It rose and fell—that seductive, terrible black—like a stingray fluttering delicately up and down just inches above the soft, sandy surface of the ocean floor. Like an eel, it fluttered and shook with a release of ripples through that deep and infinite darkness that commanded them with its gravitational effects.

Then something moved.

They watched, consumed by a morbid curiosity that was impossible to resist. A subtle flicker of movement shifted about within the heart of that vast, infinite darkness. It was white—blurry and without any distinct definition at first as it slowly moved forward, gradually coming into focus like an object slowly rising toward the surface of a dark, murky lake. Drawing closer and closer, the clarity of its details eventually coming into focus, they could finally see what it was, inauspiciously floating there right beneath the surface of that cold, dark glass.

A face.

The face of a man, to be exact. His features, calm and stoic with skin as white as paper.

His eyes were empty and black, looking like gaping holes burrowed through the pale flesh. An infinite world of endless, dark space filled the gaps within the face's body, like some illustrious, translucent phantom. The lips seemed to slowly rise and fall as the face floated in the mirror's center with a delicate grace, like a fish calmly staring at them from behind the glass of an aquarium.

"What the f—"

But before Diane could finish, a brilliant flash of light exploded across the basement like the spastic strobes of lightning across a rural field. The three of them instinctively shielded their eyes at the same time, cowering in retreat as they did so. Yet as the flash of light quickly faded, they lowered their arms and watched as the white face within the mirror burst into a million little shards of fantastic, vibrant colors. The explosive flare of light and color sang out across the basement with such intensity, they were forced to look away again, the entire room bursting with a dazzling barrage of colorful light that was otherworldly.

And then, as the vibrations and the humming engine sounds began to fade, a strange but different resonance began to sound from the mirror. It began with a deep, gargled, sucking sound as if something big, wet, and heavy were being pushed forward through the tight spacing of a large, wet tube. The bright and colorful lights beaming forth from the surface of the mirror only moments ago now subsided back into a dark, greenish black. The three of them turned and watched with a morbid fascination as a large bulge began to push forward and bubble outward from the surface of the mirror. Its flat surface now looked like a pool of bubbling tar, thick and gurgling and sputtering. Then, they watched as what looked like a basketball covered in wet tar slowly spilled forth from the mirror before carefully planting itself along the basement floor below it.

Sitting upright directly along the base of the mirror, it sat quite still, dripping and shedding that thick, black liquid as it pooled outward along its base. Floored by what they were witnessing, they watched as the shiny, viscid goo began to evaporate into a blueish-gray smoke, circling and spiraling upward before quickly dissipating into thin air. With the slippery membrane of runny black liquid now shed, the orb shaped object—now reptilian green in color—released a wet sucking sound as it began to shift and move, pushing and stretching itself until its spherical shape edged upward, gradually reforming itself before taking on the shape of a large egg. It sat about three to four feet tall, resembling some sort of a chrysalis or a cocoon; its solid looking exoskeleton shimmering beneath what little light penetrated the dark, basement room.

An eerie blanket of silence fell over the basement as the three of them stood there in stunned awe. The colorful lights that rose and fell from within the mirror, the creepy pale face floating within the space of its cold dark surface, the low steady rumbling that shook the entire house; all of it now gone. It was like some wild and vibrantly realistic hallucination that left them rattled and mystified. But as they studied the looks on each other's faces before bringing their attention back to the one thing that remained in the wake of the black mirror's fantastical feat, they all knew that it wasn't a figment of their imagination. Whatever was sitting there along the basement floor beneath the black mirror, it was real. And whatever it was, it was not of this world.

CHAPTER 16

"What the *fuck* is that?" Buddha's face appeared as though the devil himself had manifested before them from a great sky of fiery red flames. Repulsed, amazed, and completely flabbergasted all at the same time, he slowly stepped back, never taking his eyes off the thing sitting there along the cement floor.

"I don't know," Billy numbly replied, unable to peel his eyes from it himself, his mouth hanging slightly open in awe. "It's like some sort of pod, or . . . something."

And that's exactly what it looked like—some kind of pod. It stood about three to four feet off the ground, its shape like that of a giant, moisture-laden egg. It closely resembled some sort of pupa, chrysalis, or cocoon. Its entire surface (or skin), a dark forest-green in color, composed of what looked like multiple shields or layers of shell like an insect's exoskeleton. It looked like its surface was either hard and smooth or stiff and spongy, its slick texture almost glistening as if covered in a thin layer of a moist membrane.

Diane looked terrified. "So, like, I'm not having some sort of tripped out flashback or something, am I? You guys just saw that too, right? And . . . and this *thing* that just came out of the mirror? I mean . . . it's— but . . . ." Unable to conjure the words, her face went white as a sheet, stepping backwards in unison with Buddha and Billy, slowly getting as far away from the thing as possible.

"You're not tripping, babe," Billy said, the gaze along his face washed over with amazement and wonder. "I see it, too. I don't know what the hell it is, but I see it."

Whatever it was, it was quiet and still as it sat there, not even moving in the slightest. Its rounded base was shaped like the wide bottom of an egg, curved inward until it met the cement where a colloidal green slime appeared to act as a gooey adhesive in fusing it to the floor. As they continued to gawk at the unworldly cocoon-like thing while slowly making their way out of the room, it suddenly let out a soft flapping hiss as though releasing a puff of air. They all jumped when a fowl, repulsive odor began to fall upon the room. And then, the thing started slowly moving upward and down, appearing as though it were breathing gently during some strange, sleep-like state: up and down, up and down, up and down . . .

"Whoa man . . . whoa, whoa, whoa, what the fuck is this thing? This shit is getting out of control, man! I don't know about you guys, but I'm getting the hell out of here!" Turning and running through the walk-in closet, Buddha made it as far as the base of the basement stairs before letting out a startled cry, spotting a small flash of movement from the corner of his eye as it came darting down the stairs. "Whoa, what the hell!"

Just the cat. The same little stray that had been creeping around Billy's back door the last couple of days. And now, somehow, it got inside Billy's house. Looking around for a minute, it raced past Buddha's feet before coming to a quick stop along the closet door. It eyed Buddha with its little green eyes, arching its back as it began to rub its body against the corner of the open door, letting out a long and drawn-out meow as it began to slink back and forth.

"Dude, what the hell is this cat doing in here? It just scared the shit out of me!"

"What cat?" Billy hollered from inside the cedar closet, coming out to see what all the commotion was about.

"This cat right here," Buddha replied, pointing at the skinny little orange haired feline as it strutted back and forth across the doorway, occasionally pausing to arch its back and rub itself against the wooden doorframe. "It's that same one that we keep seeing out in the driveway. Must've got in some way."

"God-damnit!" Billy hissed, glancing over at Diane with a glare of anger in his eyes. "Apparently *somebody* didn't shut the door all the way when they came in."

"Hey, don't blame me!" she defensively snapped back, crossing her arms across her chest in immediate protest. "It's not my fault that your side door is a rickety piece of shit that never shuts all the way. Besides, what are you guys getting all worked up about? It's just an innocent little kitty cat. You guys should be more worried about that demon seed that just spilled out of that black mirror in your secret little basement room in there. I'd say that's the *real* priority on your hands right about now."

"I hate cats," Billy mumbled under his breath, scowling as he looked down at it with a look of disgust.

"You would," Dianne replied, bending down as she gently ran her open palm along the cat's back. "Aww, such a cute little kitty," she purred, talking to the cat in her soft, little baby talk voice as the cat closed its eyes, revving its little engine of pleasure while rubbing back and forth against her open hand. "Ohh, look what a little lover you are! Here," she said, reaching out to pick the cat up. "Let me see you."

But before she could coax the little kitty up into her arms, it sprang away, racing over toward the closet door again as it strutted back and forth along the open door frame, eventually disappearing inside.

"Shit, it's going inside the closet," Billy said, the three of them quickly following the cat to make sure that it didn't get into the backroom. "Let's get that thing out of here and put it back outside."

Buddha attempted to scoop the thing up, but it sprinted right past him, making its way into the room beyond the closet. "Damn, that thing is quick," Buddha said, pausing to watch the cat as it slowly began exploring the room beyond the closet, sniffing the floor as it moved about. It nonchalantly whipped its tail back and forth as it curiously approached the pod along the far wall, hesitantly sniffing the air from just a few feet away with its little pink nose.

The pod made a sudden yet quick sound, again like the hiss of a quick release of air, puffing itself up slightly like a balloon slowly expanding: *Pfffffft!* The cat jumped back, slinking in its stature as it stared at the pod, gradually approaching it again after a couple of seconds of silence. As it did so, four triangular flaps that folded inward to form the smooth and flush top of the pod began to splay outward. It looked like a flower blooming in fast forward, slowly and steadily peeling away from the top of its curved dome as it made a soft, subtle *hisssssss . . .*

The three of them watched in horrified fascination from the edge of the doorway, Diane cowering behind Billy while Buddha cowered behind Diane. They stared wide-eyed in disbelief as a dark green tentacle steadily slid forth from the open hole along its apex. Sliding its way down the side of the cocoon-like shell with the movement of a slithering snake, it weaved back and forth in a wave-like motion across the basement floor toward the cat's location. Like a cobra about to strike down upon its unsuspecting prey, the thin vine-like tentacle rose to the air in a tall, sloping arch. Holding its position momentarily as the pointy end of the whip shaped tentacle hung slightly downward, it began separating slowly outward as something clear and slimy began to push its way forward.

Then, as the cat began to slink backward, finally sensing that something was amiss, its hair spiky and alert, the thin tentacle came whipping downward in the cat's direction. It struck with an uncanny speed that was even too fast for the cat. The clear gelatinous thing pushing forth from the tentacle's tip expanded outward like a flattened jellyfish, slapping, and clamping down on the cat like a fly swatter striking a house fly. The animal's shrieking cries were short lived and muffled, thrashing momentarily beneath the small dome of translucent slime extending from the separated tendril. As the cat's resistance quickly ceased—its body jerking and twitching as its movements slowed— the tentacle began to steadily drag the cat back toward the pod.

As it did, the cat's fur and skin began to melt and slide free from its body as nothing but bloody muscle shined with a hazy red glow behind the grayish-yellow ball of gelatinous goop. By the time the tentacle dragged the cat back to the pod, there was nothing left but a tiny pile of bloody bones decomposing within the center of the gooey mass. They watched, stunned, as all of it eventually disappeared back inside the opening along the top of the pod.

"Ho-lee *shit*!" Billy gasped, his hand instinctively grabbing for his mouth. His voice was barely audible above a whisper as the beat of his heart seemed to resonate throughout his entire body. Transfixed on the pod like a deer that heard the sound of a snapping branch in the woods, they gawked in frozen disbelief, not convinced they really witnessed what just went down. Stunned and horrified, immediately experiencing the same dream-like state that one experiences the moment they get into a car accident. It was surreal. Unimaginable. The voices inside of their heads screamed at them to turn and get the hell out of there, yet the fear and the shock had been paralyzing; holding them incapacitated in the aftermath of the pod's grotesque consumption.

Then came the noise. It was quick and sharp, filling the air with a hard, solid crack. Like steam spewing forth from a busted pipe, it began howling through the dingy air of the once silent basement with a hissing roar. It was loud, like the sound one might imagine a dragon would make while releasing its horrible wrath upon its doomed adversary. They instinctively covered their ears and jumped backwards across the threshold of the doorway, watching as the flaps of dark green flesh along the top of the pod flayed outward again. Only this time it produced something resembling an indoor snowstorm of tiny, delicate, and violet looking flakes as the pod began to spew forth what would be forever known as "the purple mist".

It sprayed toward the ceiling with the force of a small geyser, spewing forth a million little purple flakes into the air. They watched as they floated and fluttered downward like the tiniest flakes of snow, eventually dissipating before vanishing into the air. They could taste and feel the purple mist as they unintentionally inhaled it into their lungs, choking and coughing on its almost sweet taste as they ran from the room, doing their best to get away from whatever substance the pod discharged.

Hacking and coughing and clearing their throats as they raced through the closet into the basement's main room; a heavy wave of dizzying euphoria hit all three, coming on fast and furious with staggering intensity. A magical warmth, as though a golden blanket of euphoric sunshine fluttered down from the heavens before wrapping itself around them, leaving them in a state of complete elation.

The sound of distant church bells from another world rang magnificently throughout the room, a muddled splash of rainbow-colored light casting itself across the basement like a tree's shade on a summer day. Immediately after, a gust of wind shot through the room with a giant *whoosh*, bringing with it a wave of an all-encompassing ecstasy. Their bodies felt like every single molecule had transformed into jelly. Every fiber of every muscle in every limb protruding from their bodies fell into an unusually calm state of relaxation. Any negative thoughts or energies were immediately flushed free from their minds. A loud crack snapped through the air, followed by a sedating humming sound as they slowly opened their eyes to a beautiful shade of blue, as vast and crisp as a clear winter morning sky.

"Holy shit," Billy said, his mouth hanging wide open like some drooling invalid as he gazed dazedly about the basement. "Do you guys feel that?"

Buddha slowly turned toward Billy, his eyes glassy and distant, looking like he had just taken the biggest bong toke of his pot smoking career. "Huh?"

Diane and Buddha looked toasted, shuffling like zombies about the basement; child-like and awe-struck with wonder.

"Oh my god," Diane said, slowly lifting her arm in front of her as she studied it. "I've never felt anything like this. It's so euphoric. So real. It's like . . . it's like I've just floated up to heaven!"

Her face now beamed with elation. In fact, Billy had never seen her that happy as she broke out into a bout of uncontrollable laughter.

"You see!" Billy said, excitedly spinning in her direction as he placed his hands along her shoulders.

Still laughing hysterically, she could feel a warm sensation fluttering from his fingers and almost *swimming* into her body. She smiled at Billy until her face hurt, never wanting him to let go.

"*This* is what I was telling you guys about! *This* is how it feels! *This* is what it's like when I traveled to the world inside the mirror!"

"Wow," Buddha mumbled, staring about the room as he leaned into the pool table for balance, giggling to himself as he did so. Butterflies danced within his belly as tingles of warmth skipped along his skin, tears of joy trickling down the length of his chubby cheeks as he couldn't stop smiling. "Unreal, man. Fucking *unreal!*"

"I know, right! I told you, brother. I told you. This is what it's like— this is what it's like to taste the paradise I was telling you guys about!"

As their wobbly legs felt as though they might buckle beneath them, the three of them slowly sat down, curiously gazing about the room like a trio of adventurers who stepped foot upon some strange and exotic land for the very first time.

"Holy shit, guys . . . I . . . am fucking . . . *high*!" Before Diane could finish getting the words out, Buddha and Billy burst out laughing. Soon, the laughter's contagious quality took hold as all three of them sat there along the carpeted basement floor, their faces turning red as they could hardly breathe. It was amazing. Incredible. Quite possibly, it was the greatest feeling of bliss and jubilation that they had ever experienced. A feeling of rapture. A feeling of transcendence. A feeling of absolute and unfiltered euphoria. A feeling, quite literally, they never wanted to end

CHAPTER 17

"So seriously guys," Diane said, nibbling on another crab Rangoon while leaning into the table, the fire of uncurbed excitement burning within the vibrance of her sea green eyes. "What exactly is this thing? I mean, after it sprayed that purple mist everywhere last night, everything changed. It was incredible . . . *amazing*! I don't think I've ever felt so alive and free in my entire life. The nighttime air along my skin when we decided to go for that walk to the park at the end of your street last night was almost *orgasmic*. I mean, that euphoric high, that feeling, it was just so. . . so . . . *incredible*! I've never felt anything like it. As cheesy as it sounds, it was seriously like we just strolled through the front gates of heaven."

"I told you," Billy said, scanning the dark Chinese restaurant for their waiter as he sucked down the rest of his Coke. "That's *exactly* how I felt the entire time I was crossed over into that other dimension . . . world, or . . . whatever that place is beyond the black mirror. It's unbelievable! The sights, the scenery, the sensations that you feel, it's like. . . it's like paradise."

"Totally!" Diane agreed, stirring her lemon around in her water glass with her chewed up straw. "It's like a super intense orgasm that lasts for hours. It's crazy."

"So," Buddha interjected, sipping from his cup of egg drop soup. "If the black mirror somehow acts like a portal into this other world, like Diane said, then what is that thing that spilled out of it? And, like, what's its purpose? I mean, the black mirror must have sent it for a reason, right? Like, is it some kind of an egg? Some kind of an offering? A living organism that's transforming into something greater . . . like, *what*?"

"That's exactly what it is!" Diane exclaimed, sitting upright along the worn, red leather booth. "It's some sort of gift; some beautiful offering that has spilled over into our plane of existence. Once it gives birth, you know that it's going to be something beautiful, something groundbreaking. Something epic. Something miraculous!"

"Dude," Buddha said, his attention shooting upward from his soup, his eyes wide and stoic as though something had immediately clicked inside of his brain. "That's it! That's what we *need* to do!"

"What?" Billy asked, leaning inward, suddenly intrigued with this lightbulb that just went off somewhere inside the confines of Buddha's resonated skull. "What do we *need* to do?"

"Videotape it," he said in a whisper, leaning forward now as if divulging some deep, dark secret. "Record that thing around the clock and keep a detailed video log of it. Whatever that thing is, it's here for a reason, right? And we need to be there and have the cameras rolling once it finally hatches . . . or gives birth. . . or, whatever it is that it's going to do. It'll be groundbreaking footage, man. Something that the world as we know it has never seen. Think about it—every blurry and questionable photo or video out there of a ghost, a UFO, or even Bigfoot would be blown out of the water by something like this. I mean, shit, the thing is right there in the God-damn basement and it's not even moving! We can set up shop right there and tape it around the clock. We're guaranteed to get some rad footage of this thing, especially around feeding time. We gotta do it, man. We're *gonna* do it."

A beaming grin began to blossom across Billy's face. He started laughing like a maniac as he began slapping his buddy playfully along the back, pumping his fist excitedly in the air. "Hell yeah, he's right. That's exactly what we'll do. It's genius, I tell you. Genius!"

Buddha was back. And for a while there, Billy thought that all this stuff might scare off his buddy for good. And who could blame him?

This house of his has an apparent history of black magic, suicide, hidden rooms in the basement, magical mirrors, and now, some strange, three-foot-tall pupa-looking organism that magically spilled out of the black mirror and attached itself to the basement floor. But no, not Buddha. He was back! More on board than ever, ready to record and observe the pod's each and every move. Anxious to go places that no filmmaker has gone before; grasping the moment to show the world something that wouldn't be believed.

"Dude," Billy said, the conviction stone cold in his glaring eyes, gradually staring back and forth between the two of them. "Buddha's right. If we record that thing and get the type of footage that we know we can, we could win an Academy Award. I mean, holy shit, think about it—the documentary category would be ours! It would be groundbreaking: The Pod." He smacked Diane in the arm, his excitement over the idea building quickly. "That's what we'll call it, man. *The Pod*!"

"Ouch!" She said, smacking him across the shoulder with the back of her hand. "Watch your excitement there, cowboy."

"Billy's right, though," Buddha interjected, wiping his mouth with a napkin before tossing it aside. "This will be the most groundbreaking shit the world has ever seen. I mean, can you *imagine* if we got the pod eating that cat last night on *video*? People would lose their freaking minds. They'd think that it was a clip from some horror movie on *Creature Feature with Count Zappula* or something. I'm telling you man, we're on the verge of something huge, here. We're going to change the world."

"He's right, we need to get a video camera," Diane agreed. "Like, *now*. Quickly, before we miss something. I mean, that thing could have already hatched on us for all we know. Do either of you guys have one or know how to get one? My parents have one, but there is no way in hell that they'll let me borrow it."

"Dude!" Billy said as though he just had an epiphany. "My brother has one. He and his wife got it a couple years ago, but they never use the thing. Knowing him, I'm sure he'll let me borrow it as long as I promise to take care of it. I'll give him a call this afternoon, see when I can swing by and grab it. He's totally cool about that stuff. He won't care."

"Awesome!" Buddha roared, throwing his hand up for the immediately received high five. "Looks like all we'll have to do is swing by the store and score ourselves some blank video tapes, and we're in business."

"That's right, pal. And if I can get a hold of him this afternoon, we should be up and running by sometime later today." Billy paused, thanking their waitress as she stopped by the table momentarily with his refill, waiting before she left to continue. "So, what do you say guys," he said in a hushed voice, leaning into the table again with a look in his eyes that showed he was all in. "You ready to make a documentary?"

CHAPTER 18

As the following weeks passed, the three of them had fallen into the rabbit hole of a very compulsive obsession with the pod. Work, friends, family, daily responsibilities around the house, and extracurricular activities of all kinds quickly took a back seat to their newfound addiction. Their burning urge to observe, record, and of course, *feed* the grotesquely unusual entity that now lived in Billy's basement was quickly spiraling out of control.

Buddha's daily ritual of camping out in front of the TV after work suddenly fell by the wayside. The television—once the fire to their caveman-like existence—was now nothing more than a dark, quiet box that sat in the corner of the family room, accumulating a film of dust over its gummy, dirty surface. Who needed HBO when you had PBO? (Pod Box Office), quickly becoming far more fascinating than cable could ever be.

They would sit there for hours, staring upon its cold, wet, shiny, shell-like surface. They would gaze in fascination at its thin, glistening layer of slimy film that clung and stuck to its taunt, resistant looking skin, pondering endlessly as to what lay dormant inside. They'd watch with a burning anticipation and undying wonder as it slowly rose and fell like a baby in a deep slumber, imagining freely of the wondrous imago stage that would soon take place.

And as this mysterious, insect-like cocoon continued to propel them into this spiraling obsession, their lives—once so tangible and manageable—rapidly began to crumble like a loosely assembled house of cards.

Billy Baxton, the former rock star on his sales team, now found himself struggling to hit his number for the first time since he came on board. When it came to his accounts as of late, his concentration—once razor sharp—became a mess of jumbled static. His thoughts seemed to bounce about his head like a pinball, eventually drifting off to those turquoise blue mountains and those seas of golden waves; teasing him as he sat rotting away in a world that only served so much to enslave him. He wanted it. He needed it.

He had to go back.

Having been granted a glimpse of what lay beyond the black mirror was almost a curse. Billy only experienced a sample. A mere taste. A tiny little peek into the realm of some kind of nirvana, hidden somehow from the fabric of their own reality. The defecation-like release in the wake of the pod's feeding brought with it a glimpse of paradise, igniting a relentless yearning for more that quickly became insatiable.

Diane stopped wearing makeup all together, choosing to sport an old, hole-ridden Talking Heads t-shirt or a worn-out pair of sweatpants over the stylish jeans and blouses that lined her closet. She looked tired and worn down. Her neglected hair had grown increasingly greasy looking; a permanent pair of dark circles formed under those once magnetic, cat-like eyes. The occasional pop-in and overnight visits turned into a full-time live-in situation, now spending every waking moment that she could at the house, holed up like some mindless cult member in that dark, dingy basement room.

They'd hang out down there for hours, waiting for something magnificent to bloom forth from the gift that spilled over into their reality. Desperate to capture it all on video, they had amassed an impressive library of VHS tapes in the process, filling them with hours of fantastic, mind-blowing footage of the pod. Their pre-edited material for the documentary couldn't have been any better, and they made it their mission to see the film through until whatever it was would emerge from the pod's cocoon, knowing that it would be nothing short of epic.

But getting clear video footage of a creature that the world has never seen was only part of it. It was "*feeding time*" that they really lived for. Like a smack junkie unable to resist the grip of their insatiable addiction, they had been chasing the dragon from the first taste, yearning for that orgasmic state of indescribable intensity that kicked in any time they inhaled that violet colored mist. It tasted sweet, almost morphing into something metallic as it entered the back of your throat, then quickly followed by a momentary cold tickle in your chest that was unreal, sending a fluttering chill throughout every molecule in your body. And then, just when you couldn't stand it any longer, it would bloom like a flower, a magnificent golden warmth that slowly spilled outward from the very center of your soul. It was the greatest feeling in the world, like you won the lottery on the same day as your birthday while taking ecstasy. It was something sublime that no one outside their three-man circle knew about. It was their secret, and the center of their current focus.

And boy oh boy, did the pod like to eat.

The thing would eat any time they fed it. And *anything*, for that matter. The outcome never changed no matter what they fed it—raccoons, cats, dogs, squirrels, possums, mice, hamsters, and even a few parrots. Whatever you gave it, the pod would eat it. The three of them would cower in nervous anticipation, sometimes unable to watch as they flinched away from the unfolding madness. They'd half cover their eyes as though witnessing a gruesome scene in a horror film, never ceased to be amazed by that slippery, gelatinous pad that extended forth from those vine-like tentacles, quickly engulfing and consuming its prey like that thing from *The Blob*.

But the truth was, they didn't want to kill those animals. They really didn't. Who would? In fact, they felt horrible about it each and every time, filled with a pre-game guilt over what they were about to do as their need for a fix of the ole purple mist remained paramount. Diane actually had to run over to the laundry room sink to vomit the first time she witnessed the thing digest a puppy, a cute little mutt they picked up from the pound earlier that Saturday morning. But over time, the desire for the most amazing feeling in the universe was just too much for them to resist. And there was no question about it. They had to have their daily taste.

Not to mention, finding animals to sacrifice to the pod was just too easy. And cheap, too.

You could get kittens from the classified ads in the paper for next to nothing. And there was never a shortage of pet stores and shelters in the area desperate to find loving homes for cats and dogs alike. Sometimes they took to driving around the streets of some of the rougher areas downtown, looking for stray dogs that were always aimlessly roaming the streets, coaxing them into their car with some biscuits before taking them for a ride back to the house. Whatever they gave it, the pod would eat it. And in return, it would present them with a taste of the paradise that they so desperately yearned for.

Bringing home yet another victim on a random Tuesday, Diane slipped on her shades as the sun began to creep out again from behind a large cluster of clouds. She tapped her hands to the music against the steering wheel as Madonna's *Borderline* came on the radio. She glanced over at the lazy basset hound sitting along the passenger seat beside her, finding herself frowning as he looked up at her with those sad, droopy, bloodshot eyes, as if he knew he was being driven off to some horrific fate; pleading with her as best he could with that sunken and sad gaze, hoping that it would somehow change her mind against his impending doom.

Quickly looking away while bringing her attention back to the road, she did her best to flush the visual from her head, knowing exactly what would become of the little fella in just a few minutes. An avid animal lover, the mere thought of what she was about to do sent a sick, cold shudder through her entire body, trying desperately to ignore it as she sang along with the poppy lyrics coming across the radio: "*something in your eyes is maaaakin' such a fool of meeeeee . . .* "

Turning onto Hickory Leaf, she spotted a group of happy looking kids shooting baskets and riding bikes on the corner. They laughed and played while having what looked like the time of their lives, completely oblivious to the grotesque horror that was about to unfold within the basement confines of a house along this very street.

As she neared the house, she could see that Buddha was already home, his piece of shit Toyota parked in the driveway in its usual spot. It was the same brown Tercel that he'd been driving since high school. It was a real piece of junk, covered in faded WRIF stickers along the back while random patches of orange rust expanded like a cancer across the surface of its shit-colored paint.

"Fuck," she hissed, tossing her Honda into park with a bit more force than she normally would have, annoyed to see that Billy wasn't home yet. *Of course he isn't, and why would he be?* She was pissed knowing they'd have to wait until he got home from work to get high now.

Everything was always on his schedule. It drove her nuts. She felt like she was going to explode, boiling over with an unbarring frustration from another shitty day. And the fact of the matter was quite simple: she needed to get high. Like *now*.

Running her fingers through her hair while momentarily tempted to rip it free from her scalp, she took several deep breaths, glancing back over at the lethargic looking dog beside her as he looked over at her. "Don't do that," she snapped, her heart breaking at the sight of those droopy, sad, sleepy eyes that seemed to plead desperately for her mercy. "Ugggh, I hate that!"

Getting out of the car and walking over to the other side, she opened the passenger side door as she tried to coax her little buddy from the Humane Society out of the vehicle. Reluctantly hopping down from the passenger seat onto the driveway, the chubby little dog looked up at her again as she did her best to ignore it all. "Come on, buddy. I hate to do this, but we gotta get this over with. I'm sorry. I really am."

Heading over to the side door normally left open, she pulled out the spare key that Billy had given her and let herself in. The port little basset hound waddled in behind her, completely oblivious to the horrible fate that awaited him on the other side of the door. Stepping into the kitchen, she was immediately greeted by a smell that was absolutely putrid. If forced to put her finger on it, it smelled like the rancid hybrid of rotting fish and sour milk, so strong that she almost gagged. A pile of dirty dishes caked with dried, crusted on food sat in the sink, stacked so high that the top plate was hitting the faucet. A small cloud of tiny fruit flies buzzed aimlessly around them. Old newspapers and junk mail lay scattered across the gummy, sticky counters as if blown across the room by a heavy wind. Even a few dirty sweat socks sat discarded in random spots across the kitchen floor, right next to a couple of empty bags of potato chips and a couple of empty Domino's Pizza boxes.

Though the place looked like the aftermath of some huge, destructive bash, the house was eerily quiet in its neglected state. Sure, Buddha's car was in the driveway, but she couldn't hear him. That, and the smell of marijuana wasn't wafting upstairs and into the kitchen. *Weird*, she thought. *Very weird . . .*

Coaxing the dog to follow her, she began heading down the basement stairs, calling out for Buddha while anxiously chomping at the bit to feed the pod and get fucked up. "Buddha? Hey Buddha, . . . Buddha, you home?"

Reaching the bottom of the stairs with her little friend in tow, she looked across the basement to find him crashed out along a beanbag in the corner of the room. A burnt-out roach sat balanced along a big, glass ashtray sitting along the floor beside him. The red light along the top of the camcorder dimmed out, a dead giveaway that the tape ran out and it was no longer taping. *Great*, she thought with an exhausted huff. *So typical!*

She looked around, a disgusted look along her face. Quite reflective of the state of the kitchen upstairs, the basement was equally trashed. No longer able to see the green felt surface of the pool table, it sat covered in piles of empty pizza boxes and crusty Styrofoam carryout containers. The discarded boxes of food piled so high they started to topple over and spill onto the carpet. Wrinkled sleeping bags, pillows, empty bags of Doritos along with several drained cans of beer and Tab lay scattered across the floor as though there were no such thing as garbage cans inside the place. The house was completely trashed, and all while Buddha snoozed away comfortably, enjoying the benefits of a nice afternoon siesta as though there wasn't a single worry in the world. *Lazy fucker*, she thought as she marched across the basement in his direction. *The pod could have hatched, you dumb ass!*

Stomping over to where Buddha sat sleeping, she swung back and kicked his feet, startling him awake as his glassy eyes started darting about the room. Wiping a string of drool from the corner of his mouth, he pushed himself up as a cross look narrowed its way onto his chubby face.

"*Dude*, what the *hell*," he mumbled, glancing up at her as he rubbed the sleep from his itchy, bloodshot eyes.

"Oh, I'm sorry," she snapped, her voice sharp with irritation as she threw her hands up to her hips. "Did I interrupt your nice little nap, there? You're supposed to make sure that the camera is recording at all times, so we don't *miss* anything. It was *your* idea, remember? Oh, but here you are, taking an afternoon snooze while the fucking camcorder's tape has run out."

"Dude, chill."

"*Chill*? How 'bout you get up off your ass and get a blank tape in that thing. I don't know if you noticed, but I picked us up something here after work and I want to get high. Come on, let's get this thing all set up."

He glared at her with a look of disgust, slowly pushing himself up from the beanbag as he made his way over to a large cardboard box full of blank VHS tapes sitting along the corner.

Fucking bitch, he thought, loading the tape into the camcorder as he turned it on, zooming a nicely centered shot of the pod in the camcorder's viewer. *Who the hell made you the boss of this entire project?* Making sure that everything looked just right, he watched the pod for a moment as it rose and fell gently. Satisfied that he had a perfectly lined-up shot, he turned momentarily from the camera toward Diane, appearing puzzled or as if something were perturbing him. "What about Billy? He called to say that he'd be home from work in about an hour. Shouldn't we wait for him?"

"Seriously? An hour? Dude, I don't know about you, but I don't think that I can wait that long. Come on, make sure that the camera is rolling and let's get this dog in there. Besides, if he's pissed that we went ahead and did this without him, there's still plenty of those kittens that we picked up the other day. Look around, they're everywhere!"

Buddha scratched his head, knowing damn well that the amount of mist generated by a little kitten just wasn't the same as a substantial sized dog like the one she brought in with her.

And if he knew Billy, he'd be livid that they went and partook without him. "Man, are you sure? I don't know if you've noticed, but the guy hates cats. And if I know Baxton, I'm pretty sure the last thing he'll want to do when he gets home is chase down one of those squirrely little fuckers. I'm telling ya, I know the guy. He's gonna be pissed."

"Well, if he hates cats so much, all the more reason to feed them to the pod. Come on, stoner boy. Let's get this hound in there and get this show on the road."

Reluctantly giving in to Diane's relentless insistency to do things her way, he walked over and grabbed an axe from the wooden weapon rack that Billy had set up by the closet door. Ever since witnessing the pod gobble up that stray cat who found its way inside that one day, the three of them quickly agreed it could very well try eating one of *them*, as well. This being the case—and a very *realistic* one at that—they agreed to carefully arm themselves each and every time they opened that door. And in addition to arming themselves with weapons, Billy also installed a door complete with a deadbolt lock and a plexiglass window along the center to allow for continued observation and recordings while keeping themselves safely separated from the pod.

Standing guard, Buddha patiently waited for Diane as she tried to coax the dog into the closet with a couple of biscuits that she fished from her purse. Cautious, yet clearly interested in the crunchy treats, the sleepy-eyed dog hesitantly stepped into the closet's adjoining room, sniffing at the ground as his pudgy body wiggled back and forth. Lapping and crunching up the first biscuit, wet little pieces falling out the side of his hanging jowls, he sniffed his way toward the second one that landed no more than three to four feet from the pod.

They both nervously watched as the dog suddenly froze in its tracks, hearing that awful hiss spill forth from the pod as those wet, dark green flaps along its top began to fold outward like a paper fortune teller that the kids made at school. The dog quickly flinched backwards, startled by what sounded like steam spewing forth from a busted pipe as a tentacle like a wet vine slithered down from the opening along the top of it. As the curious canine quickly regained his courage and began to explore the room further, the thin tentacle extending from the pod slithered and slid its way across the cold cement floor like a sidewinder scurrying along the desert sand. The dog began barking and pushed its ass upward as his tail dropped. Right then, the tentacle slowly rose to the air like a jungle vine magically coming to life, the pointy tip of it now wiggling seductively back and forth like the tail of a playful cat. Next, they both heard a wet clicking sound, the insect-like exterior of the pod appearing to move with such a subtleness, they almost questioned if they saw it at all. As the back and forth wiggling of the pointy tentacle came to a sudden stop, four sections along the end of its pointy tip slowly opened as they always did pre-strike, the dark green of its focused tip blossoming into something bright and pink. A bubble of that translucent looking jelly began to expand outward from the small opening of shiny, pink flesh. And then, with the lightning-quick speed of a blinking eye, the tentacle swung downward like a cracking bullwhip, its gelatinous end hitting the dog like a swinging hammer striking the head of a nail.

Buddha and Diane wretched in disgust as they heard the snapping of several bones; a howl like nothing they had ever heard stabbing at their ears as shivers as cold as ice traveled across their skin. Thrashing and catapulting into a desperate spasm, the foggy colored jam slowly expanded and engulfed the dog entirely, eating away its fur and its flesh with an ease they saw countless times before. Dwindling in resistance as the pod began to slowly drag the dog across the cement floor, they watched with the fascinated horror of a rubbernecker at the scene of an accident. They watched as it quickly turned into a small pile of mushy, red flesh inside the center of that jellyfish looking dome of yellowish-white slime. Buddha clamped his hand across his mouth, desperately fighting back the overwhelming urge to vomit, watching as the pod reeled in the dog's remains; bloody and decomposing bones slowly vanishing into that shrinking orb of a pus-like yellow. The dark, wet flaps encompassing the mouth along the top of the pod eventually folded inward on top of it all as the well-fed pod now swelled outward like an expanding medicine ball.

"Hold on tight, stoner boy!" Diane looked over at Buddha with the gleaming grin of a little kid about to hit the apex of a rollercoaster. Staring back at her, he spotted a sparkle of madness within the vibrance of those fading green eyes. The thing howled throughout the basement with that awful hiss as it released a plethora of glittering, fluttering, smokey purple flakes into the air, lifting and dancing through the basement like some magical snowstorm. "It's showtime!"

V: THE KEY

CHAPTER 19

From the moment he got home, Billy could tell that Buddha and Diane fed the pod and got high without him. The look on their faces and that glee in their eyes were a dead giveaway. And it was just the way his shit-ass day was going, too. After getting stuck on the phone with some asshole customer while he was trying to get out the door, he got stuck behind some accident along Maple that brought traffic to a standstill. Not to mention, some old bag that looked like the lady from the "where's the beef!?" commercials gave him the finger for no apparent reason as he pulled into the neighborhood. So yeah, needless to say he was ready to feed the pod, suck on some mist, and call it a day. He was beat. Spent. And the last thing that he wanted to deal with as he walked through the front door was the never-ending narcissism of his so-called girlfriend and her ever-expanding micro-management over the whole pod situation.

Tossing a handful of mail onto the already cluttered kitchen counter, he grabbed a cold one from the fridge and cracked it open. He sucked a long swig before releasing a wet belch, running his fingers through his tousled hair, surveying the room that suddenly looked ransacked by a gang of restless burglars. *Jesus Christ*, he thought, rubbing a finger along his stubbled chin. *How did I let this place become such a shithole?*

It was inconceivable that they even allowed the place to reach such a state, looking around in disbelief at the horrible condition of his house—the dirty dishes, the empty wrappers and tossed aside newspapers, the pizza boxes, the empty fast-food bags and Styrofoam containers; all of it scattered randomly about his kitchen as though it were a garbage dump.

Pushing his way past a couple of chairs pulled away from the breakfast table that were completely covered with junk mail, empty beer cans, and a bunch of old, crumpled up Burger King wrappers, he followed the muffled sound of the stereo blaring from somewhere down below, ready to see what the hell was going on with these two.

Reaching the bottom of the basement stairs, his hunches were immediately confirmed. It didn't take a genius of human observation to realize that they were both stoned out of their damn gourds. The sweet smell of the pod's purple mist-like secretion lingered throughout the air like cigarette smoke through a bowling alley.

Buddha camped out along a beanbag playing with a candle, slowly running his hand over the top of its flickering flame. He watched through glassy eyes of mystified wonder as the tiny flame flickered back and forth from the movement of his hand. Diane was rocking her head slowly back and forth as she stared wide eyed into the ceiling, singing along with Til Tuesday's *Voices Carry*, belting out the wrong words to the song like some happy, oblivious mental patient: "Hush, hush . . . keep it down now . . . your voice is scary."

Taking a swig of his beer, he let out another belch, and stepped into the room as both Buddha and Diane finally acknowledged his presence. They looked startled yet lethargic in their movements, their eyes glazed over and spaced out. "Well, well, look at you guys. . . sitting around, sucking on some pod mist, having a good ole time. Thanks for waiting for me guys, I really appreciate it. You at least remembered to toss a blank tape into the camcorder when you got home, right?"

"Dude, take a chill pill," Diane snapped, a slight slur to her voice signaling the fact that they were hit by the stuff. "I mean, like, we totally waited for you, but it looked like you weren't coming home. For all we knew, you were out sucking down some beers at happy hour with your co-workers or stopping by your brother's house to work on his Camaro or something. How were we supposed to know?"

Billy's eyes widened as he took another sip of his beer, slowly leaning into the wall as he did so. "Take a chill pill? Diane, this is my fucking house! If it wasn't for me, there wouldn't be any basement to chill in, or pod to watch, or documentary to tape, or purple mist to suck on all day so you guys can sit around and trip out. The least I could get is a little respect around here for once. I'm sure it wouldn't have killed you to wait a few more minutes until I got home. Seriously, you guys are like a bunch of fucking smack junkies all of a sudden. It's getting old, dude. It's getting really fucking old."

"Dude, Billy, I tried to tell her to wait, but she totally insisted—"

"Oh, what-the-fuck-ever, Stoner Boy! I didn't see you objecting all that much when I suggested that we go ahead and toss ole Flash from Dukes of Hazard in there for a little afternoon buzz. It's not all my fault, so don't go blaming me. Besides, there's plenty of those kittens roaming around here somewhere. I figure that there's got to be at least three or four of them left from that litter we scored off that ad in the paper."

"Yeah, and those are so easy to catch," Billy replied with the shake of his head and the roll of his eyes. "And besides, that's another thing—I don't like cats. In fact, I fucking hate cats. And the last thing I wanted was a bunch of those little fuckers roaming around here, acting all sneaky and shit, pissing all over my laundry and stuff. I'm done. I'm fucking sick of it. Enjoy your nice little trip, guys. I'm going upstairs."

Not even slightly in the mood for the onslaught of Diane's relentless rebuttals, he nonchalantly tossed his near-finished beer can into the corner of the basement. The can hit the wall with a soft tink as leftover swill and backwash dribbled out the top of the can onto the carpet. Without skipping a beat, he turned and stomped his way back up the creaking stairs.

171

Diane started in again as he simply ignored her rambling of endless excuses, slamming the basement door behind him as he left them to their world of psychedelic wonder.

Billy shook his head as he looked about the kitchen again, scowling at its nasty stench, noticing that it smelled much worse than when he initially walked in. It was gross. So foul that he almost gagged, wondering how they had been living like this. As though overnight the place became an absolute pit, a product of their neglect as they continued to fall into an unhealthy obsession with the pod.

Both the mirror and the pod were powerful, there was no doubt about it. There was a dark compulsion that called to them that they couldn't explain to outsiders. A compulsion to know. A compulsion to feel. A compulsion to become witness to something that no living person on Earth had ever experienced. Yet as consumed as they were with the pod, it looked like Buddha and Diane were a little too consumed at this point in the game.

Ignoring the squalor that took over his house like a living cancer, he stopped by the fridge for a fresh one before disappearing down the hall and into the seclusion of his bedroom. He needed a break from those fucking leeches, deciding to relish in the solitude of his own four walls of momentary privacy for a bit, deciding that he'd deal with those bozos and the mess that they've created later. For now, he just needed to relax.

Setting his beer on the nightstand, he plopped himself down on the bed, the weight of his body bouncing along the mattress a few times as he let out a long and tired sigh. He felt numb. Empty. Off. He couldn't put a solid finger on it, but for some odd reason, he just wasn't himself.

Slowly grabbing for the clicker on the other side of the bed, he turned on the TV, deciding to zone out on some tube for a while and allow his restless mind to ease itself a bit. Flipping past a bunch of low budget music videos, news reports, and a slew of migraine inducing talk shows, he eventually stopped on some nature show about sharks along the coral reef hosted by some guy with an over-the-top Australian accent.

"What a day," he whispered aloud, lazily shaking his head back and forth as he rubbed his tired eyes. "What a fucking day."

Laying along the top of the fluffy comforter while gazing mindlessly at the ceiling, he began to notice a festering itch working its way along the inside of his forearm. It was the same spot where he found those bumps on his skin in the shower. Unable to resist, he started scratching at what felt like a cluster of mosquito bites huddled together beneath the sleeve of his dress shirt. And just like mosquito bites, it seemed like the more that he scratched at it, the more that it itched. And damn, did it ever itch.

Deciding to get a better look at it, he propped himself up in his bed and began working at the set of buttons along the end of his dress shirt's sleeve. Loosening them up, he slowly slid his shirt past his forearm, his skin suddenly feeling sensitive to the delicate touch of the cloth along its surface. It stung a bit, yet ticklish at the same time. It even burned a tad as he revealed what was going on along the inside of his arm; the exact location of that mysterious "bite mark" that he received from his brief journey into the mysterious world on the other side of the black mirror.

Seventy-five percent of the surface of his forearm looked pink and irritated, resembling a rash or something similar. The center of the affected area was darker in color, almost red. The skin around it took on a flakey, crusty texture. Near to the two initial "punctures" in his skin sat a small cluster of red bumps—tiny and dome shaped, looking like the dimples of a rash or the breakout of hives. Looking closer, he could see that some of them were slightly larger and appeared almost moist in the glint of the lamp's soft light.

"Fuck," Billy whispered, unable to repel the burning urge to scratch at it further as he raked the tips of his fingernails over the itchy, burning, bumpy pink flesh that scorched with a discomfort unlike any irritation or allergy he ever experienced.

Deciding to get a better look at it beneath some brighter lighting and maybe put a bandage over it, Billy got up and headed across the hall, ducking into the bathroom for a closer inspection. Disrobing his shirt, he sat down on top of the toilet seat and twisted his arm so he could get a better look. He could feel the affected area throbbing now, the two red dots in its center appearing even darker in color than they looked just a moment ago.

Noticing a faint yellowish-white head along the top of some of the rash-like bumps, his curiosity suddenly got the best of him, deciding to give one of them a little squeeze like you would a zit. Careful as he did so, he began to apply a slight increase of pressure with the tips of his forefinger and his thumb. Upon reaching the tiny red bump's threshold, he could feel a soft pop as a thin string of a yellowish liquid shot outward with the speed of a cork popping free from a champagne bottle. The puss-like substance hit him along his right cheek as he instinctively flinched backward, almost falling off the toilet seat while frantically wiping at his face in disgust. "Eww, what the hell?"

Jumping to his feet, he quickly turned on the sink's faucet and began splashing water against his face in large, heaping handfuls. Satisfied that he washed away the warm, yellow fluid that squirted him, he grabbed a hand towel and carefully padded his face dry before quickly checking himself in the mirror.

Pulling open the medicine cabinet and grabbing a small tube of Neosporin from the top shelf, he closed the glass plated door and began hunting through the vanity beneath the sink.

Quickly growing irritated again with the level of Diane's stuff he'd begun to find around his house as of late, he began tossing aside hair dryers, crimpers, brushes, and hairspray bottles that began taking up most of his own bathroom space. Continuing to push his way past a box of cotton balls, a spray bottle of 409, some Comet, and some extra bars of soap, he soon found what he was looking for: a box of larger sized band aids hiding in the vanity's back corner.

Figuring that the best thing to do would be to put some ointment on it and keep it covered until he could schedule a trip to the dermatologist, he carefully applied some Neosporin to the affected area before carefully concealing it with a wider sized bandage. Once done with that, he sat there on the toilet for a minute as he let out a long and tired sigh.

Deciding not to invest too much worry into it until he had the thing looked at, he eased himself back onto the comfort of his bed and his propped-up pillows along the headboard, welcoming the lucidness brought on by the beer. He didn't eat much at lunch, and he could already feel it slightly in his head. He began to lose himself in the subtle buzz and the distraction of the glowing television, all of it beginning to take his mind away from his arm and the pod downstairs. Not to mention, his roommate and his girlfriend who—once again—took advantage of his resources to get fucked-up without him while letting his house slowly turn into a pigsty.

About halfway through his second beer, his eyelids began to feel heavy. They would slowly dip, catching them suddenly as he held them open, staring at the TV a moment longer before they gradually dipped again against his will. Yet fighting it as he did, the soft blue light of the television flashing in the dark room slowly began to lull him into a half sleep, still able to hear the muffled sound of Diane and Buddha's laughter in the basement below.

Chapter 19

Falling even further still into a state as close to sleep as one could reach, he thought he could hear Diane's laugh again, only this time, it was closer. Much closer. In fact, it sounded as if she came into his room. *But did she?*

She sounded so close, yet at the same time, distant enough that it was hard to tell. "Billy," she whispered softly, like a ghost communicating from another world. "Billy . . . Billy, wake up. . . "

It was then that he could feel her hands moving gently along his stomach. The tips of her delicate fingers were soft and warm, barely touching him as they slid their way across the surface of his belly toward his chest.

He stirred, exhausted and unable to move as his mouth hung lazily open. "Diane?"

"Yes," she whispered, sounding no more than a foot away, a puff of her breath tickling the lobe of his ear. "It's me. . . I'm here. . ."

"Diane? . . . babe, is that you?"

"Shhhhhh," ordered her whispering voice again, so comforting and calm, only this time closer as he lay there in the darkness. "Yes baby, it's me. Shhh. . . just lay down and relax . . . it's okay. Just close your eyes."

Too tired to open his eyes as he lay there, she began to use her mouth, her tongue, and her fingers as instruments of pleasure in ways that she never had before. He rolled his head back even further into the pillow, little waves of euphoria fluttering through him as he fell subject to her pleasuring. Before long, he could feel her climbing on top of him, slowly straddling him completely as she began to guide him inside of her.

"Is that nice?" Her words hushed, and breathy as they echoed delicately throughout the narrow cavern of his ear.

"Yes," he gasped, unable to remember when this ever felt so good, relishing in the warmth of her.

"Keep your eyes closed," she whispered, beginning to gyrate her hips into a nice, fluid rhythm as their breathing joined together in a heavier, animalistic moan. As he moved his hands up the length of her hips, eventually cupping and squeezing her breasts, he eventually opened his eyes and gasped; shocked to find that it was not Diane at all who seductively led him into this incredible dance of primal fornication.

Straddling on top of him was something that wasn't human, though exotically beautiful and like nothing he had ever laid eyes upon. Its skin was incredibly soft, shiny, and green in color, though as warm to the touch as human flesh. The shape of its body resembled that of a beautiful woman—picturesque and without flaw in its every curve and detail. Yet its eyes were yellow and like that of an insect's, magnetically powerful as Billy found himself unable to look away. And though its face possessed the details of a gorgeous runway model, its features were fiercely exaggerated, high-arching eyebrows, prominent cheekbones, a long pointy nose as if someone had stretched the flesh outward like clay with two antennas extended from the top of its forehead. A cracking sound like the snap of a bullwhip ripped through the air with a quick puff of wind as the exquisite creature spread its magnificent set of wings, gleaming and shimmering with a fantastic spectrum of dazzling color.

It was then that he came. The orgasm, so powerful and intense, it felt as though his body transformed into a firework, exploding across the canvas of dark sky like a web of expanding and sparkling color. Every cell within his body seemed to tingle and wither with delectation. He could feel himself falling into a chasm of endless pleasure, opening his eyes to see that the creature vanished, now plunging deeper and deeper into a pit of endless light that pulsated with brilliant shades of blue and purple.

And then, as quickly as he closed and opened his eyes again, everything went completely black.

He opened them to find that he was no longer in his bedroom, yet inside the family room of his parent's old house. It was the same house where he grew up as a child, with the same furniture, the same smell; everything about the place was exactly how he remembered.

Looking around, he found himself sitting cross legged along the orange shag carpeting, camped out in front of the old television that dad always referred to as, "the boob tube." A bowl of Fruit Loops floating in a sugary pool of blueish milk sat in his lap as *Hong Kong Phooey* was driving around in the Phooey-mobile on the TV. *Where am I*, he wondered, reluctantly eating a spoonful of Fruit Loops, hoping to convince himself that he was simply dreaming. Surprisingly, he could feel the crunch of the cereal beneath his teeth, tasting every bit of its sugary flavors along his tongue, washing away any lingering doubt that this was all just some fantasy or dream conjured by his wandering mind. It all seemed so authentic; so implausibly real, as if he jumped into a time machine, bending the bounds of physics and time as it miraculously carried him back to the days of his childhood. *But how*? Billy wondered, struggling to understand how he got there. *What the hell am I doing here? What in the world is happening?*

Reaching his spoon back into the bowl of cereal, he noticed there was something submerged in the sugary milk, fluttering around beneath the surface. *What the hell?* Investigating further, he felt the tip of his spoon touching something a bit more solid than the soggy rings of cereal as he slowly lifted it to the surface. He flinched wildly, a disgusted shiver rippling through his body as he dropped the bowl to the floor, instinctively repelled in disgust. As the soggy remains of the cereal and milk splashed onto the carpet, he watched a couple of cockroaches scurry away from the cereal bowl, taking refuge and disappearing beneath his mother's old, yellow couch.

Repulsed and more than a bit freaked out, Billy jumped quickly to his feet, glancing around nervously to see if there were any more roaches in his vicinity. He suddenly felt fidgety, his skin all itchy. Spotting a bit of movement along the top of the television from the corner of his eye, he looked over to see about six more cockroaches scuttling about its wooden surface.

Overtaken by a horrible panic that began to boil rapidly inside of him, he ran up the stairs in big, leaping bounds before racing as quickly as he could on his little legs toward his parent's bedroom. He screamed frantically for his mother, wondering where his parents and his brother were, greeted by the hollow silence of an empty house. Swinging open the bedroom door and stepping inside, he froze immediately in his tracks while gasping audibly, quickly stepping back again across the threshold of the doorway as he witnessed what was on the other side.

There were hundreds of them—thousands, even. He watched with disgust and horror as a multitude of cockroaches scurried about the surface of his parent's bed, the adjoining nightstands, and even the big wooden dresser that sat along the opposite wall of the room. They were everywhere. Big, ugly, brown bugs randomly scuttling about as he listened to those whispering little hisses that they generated.

Trying to capture a scream within the pit of his lungs, he conjured nothing but silence. He could feel that familiar and painful lump in his throat as warm, salty tears began to fill his eyes and run the length of his face. He ran from the room crying, a little boy gripped with fear, scream-ing bloody murder for his parents and his brother as he began to notice that there were roaches all over the walls and scurrying about the hall-way's carpet. His prepubescent wails, echoing down the short hallway, feeling the soft crunch of the cockroaches beneath his feet as he moved as quickly as his young legs would carry him. They were everywhere, growing rapidly in numbers throughout the house as though they were magically multiplying by the thousands as he bounded down the stairs and raced for the front door.

Grabbing the doorknob with his sweat laced hand, he desperately turned and yanked it, eventually pulling it open when he met with a horror that far exceeded what he already witnessed inside the house. It was terrifying. Paralyzing. He stood there upon the front porch stunned, unable to catch his breath for a moment as he struggled to comprehend what he was looking at; his eyes glazed over in grotesque wonder.

They were everywhere. All that he could see from his parent's front porch—the streets, the trees, the houses throughout the neighborhood— were smothered in dark, rolling waves of a horrible, shiny brown. The summer air hummed with that awful high-pitched hiss as he stood there transfixed and stunned. The world, as young Billy Baxton knew it, was completely infested with bugs.

CHAPTER 20

Billy Baxton knew that there were other worlds that existed beyond our own. There was much more to this. So much more. He saw it. Oh yeah, he saw it alright. Unknowingly and unintentionally, he stumbled upon a whole other world that appeared to exist on top of their own. Somehow, though he still didn't know how, it was *right* there. Right there beyond the mirror's cold, black surface; still hanging there on the wall in that secret room down in his basement. God, how he had gazed deeply for hours into that endless and horrible sea of black! It was something dark. Something awful. Something gorgeous. Something abhorrently seductive, slithering and waiting on the other side, eagerly anticipating the hatching of the one and only pod.

But unlike Buddha and Diane, Billy knew all about the world on the other side of the mirror. He went there. He experienced it. And it was like nothing he had ever imagined, immediately enthralled with its exotic beauty the moment he stepped foot within that magical microcosm that somehow paralleled their own reality. He witnessed its topography, its magnificent and boundless landscapes visually eclipsing anything here on Earth. The vividness and richness of its colors held a vibrance and life that were beyond anything witnessed within their own spectrum of colors. His lips and tongue tasted the sweetness of its exotic fruits, the flavors falling upon his tongue wonderfully foreign, bringing with it a pleasure to his sense of taste that the palette had never experienced.

And as he watched a handful of orange leaves dancing in the grip of an Autumn wind outside his office window, his thoughts circled back to this phantasmagorical place, recalling every whimsical detail as though he just returned. He could still feel the grit of sand in his mouth, stirred slowly awake by the soft roar of waves smashing gently into a shore that sounded close in proximity. The sand crunched beneath his teeth, wiping away the tiny grains that clung to his mouth and the moisture along his face. He spat pathetically, watching a tiny string of saliva hang between his lip and the wind before eventually falling and disappearing into the beach below.

Pushing himself up, Billy looked around, squinting his eyes against a sea of color that was wildfire to the human eye. It instantly took his breath away, quickly surpassing anything that he had ever seen, even on his most incredible adventures out west: the texture, the vibrance, the range in shades of those fantastical colors. It was incredible. Absolutely breathtaking.

A giant sea of magnificent golden waves crashed upon a gorgeous beach of white sand, stretching infinitely in both directions. The sky above blazed with incredible shades of lavender and violet, its colorful splendor exceeding expectations, even for the most beautiful sunset he has seen so far. Beyond the forest of towering trees that hugged the outside edge of the beach a good hundred yards out, giant mountains of a magnificent blue stretched toward the alien-like sky in the distance, so tall that they extended into the clouds as they seemed to reach towards the heavens above.

Dazed and dumbfounded, wondering how he got here, he stood along the tropical shore, gazing wide eyed upon this strange, fantastical world. How had he gone from the confines of that tiny basement room to somewhere so breathtaking. *It's the mirror*, he thought, brushing off the excess sand as he began to stroll along the length of the beach, staring admiringly at the spectacular sky above. *It just has to be. . . the mirror has teleported me here!*

Lost in a fog of wondrous daydreams as he marveled at the world around him, he suddenly heard something coming from the tropical forest off to his right. *What was that?* He froze in his tracks, wondering for a moment if he even heard something at all or if it were merely a ruse of his imagination. But then, as he paused along the stretching beach and listened intently, he heard it again. It came soft and subtle, blowing gently in the breeze as though the forest itself had come alive while calling his name.

Billyyyy, it whispered, a gentle purr so faint that he wondered if he had merely heard the rustle of the tropical foliage blowing softly in the grasp of the warm, gentle wind. But then, like a ghost calling softly through the walls of an old, haunted mansion, he heard it again—*Billyyy*.

Watching as the plants danced fluidly in the ocean's breeze, he began to walk in the direction of the lush, tropical forest. There was something beyond all that greenery that called to him; slowly luring him deeper and deeper into the dark depths of this mysterious, alien jungle.

Maneuvering his way through a maze of vines, roots, stretches of slippery mud, creeks, and dangling branches from the endlessly looming trees that stood in his way, he marveled at the magnitude and variety of insect life stirring about the heavily wild area. Startled and slightly jumping at the sudden sound of something buzzing loudly around his head, he quickly ducked down, glancing up to catch a couple of dragon-flies the size of pelicans zooming by just a few feet above him.

"Sweet Jesus," he whispered, watching as they zipped and weaved in and out of the trees like a couple of rockets before flying off and disappearing into the jungle.

Traveling deeper and deeper into the jungle as he continued to follow the mystifying whisper, he began to hear a wet slurping sound to his left, spinning on his heels to locate its origin. "Holy shit!" he said aloud, his eyes widening as his jaw fell open. He couldn't believe what he was seeing. They were everywhere. Easily hundreds of them, if not thousands. They resembled large blue beetles that looked to be about the size of a football, yet their bodies slid along the surface of the tree bark on some flat, gelatinous pads that sat right beneath their hard, shiny, shell-like bodies. They sounded like someone slurping on a melting popsicle in the summertime, their long thin antennae moving up and down as they traveled the surface of the massively wide tree trunks with a slow, lethargic speed.

"Wow," he whispered as he stood there utterly amazed. He bent down and moved in for a closer look as he studied the unearthly looking insects slithering about the blueish-grey bark. "Unbelievable!"

Continuing on, Billy was like a sponge, carefully observing. There was just so much to take in, too—the array of strange wildlife, the wild fruits that hung from the trees and bushes, the collage of colors exploding through everything within its natural landscape. And as he walked along, marveling at it all, he felt filled with a radiant joy like nothing he had ever conceived in his wildest dreams. Like an untapped utopia, a formidable world of paradise man had not discovered nor imagined.

And then, he heard it again. That soft, seductive whisper that called to him from the darkness of the forest beyond the tropical path: *Billyyyyyy . . . Follow meeeeee, Billyyy . . .*

Moving in the direction of the whispers, he pushed and traveled on through the ever- thickening forest, the voice pulling him onward with the strength of a lasso pulling a fleeing cow. Yet unlike a bucking young steed that resisted its harness with every bit of strained strength, Billy trekked onward with an eager willingness, more desperate than ever to locate the origin of this mysterious voice calling to him through the endless foliage.

Pushing, stepping, and ducking his way past the jungle's greenery as the density of the forest increased as he went, Billy finally reached an opening past a concentration of towering palms the height of skyscrapers. The path where he was dumped by the whispering voice showed a glorious field of the lushest grass he'd ever seen, encompassing a giant

U-shaped waterfall that would rival that of Niagara Falls. The roar of the falling water sang out into the clear skies like the song of angels, a fine mist rising and dancing throughout the air as though it were alive, resting pleasantly along the surface of his skin.

"Beautiful," Billy whispered as he began to smile, walking even further into the luscious clearing, basking in the golden beams of the sunlight coming down. Closing his eyes, he slowly stretched his arms outward, enjoying the waterfall's cool mist as it continued to gently fall upon the surface of his sweaty skin. "Absolutely beautiful."

But then, he heard the scream—a shrill and high-pitched cry, it rang out from beyond the edge of the canyon, echoing over the roar of the plummeting river as its glorious song filled his ears like a thousand ringing church bells. Momentarily wondering where the sound came from, he watched as it suddenly rose into sight from somewhere below the cliff, lifting to the air like the great Phoenix rising from the fallen ashes of its once great glory.

Its body was humanoid in shape. Its skin, green like an emerald stone as it glistened in the light of the dual suns shining down from the violet sky. Spreading its massive wingspan outward as it began to glide closer to the ground, the light shining through their thin membranes intensified their color like the light coming through the stained-glass windows of a church.

Shades of reds, greens, oranges, yellows, and purples shone magnificently across the surface of those mammoth wings. It was like some kind of mythical butterfly from a distant galaxy somewhere far across the universe.

Its face looked like an insect's. Several plates, appearing to possess the hard shell of an exoskeleton, connected to form the majority of its large, spherical head. It titled and gazed curiously down at him with a pair of red compound eyes the size of basketballs. Two substantial hook shaped mandibles slowly unfastened and bloomed to expose its maxillae of various moving teeth-like mechanisms and tiny hairs that wiggled and moved about its flower- like mouth.

Though a powerful grip of fear should have seized him, he found himself unusually calm, watching as the humanoid looking insect slowly came down along the vast, grassy field that looked like emerald hair blowing in the wind. Bending its knees upon initially landing, Billy watched as the creature slowly stood, standing at least seven feet tall as it steadily and hesitantly began to approach him. Its eyes flashed a brilliant red like a railroad light before quickly going dark, those incredible looking mandibles opening and closing again in an unsettling rhythm. A tendril-like tongue in the shape of a pink colored serpent fell from its mouth, slithering and sliding across the grass toward him.

Billy's heart pounded rapidly beneath his chest, suddenly frozen with a morbid fascination as he watched it lift into the air. The pink colored tongue began to thrash and whip about wildly with a life of its own, suddenly striking down as it slapped Billy along the inside of his arm. The slap was hard but quick, like the strike from a very large rubber band being shot against your skin at close range. Though delayed by a second or two, a quick, warm sting shot across the surface of his forearm, hot yet fleeting like a needle momentarily poking through his flesh. "Ouch!" He hissed, reactively pulling back as he glanced down at his arm, noticing a couple of purple dots that slowly came into view along the pale flesh of his forearm.

The creature stood still a moment, almost statuesque in its stance, slowly and gracefully stretching its arms outward. Like a sailing ship rising its magnificent mast, its impressive wingspan quickly fanned outward again with a powerful snap. Its arms rose toward the sky above as it released an incredible scream into the air, sending a thundering echo throughout the canyon below. As it rose, the natural light sent a spectrum of fantastic color through the translucence of its wings across the entire valley. Then, as quickly as it appeared, the creature was gone, shooting into the air like a rocket, watching with fascination as it vanished into a crisp universe of lavender above.

"Billy," a voice called as he inspected the tiny marks along his arm, wondering just what the hell that thing did to him. Diligently sliding his finger over the tiny purple bumps along his skin, he heard it again, slowly growing louder as it finally snapped him from his daydream of the other world: "Billy. . . Billy . . . *Billy*!"

Billy swiveled in his office chair away from the window to find his sales manager, Jimmy Collins, standing there beside his desk. "Ground control to Major Tom. What's going on there, buddy? You alright?"

"Yeah, yeah I'm good Jimmy. What's up?" Billy rubbed his eyes quick before taking a swig of coffee from an orange Garfield mug that he adopted as his own from the office kitchen. Billy was pretty sure it was Carol's, the cat lady that used to work in accounting who got fired for drinking during lunch one too many times. Collins—who was wearing that same pale yellow Polo shirt that he wore every Monday— leaned casually into the corner of his cube wall, appearing as though he needed something.

"Mark Tweedy over at Vector Designs left a message on my machine saying that they're still waiting on those specs for that big project that they've got coming up. Did you ever get back to him on that? If not, they need that shit ASAP, brother. As in, today." Jimmy raised an inquisitive eyebrow as he stroked his mustache, pulling up his dress pants with his other hand as his beer belly seemed to push them further down. At first glance, the guy didn't look much different than a used car salesman or a gambling degenerate that spent a little too much time down at the track. But the truth was, the guy was a company legend. Not only was he the best salesman in the company's history, but his sales team was the highest producing team in the company for five years straight. That fact alone—along with his good ties with upper management—made him a shoo-in for the VP of sales position that would be opening at the end of the fiscal year. He was hands down the best sales manager to work for in the company, but the guy expected results. And considering that Billy's numbers weren't exactly up to par as of late, the last thing he wanted to do was let the guy down.

"Yeah, I actually drove by their office and dropped those off for him this morning," Billy replied, assuring his boss that he took care of it. "He should be all set."

"You did?"

"Oh yeah," Billy said, taking another sip from his coffee. "They're good to go. I gave them to his secretary while he was out of the office, but she said that she would make sure that she would get it to him. I'll give him another call right now to make sure that everything's all set."

"Alright, so you're on top of it. Good to know."

"Oh yeah, they're all set."

"My man," Jimmy said with a playful slap across Billy's shoulder. "That's a big ass project that they've got coming up, and we need to make sure that these guys are happy. Your number for this quarter can't afford for these guys to get pissed-off and jump ship."

"Not to worry, boss." Billy said as he picked up the phone and gave Collins a confident wink. "I'm all over it."

"Good stuff," his manager calmly replied with a thumbs up as he slowly turned to walk away. Pausing momentarily as he did so, he spun back around and brought his attention back to Billy, crinkling his face as he pointed at a big wet spot along the sleeve of Billy's shirt. "Dude, what the hell is *that*? Your boyfriend jizz all over your shirt again or something?"

"What? Oh . . . uh . . . yeah, I've got this really bad rash on my arm, and it seems to be getting worse. Not sure if I brushed against something nasty while doing some yard work at the new house or what. I put some shit on it earlier and bandaged it up good, but it looks like I need to put a fresh wrap on it."

"Yeah man, you might want to run to the bathroom and take a look at that. Whatever you got going on under there, it doesn't look good."

"Damn," Billy replied, poking the end of his finger at the wet sticky area of his shirt where the puss and blood had clearly soaked through. "I guess you're right. Let me go take care of it real quick."

Taking his boss's advice, Billy put his follow up call to Vector Designs on hold for a minute before heading off to the men's room to take another look at his arm. The unbearable itching subsided substantially but it looked like the infected area already leaked through the bandage he applied earlier.

Ducking into an open stall and taking a seat, he began rolling up his sleeve, noticing right away that the white gauze covering the strange rash became completely saturated with a reddish-orange liquid. A crusty, yellow ridge of flaky skin was expanding outward below the gauze, perfectly outlining the affected area. Carefully pulling back on the tiny pieces of tape that held the bandage down—the adhesive sticking and pulling at his irritated skin as it reluctantly let go—slimy strings of a yellowish puss clung to the peeled back bandage as he gasped, finally exposing the wound that was festering underneath.

It looked worse. *Much* worse.

Incredibly, the affected area looked like it was way more irritated than hours earlier when he dressed it before work. *But how*, he wondered. *How did the infection get so bad in such a short amount of time?* What had been nothing more than a few red, itchy bumps only days ago was now a fleshy red wound that covered more than forty percent of his forearm's inside. The two tiny puncture wounds where that strange creature stung him swelled into a couple of large bumps, throbbing and burning at the center of the wound. They were hard yet glistening with a yellowish-clear goo that oozed over, glazing over the rest of the irritated area with a slimy liquid: a field of bumpy, hard, sensitive flesh encompassed by a ridge of flaking, decaying skin.

"Holy shit," he gasped, realizing that he would need to have it looked at immediately. "I need to get to a doctor."

CHAPTER 21

Grabbing his stuff and high tailing it out of the office, he quickly headed home to check in on the pod. Ensuring that it was still "breathing" in that slow, consistent rhythm, he popped out the tape, labeled it with the date, stashed it away in chronological order with the others, and popped a fresh VHS tape into the camcorder before pressing the record button. *Any day now*, he thought, watching while praying that it would be hatching soon. *Any day now . . .*

Heading back upstairs, he tossed open one of the cupboard drawers, fished out a copy of the white pages dropped off at his front door, and began looking up some dermatologists in the area. After calling a couple that were closed and a few that didn't have any openings for that day, he eventually found one that was just a couple miles down the road. And not only was the office right by his house, but they actually had an opening and even honored his shitty-ass health insurance.

Oh, thank God! Looks like I'm in business.

After finding the place and filling out a stack of forms while waiting across from some nerdy looking kid with horrible acne flipping through a *Dungeons & Dragons* manual, Billy finally met with a short little doctor who looked a lot like Danny Devito. After examining his arm, the doctor prescribed him an ointment to apply daily and scheduled a follow-up appointment in a few weeks before sending him on his way.

Stopping by the corner drugstore just a mile down the road from his house, Billy got his prescription filled before heading home to enjoy the rest of his day off. Not having much of a plan and knowing that he didn't have to head back to the office, he figured he would spend the rest of the afternoon picking up around the house while observing and feeding the pod.

He didn't quite know how, but he knew it would be any day now. Something tremendous was happening. He could feel it. He could sense it. *Any day now*, he kept telling himself, suddenly smiling as he tapped his hands along the steering wheel to the Bruce Springsteen song belting out over the radio. *Any day now . . .*

The pod even looked different over the last couple of days. Yep, there was no doubt that it was getting bigger. It was morphing. Transforming. Preparing itself to give life to a mysterious greatness that was growing within the confines of that hard, slimy, protective shell. Its round body was much more bloated and swollen than over the last week or two. Its taunt, dark green skin seemed to glisten with its slimy coating that looked much thicker than just forty-eight hours earlier. It looked healthy and ripe, like an organic piece of fruit ready to be picked from the vine.

It's almost time, Billy, he heard a voice call to him, whispering from someplace far from their own. *It's almost time . . .*

And it was almost time. And being that time was of the essence, that was exactly why he wanted to get home and check up on everything before Buddha and Diane did. They were becoming a predicament as of late. An issue. A real problem. And frankly, Billy was beginning not to trust Tweedle-Dee and Tweedle-Dumb to complete even the simplest of tasks surrounding their project. They were constantly getting way too high off the pod's purple mist; hooked beyond control, constantly forgetting to reload the camcorder with a fresh tape or even store away the old one in its proper place. They threw any form of responsibility out the damn window, treating his place like it was nothing more than a garbage can, forgetting that this was *his* house and *his* God-damn basement. Besides, if it wasn't for him, there wouldn't even be a pod in the first place. And from here on out, until this thing went through the finality of its complete metamorphosis, *Billy* was gonna be the one running shit. *Billy* was going to be the one in charge. *Billy* was going to be the one calling the shots. And once he instills some sense of order back into this project of theirs, it will be smooth sailing from now on as they await the grand metamorphosis.

Pulling into the driveway, as expected, Billy immediately noticed that he was the first one home, steadily bringing the Grand Prix to a slow stop into his usual spot. *Thank God*, he thought, realizing that he would actually have some time to himself, regretting his terrible decision to provide Diane with a spare key to the place. He was an idiot. A real moron. He had given it to her during a moment of weakness, the two of them blasted out of their fucking minds when he decided to let the suggestion spill forth. Seeming perfectly feasible and reasonable at the time, all cuddled up on a beanbag in the basement, tripping hard on the purple mist after they fed the pod an English Springer Spaniel.

"Yeah, yeah, babe," he mumbled with a slurred delivery, slightly nodding off as he sunk further and further into a state of sedated intoxication. "That's a great idea. That way you can get in here when we're not home. We need all the help with the pod that we can get."

Yeah, great idea, Billy, he thought, now shaking his head in complete disbelief at the utter stupidity of his decision. *Just give her the whole damn key to the castle; complete and full access to the bachelor pad anytime she wants*! Yep, without thinking the thing through in the slightest, he provided her with an all-access pass, totally leaching himself of any sense of privacy or freedom that his new house afforded him. In retrospect, he realized that he created an open-door policy that would be abused on a regular basis. It wasn't long before she started acting like she owned the place—bossing the two of them around, getting high off the mist when they weren't home, leaving the place a constant mess, smoking those nasty-ass cigarettes inside the house, not to mention, she even ate the last of his Klondike bars from the freezer the other day. It was getting old. It was getting *really* old, *really* quick. And the more he thought about it, the more he questioned what in the hell he was even doing with her in the first place. He realized now that this whole reconciliation with their teetering relationship had been a huge mistake. In fact, if he had it his way, he would get the key back and boot her ass out for good.

Kicking a bunch of rolled up newspapers in their plastic bags off the step along the side door, he let himself in and closed the door behind him. Tossing his keys onto the kitchen table, he was greeted immediately by that god-awful smell, scanning the mess that seemed to overtake his house.

But that was all right. Billy had the entire rest of the afternoon to pick up and get at it. Plenty of time to go check on the pod, make sure that everything was in check, and begin his endeavor into some serious and long overdue house cleaning.

Heading down into the basement for a sec, he reactively jerked backward and almost tripped on the stairs as a black cat came jetting right past him. Still unaccustomed to the things running freely about his house, it scared the living shit out of him, racing past his feet like a bullet before hitting the top of the stairs and vanishing into the kitchen.

"God-damn cat," Billy hissed, holding his chest a moment while taking a deep breath. He grew more than a bit irritated with the growing number of animals living in the house that Diane liked to hoard for pod food. Especially the cats. They were a lot harder to catch, and the buzz just wasn't as intense anymore. Buddha had been driving him crazy, too—constantly buying hamsters from the pet store—but not to the extent Diane did. She was the worst. And at that point he had to admit, just like all the god-damn cats around his house, Diane needed to go.

Ducking into the closet leading to the pod's lair, he knelt slowly before the plexiglass window along the observation door, glancing inside to see that not much had changed since he left for work.

It was still sitting there in its usual spot, rising and falling steadily with that cool, beautiful rhythm. But still, no signs that it was hatching just yet.

He touched his hand to the plexiglass as he leaned in closer, the tip of his nose softly pressing into the transparent door, a circle of condensation blooming outward before his mouth. Though it was unexplainable, he felt so connected at that moment. Somehow telepathically hit with the validity that the pod's hatching was something monumental, truly vital to the ways of the universe. And then, just like so many times before, that all-too-familiar female voice began calling to him; soft and subtle with its usually seductive whisper: *Billyyy. . . you've been chosennn, Billyyy . . .*

Trying to snap himself out of it and wondering if the whispers were simply in his head, he checked the camcorder on the tripod to find that the tape inside was almost full. "Yep, just as I thought," he said, deciding that it was a good time to stop recording and replace it with a fresh one before they missed something. "Time to reload."

Grabbing the cardboard box along the floor that housed the blank tapes, Billy noticed it felt pretty light, opening it up to find that either his self-obsessed girlfriend or his stoner roommate decided once again to take the lazy route. "Great," he said, dropping the empty box to the floor as he let out a tired sigh. "Lazy fuckers. Out to the garage I go to grab a fresh box."

But before grabbing a fresh box of videotapes from the garage, he figured he'd swing out to the mailbox to grab the mail. He fumed with frustration as he strolled down the driveway, his mind churning over all the bullshit that began to pile up onto his already overflowing plate.

Sure, their plan should have been simple enough: feed and record the pod until the thing finally hatched. That's it. Nothing more. It was full proof. Perfect. An absolute no brainer that would be as simple as tasks came. But as usual, things were always easier said than done. And lately more than ever, Billy Baxton felt like the ever-necessary glue that was now barely holding this entire thing together.

First of all, he had a roommate who was a fucking slob. A pig. A sloth. A fat, sweaty, smelly mammal of a man that surfed through life as though it were merely a vacation without an agenda. A guy that lived like a college kid, existing in a time warp as he treated the house like it was some old, beat up and battered frat house. A guy who never took challenges in life and immersed all his free time into things like slasher movies, comic books, weed, new wave bands and Star Wars. A single guy who never put any effort into meeting chicks, simply happy with the scraps that usually fell off Billy's plate and onto his lap. Besides, even if he did bring a girl home, where would he take her? His room was a fucking pit and reeked of weed, patchouli oil, and sweat socks. He was simply a guy that was never going anywhere in life. A guy who would always be content, even if forced to live in the squalor of his own filth.

And then there was his lover. His sweet and wonderful Diane. The queen of her imaginary kingdom who cared about no one in this cruel, unfair world but herself. A user and a bottom feeder who was the epitome of a narcissist. A girl who skated comfortably through life on her looks and her witty humor that made her seem like one of the guys. A taker. A manipulator. An artist who did what she did quite well, weaseling her way in and out of men's lives while getting what she wanted before sailing on. It was a craft she would continue to polish and hone until the day that time finally decided to rob her of her beauty. The girl was a bitch, plain and simple. A horrible human being who used him for the greatness that would hatch forth from the pod and the riches that would soon follow. And all while she was fucking that asshole from Club Zero for coke while she swore up and down that she was finally fully committed to Billy. *That bitch*, he thought as he reached the bottom of the driveway. *That fucking liar*! He was sick of her walking all over him like he was nothing but a beat up, dirty doormat. It was time, once and for all, that the tides were turned.

Bitching and moaning beneath his breath as he pulled a huge stack of bills and newspaper printed advertisements free from his overstuffed mailbox, he turned and moseyed his way back up the driveway. Yet as he reached the walkway that led to the front porch, he began to hear a very low revving engine coming from somewhere down the street. Wondering if it was that bad-ass Trans Am with the souped-up engine he spotted cruising through the neighborhood a couple of times, he paused along the front porch and glanced down the street in hopes of catching a glimpse of his dream car. But as he did so, he could see that it wasn't the Trans Am.

It was Gary, that fucking loser who works at Club Zero, driving that shitty navy-blue Bronco of his with the busted-up muffler. But what the hell was he doing on his street? And why in the hell was he pulling up to the curb just a few houses down.

What the hell? Billy thought, ducking back a bit behind the wall that covered the porch, doing his best to get a good look at just what the hell was going on. Peeping his head out ever so slightly from behind the corner of the brick wall, Billy watched anxiously as the passenger side door slowly opened.

"You little fucking tramp," he whispered aloud, watching as Diane got out of the car, giggling and laughing as she blew him an imaginary kiss goodbye. Swinging her purse over her shoulder, she began heading down the street toward the house as he pulled the Bronco around in one of the neighbor's driveways before driving off in the opposite direction down Hickory Leaf. "I'll be damned," he hissed, gripping the mail beneath his tightening fingers as he could feel the acceleration of his heartbeat beneath his chest. "That lying, cheating bitch. I was right all along."

Disappearing back inside so she wouldn't see him, he tossed the mail onto the already cluttered counter, grabbed a box of blank VHS tapes from the garage, and headed back down into the basement to carry on with his duties. Unlocking the door that separated the pod's lair from the rest of the basement, he moved the camcorder up a little past the threshold of the doorway for a better angle, lining everything up to ensure that he had a nice close-up shot of the pod. Once centered inside the viewfinder, he popped out the old tape, dated it with the black sharpie that he kept by the video tape library and filed it away with the rest of the recorded footage. Opening the package of fresh tapes, he heard the side door opening and closing, quickly followed by the sound of Diane bounding nonchalantly down the basement stairs.

"Uhhh, hey, what's up?" Diane asked, leaning into the closet's doorway as she took a sip from a 7-11 Big Gulp, tossing a lock of hair out of her eyes.

"Not much," he replied, refusing to look up at her as he slid the blank tape from its cardboard sleeve before popping it into the side of the camcorder.

"What are you doing home from work?"

Her tone sounded a bit cautious and concerned. He could sense a bit of worry in her voice, missing that usual edge of confidence that always shined through with an egotistical pride. "Oh, I took off early. Swung by the dermatologist to get my arm looked at. Hey," he said, finally turning around to face her. "If you parked behind me, you might want to move. I gotta swing up to the store for a minute to grab something."

"Oh, uh, no, I didn't drive my car here . . . Kelly dropped me off."

"Why?"

"The Honda's in the shop. Getting my brakes looked at."

"Kelly, huh?" He slowly rose to a full stand, cocking his head a bit as he studied the change in her eyes. "I'm not sure I believe that. Call her."

"Excuse me?"

"You heard me. Call her ass up. I want to hear if she really dropped you off."

"Dude, how can I call her? She just fucking dropped me off. She's not even home yet."

"Then call her and leave a message telling her to call you back. I want to hear her say that she dropped you off."

"Jesus Christ, what the hell has gotten into you?" Diane's face twisted into a scowl of frustrated anger. Billy loved it as the gloves finally dropped, sizing each other up like two goons on the ice getting ready to dance. No more mister nice guy. It was time to lay it all out there.

"I don't know, but I know what's gotten into you. It's something powdery and white and it goes right up your nose."

"Oh please, Billy! I don't do as much blow as you think. In fact, I haven't had a bump since the other weekend."

"Really?"

"Yes, really!"

"If that's so, then how come the edges of your nose are brighter than Rudolph the Red Nosed Reindeer's? You probably just did a bump off Gary's dick before he dropped you off."

"*What* the *fuck* did you just say to me, asshole?"

"Ya know what's worse than an arrogant, know it all bitch who treats everyone around her like dirt? A whore that drops her panties at the mere sight of a freshly cut up line. Now drop your key off on the table out there and get your ass out. We're done."

Chapter 21

Diane's eyes looked like they just watched Moses part the Red Sea, her face turning a shade of red as bright as an Arizona sunset as her arms and legs began to tremble. Watching her reaction, Billy half expected to see trails of soft smoke shooting from her ears like steam spewing from a warmed-up tea kettle. Yep, if he was trying to get her to snap, he surely did good. Mission accomplished, Billy boy. Mission accomplished.

"You mother fucker," she hissed, swinging an open palmed shot with a speed that would have taken Sugar Ray Leonard off guard, catching him perfectly across his left jaw with the sound of a loud pop. It stung like a bitch too, stunning him pretty good as he instinctively brought his hand to his face, feeling the warm tingle of its after-effect. Taking in a slow, deep breath, he glared back at her with a fire of hate in his eyes that he felt could have burned a hole right through her.

"What do you take me for, some kind of a fucking idiot? I know that you've been fucking him!" He stepped a few feet closer now, ready for the block this time if she wanted to swing at him again. "See, I know what you are now, Diane. You're nothing but a slut. A fucking whore." He then hocked up a good-sized ball of phlegm in his mouth before spitting it right at her, watching her reaction of repulsion and absolute lividness as it hit her square in the face.

A rage fueled noise rose from within her like the pressure building inside of a powder keg, wiping her face before springing at him in a frenzy of wild rage. Her arms flailed at him as Billy did his best to block her blows. Retreating into the basement room to avoid her barrage of swinging fists, her nails caught him suddenly in the side of his face, his cheek burning with a sharp sting as he fought to deflect her ongoing assault.

"I hate you! I fucking hate you!" she screamed; kicking, and punching, and slashing and scratching with everything she had.

"Get the fuck off me!" Billy yelled, giving her a hard shove as she went fumbling backwards, hitting her back against the brick wall before losing her balance and falling to the floor.

As she turned and glared in his direction, her eyes suddenly shined with a wild lunacy that gave him chills. He then watched as her face contorted into something ugly and hateful, her teeth barred together like some rabid creature foaming at the mouth. Brushing a strand of sweaty hair from her face, she grunted and slowly pushed herself up from the basement floor, staring at him with a fiery glare of fury in her eyes. "You. Fucking. *Asshole!*"

Finally getting back to her feet, the concentrating look of rage in her eyes was suddenly eclipsed by that of shock and terror. Looking like they might shoot straight out of their sockets, her eyes quickly widened to the size of golf balls. Her jaw fell open and at the same time a harrowing scream began to build from somewhere deep within her gurgling throat. In the excitement of the struggle, neither of them noticed the pod extending one of its tentacles from the tiny opening along the top of its slimy dome, slithering about the floor like a sneaky snake before wrapping its way around Diane's calf.

Billy gasped, watching as it began to squeeze and coil her leg with the strength of a python. It spun its way around several times over as the tentacle's tip flayed outward, releasing a blob of that clear, gelatinous goo that began to cover the surface of her entire leg. She screamed frantically, her shrill cries filled with desperation and anguish, sending rows of gooseflesh traveling over the length of Billy's arms.

He tried to move, but he froze. He couldn't budge. He watched in a horrific state of stunned disbelief as the skin along her leg slid free like wet paper, the glistening, red muscle and tendons shining beneath that viscid goo.

"Billy!" Diane hollered through her desperate sobs and frantic screams, hysterically reaching her shaking arms toward him as the pod continued to reel her in; all while continuing to consume her with those abhorrent tentacles. "*Help* me! Please! It hurts! Oh my God, it hurts! Jesus Christ, it's got me, Billy! *Please*! *Help me*!"

Yet as badly as he now wanted to reach out and grasp her trembling hand within the grip of his own in hopes of dragging her free from the pod's deadly grasp, something powerful from beyond their own world trapped him dead in his tracks, holding him in place. He was suddenly useless and completely inept, unable to move his feet, watching as this otherworldly organism living in his basement now aggressively fed upon Diane's human flesh at a rapid rate.

"Diane!" He gasped, reaching his hand out as his feet felt like they were anchored in wet tar. He watched as the jelly-like extension along the end of the tentacle bubbled and sizzled while it consumed her leg, eventually tearing free from the rest of her body with slippery ease, strings of bloody muscle and tendons sliding along the basement floor. Being dragged back toward the pod, the entire mass of her leg—skin, muscle, tendons, cartilage, and bone—slowly digested into something mushy and red beneath the translucent bubble that hung from the end of that slimy, green tendril; eventually disappearing into the belly of the pod.

Watching the horror unfold as if it were some terrifying nightmare, Billy tried desperately to block her chilling screams, thinking that he momentarily heard the sound of that familiar female whisper coming from the cool, raven-black glass. *Billy*, it whispered like something passing subtly like a gust of blowing wind. *Let it go, Billy. . . let it happen . . .*

As she frantically tried to get to her good knee and crawl away from the pod, a second tentacle whirling and waving through the air came slapping downward, releasing another ball of that yellowish-white goop. This time it came clamping down over her head with the speed and grace of a striking cobra, violently yanking her head back while immediately eating away the skin along her face and neck.

Billy shrieked like a little girl as the pod began to pull more aggressively in its direction, thrashing her body around like a rag doll. He couldn't believe his eyes as the features of her once beautiful face quickly transformed into something resembling a grotesque Halloween mask. By the time the pod dragged her to the gooey base of its slimy green cocoon, her face and head were nothing more than a bloody skull that seemed to smile with a nefarious grin. Slowly deteriorating before his bewildered eyes, her thrashing arms slowly ceased their flailing as her bones quickly decomposed into that bloody, gritty pulp. Within seconds, the pod had completely pulled what remained of Diane inside of it through the aperture along its top; the thrashing and screaming and fighting that once filled the small basement room coming to a deafening halt, leaving in its wake an unsettling silence that chilled Billy to the core of his bones.

As the pod slowly stretched and swelled outward like a filling bladder, it suddenly rang out with the sound of a screaming tea kettle. Shooting a geyser of purple secretion into the air like an erupting volcano, Billy—still stunned and horrified by what he witnessed—watched as the tiny particles of mist gracefully floated and drifted all around him like a lavender colored blizzard. It was as if he were standing in the center of a giant snow globe, watching as they crackled and vanished into the air like the tail end of a firework. He could feel it entering his lungs like a thick, sweet stream of smoke. He choked, coughed, and spit in reaction to the intensity of the purple mist, suddenly much stronger than ever before. Sure, the high it produced after they fed it random cats and runaway dogs was intense to say the least, but it was nothing like this.

The overwhelming sense of euphoria began to take effect almost immediately, hitting him like a frying pan over the head and hurtling him into some hallucinogenic, mind-bending universe that overtook his entire basement. Colors flashed, popped, and melted before his very eyes as music of angelic design from the heavens above played to him with sounds that were not of this earth. It made Mozart sound like a bad disco track. It was magnificent. Enthralling. Even in the wake of something so revolting and tragic, he never felt so incredibly jubilant and alive as he did right then, basking in yet another taste of the unfathomable utopia that was soon to spill over into their own world.

"Holy shit," he whispered, attempting to walk as the floor below him felt like it was halfway between solid and liquid. "I'm fucked up!"

And though he just lay witness to something so grotesquely horrifying that it would have put most into years of heavy therapy, Billy began laughing uncontrollably. Howling hysterically like a complete lunatic, he struggled desperately to contain himself. He watched the pod kill and eat Diane. There was no denying it, he saw it with his own two eyes. He witnessed her disintegrate into a digested pile of bloody, pulpy mush before being sucked into the pod's belly. Yet for some reason he was not afraid, clumsily approaching the pod as he slowly reached out with his wavering arm. "You ate her," he said, struggling not to laugh as he swayed back and forth like a drunkard after a long night of celebrating. "You fucking ate her!"

The pod simply sat there fused to the floor in its usual spot. Quiet. Still. Silent in the calm aftermath of its violent consumption. Billy could see a soft hue of a golden light emitting off of it, surrounding it like a heavenly shroud of amber. He was no longer afraid. He wanted to touch it. Feel it. Whatever this magnificent, alien cocoon-birthed from the all-great-and-powerful black mirror, he wanted to connect with it.

And so, he did. Without much hesitation, he reached out and touched it. Its surface was warm and slick beneath the tip of Billy's forefinger. Moist, as it appeared, but not as slimy as he imagined. There were coarse little hairs poking forth from its surface, standing spike-like sporadically along its skin. It felt much more solid than he envisioned, hard like a rock or the shell of a large tortoise. The majority of its skin (or shell) was smooth, broken up by the uneven areas where sections of its strange exoskeleton met and interchanged with its other plates.

Like bath water, the sensation of comforting warmth swam its way up the length of his fingers and into his hand. He was dancing in perfect unison with the universe, feeling one with the pod in unimaginable ways. There was a connection. A bond. Some sort of destiny behind it all that he couldn't even begin to understand. The house. The basement. The hidden room. The black mirror. And now—the pod. All of it falling into place as though mapped out by something greater than he could ever conceive.

Billy, he heard that soft, sensual voice whisper as though it were just inches from his ear, *you must go, Billy* . . .

Like a piece of glass violently shattering, Billy broke from his metaphysical connection and snapped to, realizing the magnitude of what was going down. "Oh shit," he said, yanking his hand away from the pod and running it through his hair, trying not to laugh while trying not to cry at the same time. "Oh fuck. Diane! Diane's dead! Fuck. . . fuck. . . fuck . . . fuck . . ."

His mind immediately began to assemble a mental checklist, focusing on quickly getting his shit together and putting his ducks in a row as his brain felt like it was being sucked into a tar pit of psychedelic madness. *Shit, shit, shit, what do I do*? *What do I do*! *I gotta get my facts straight, I gotta get rid of some things* . . .

Deciding to quit pacing while doing his best to fight off the formidable effects of the purple mist, he sprang into action. He had to act now, knowing damn well that if he decided to plop down into one of the beanbags along the basement floor, he'd be lost for hours inside a tornado of its intoxicating aftermath.

Alright, first things first, he thought, carefully grabbing the railing as he steadily made his way upstairs. He was fucked up beyond belief, his entire sense of balance turned upside down. The basement steps beneath his feet were twisting and bending like rubber. *I need to get my hammer from the garage, and I need to smash that VHS tape. I can't let there be any evidence of the pod eating Diane! And once I smash up that tape, I'll make sure to burn it* . . . *that's it! That's exactly what I'll do* . . .

And that was exactly what Billy did. Popping the tape out of the camcorder and bringing it to the garage, he grabbed his hammer from his toolbox and began smashing it with all his strength: *BAM! BAM! BAM! BAM!* Bringing the hammer down again and again, he watched as a plethora of plastic chunks and pieces shattered, spun, shot, and crumbled beneath the force of those repetitive yet powerful blows.

Satisfied with the level of its destruction and demise, he grabbed a dustpan and swept up what he could, tossing all of it into one of the metal trashcans as he went to find some lighter fluid. *There*, he thought, marching through the house as he licked his lips nervously. *Now there won't be anything to tie me to any of this shit . . . As far as anyone will ever know, the earth just up and swallowed her whole! She ain't never coming back, that's for sure. She ain't' never coming back.*

Returning a couple of minutes later with a shiny little can of lighter fluid in hand, he splashed a bit into the metal can, finishing it off with a well-lit match as he watched it go.

Whoosh went the flames as the lit match hit the doused remains of the tape, watching the fire dance before him, bringing the recordings of her horrifying death into a state of ash; the proof of her incomprehensible fate forever vanished from the face of the earth.

Next—I need to get all her shit and get it out of here! The less time that the police think she spends here, the better. Billy knew that Gary dropped her off and that the odds were good that Gary was the last person she was spotted with. He also knew that Diane was clearly getting cocaine from Gary and whoever else she hung around with in that whole seedy Club Zero underworld. And the more that the cops poked around, the more they would uncover just how deep she was into that shit. Hopefully, that would take most of the heat off Billy.

However, Billy *was* technically the boyfriend and the first person that the cops would start questioning in the initial stages of their investigation. But he also had to consider the fact that the pod devoured her alive. They will never find or hear from Diane Zajnecki ever again, whether he liked it or not. Never. But not only that, he didn't have a motive in the world to kill her; therefore, the chance that Billy can somehow get pinned for her murder would be impossible. No motive, no weapon, and most importantly, no body. It would be as if Diane took off to hide from the world on a tiny, private, island somewhere in the South Pacific. And as long as he played it cool with the knowledge that she was gone forever, he had nothing to fear.

But he did, however, have to go over the facts in his head and get this entire ordeal figured out. He didn't have a choice. There wasn't much room for error in all of this. Diane was dead, and there was no going back on that now.

Fact: she was a longtime on-again and off-again girlfriend of his who spent a lot of time at his house, though he would never bring up the spare key unless they brought it up first. Fact: though their relationship has always been up and down, there was never really a big blow up in public and nothing involving the police during their domestic spats. Fact: he had absolutely nothing on his record that would expose some dark skeletons hiding out in the closet of his past. No erratic behavior, no psychological issues, no problems with drugs (well, alcohol), no gambling addictions; and amazingly enough, not even a single drunk driving on his record.

Nope, as far as they would know, he was just a regular guy who worked a regular job and got along with most people he knew. He was good to go. All he had to do was stay calm and level-headed, and he had nothing to worry about.

Sure, there was always the possibility that a neighbor spotted Diane walking into the house that afternoon while his car was in the driveway. Yes, but he could just say that he'd taken a long walk, claiming that if she came by, he didn't see her. He'd play dumb, plain and simple. *Ask her friends*, he'd tell them. *They were drinking and dancing up at Club Zero every weekend. She hung out with nearly everyone that worked there . . . in fact, she started hanging out there more than she was ever over here . . . hardly even saw her anymore . . .*

He had to gather all her stuff and he had to get it out of there. Like now. The less domesticated, dedicated, and serious their relationship appeared from the outside, the better. And with Buddha arriving home from work in about an hour, the clock was quickly ticking. If he is going to do this, the time is now.

Swinging open one of the kitchen drawers, he ripped out a huge, plastic Hefty bag and staggered sloppily down the short hallway. Stopping about halfway down and ducking into the bathroom, he started tossing everything that he could find of hers inside the bag: her hair dryer that she kept on top of the toilet, her makeup bag from the medicine cabinet, her eye cream, tampons, toothbrush, lotion, and even her Paul Mitchell shampoo that always made her hair smell like coconuts. The mere whiff of it used to make him horny as all hell, but he couldn't think about that right now.

After combing the house and collecting every last bit of her junk, he opened up the garage, started up the car, and slowly backed it in before shutting the garage door behind him. The last thing he needed was some astute neighbor telling the police, *"Actually, officer, I do remember seeing him carrying some big garbage bag out to his car and tossing it in his trunk before taking off somewhere."*

"Hell no," he said to himself, closing the garage door as he popped open the trunk and dropped the plastic garbage bag inside. "Not gonna happen."

Slamming the trunk shut and ensuring that it closed securely, he went around to the driver side, slid behind the wheel, and fired up the rattling engine. Ready to leave, he opened the garage. It churned and moaned like some prehistoric beast, rising steadily as he slowly pulled out into the early evening. "Alright," he said to himself as he eased down the driveway, content that he properly flushed his house of all things Diane. He was well on his way. And he knew that once the dust finally settled on all of this, everything was going to be okay. "Time to take care of business and stick with the story."

The evening was pleasant but cool, a nice breeze blowing through the rolled down window as Billy focused intently on the road stretched before him. He took a deep breath, holding the wheel steady with his sweaty palms in the ten and two position, still pretty wrecked by the aftereffects of the pod's purple mist.

An inky darkness began to fall over what still felt like late afternoon, the length of the days growing shorter as time marched on through the final days of October. The smell of wet leaves wafted through the crisp wind; pale yellow beams from the car's headlamps guiding the way down the north bound path of a rural highway. He had been driving over an hour now, figuring it was about time to choose an exit, ditch the garbage bag of her stuff, and head on home. The tedious drive back would allow him plenty of time to think and formulate his alibi if the cops came sniffing around with a bunch of questions aimed at tripping him up. *Not that it really matters though, right? No body, no crime.* He had to keep telling himself that as he stared at the vanishing yellow lines ahead, whizzing underneath him as he continued on, deeper and deeper into the night.

After driving past another state rest stop and an exit that laid home to an A&W, a Shell station, and an old Arby's, he opted for the next one— a town about two miles further that housed a SEARS along with the usual scatter of gas stations and places to eat.

Billy let out a deep breath as he pulled into the SEARS parking lot, the light from its huge, illuminated sign shining through the car's windows. It was just as busy as it needed to be—a few cars here and there but not too many, scattered evenly about the acres of dark asphalt and humming fluorescent lamps that barely lit a thing. Driving casually along the back row of the parking lot's fringe, he eventually pulled into a spot near the dumpsters out back. Killing his lights as he put the car into park, he took a deep breath. He sat there for a moment in the dark car, listening to Fleetwood Mac on the radio as he steadied his breathing: "*If I live to see the seven wonders, I'll make a path to the rainbow's end.*"

"Alright, Billy Baxton," he said, glancing at his reflection along the rearview mirror while taking a deep breath. "It's showtime."

The streetlamps casting soft amber pockets of light across the barren parking lot buzzed softly in the quiet night as Billy lifted the garbage bag from the car's trunk. Slamming the squeaky trunk shut with a hefty thump, he shuddered momentarily from a gust of brisk wind coming through, opening the dumpster's lid with his free hand as he heaved the bag inside. *I can't believe she's really gone*, he thought while sending the dumpster's lid slamming shut, saying goodbye forever to the last of Diane Zajnecki. *She's gone. She's really gone . . .*

Standing there for a brief second, Billy let out an exhausted sigh. The drive out there allowed his intoxicated state to fade a bit, leaving him with that lethargic feeling that usually accompanied the come down. Running his fingers through his layered hair, he looked momentarily toward the swirling dark sky. Knowing that it was time to head back, he casually got into his car, started up the rattling engine, and took off.

The night grew cold as he drove back. Choosing to leave the window open a crack, the brisk air kept him awake and alert as he formulated his game plan. He was tired and his head was still a bit foggy from the mist, though it was coming back to him. After driving down the dark freeway with the radio off for a good twenty minutes, it finally came to him like a splash of cold water to the face.

That's it! His mind started growing sharper again as it all came together. He knew where he would say he was all evening if anyone asked.

His parents had been up at their family cabin on Tawahasse Lake for the last five days and would be coming home tomorrow. And being that he had a key to the house, he'd simply say that he was over there getting the mail, bringing in the newspapers, turning on a few lights for security, and just generally making sure that the house was in order before they got home. Shit, he'd even stop by right now and leave a note for his folks, so they had physical "proof" that he was actually there. Their private driveway was secluded by a wall of trees that blocked the view of any nosey neighbors, so it would really come down to his word against no one if anyone chose to challenge him on the validity of his alibi's timeframe. It was perfect. It was sure to work, as solid of an alibi as any he could come up with.

Smiling to himself now that he had a plan, he rolled up the window and turned the tunes back up, listening as the spacey, eerie, synthesizer-laced intro to Red Rider's Lunatic Fringe came on the radio. Billy watched the night whisk past him as the spooky, mysterious build-up got interrupted by two short strikes of Thomas Cochrane's electric guitar before plunging into the dark, pulsing rhythm of the song's body.

Although he never really wanted her to die, what was done, was done. Diane was gone and gone for good. Never to be found and never to return. It would be as though she magically vanished from the face of this very earth. Gone. It was such a small, simple word with such a mammoth, imperious meaning and reality behind it.

Gone.

And for the first time in a long time, sitting there behind the wheel of the dark car as it raced down the freeway, Billy Baxton felt free. Truly and purely free. Free of all her high maintenance demands and her nagging, annoying ways. Free of hearing her daily outpouring of personal drama and trivial issues that usually centered around herself. Free of her mood swings, her snapping, her arguing, and her constant screaming.

Free of her narcissism and her horribly selfish ways, her amazing ability to spin any argument and make everything center around her. Free of her always hanging around his house, bossing him around, belittling him, and using him for the powers that the pod possessed. Free of her sneaking, her hiding, and her snowballing world of never-ending lies that were only getting worse. Free of her infidelity and her constant cheating, the exchange of her body for a drug that changed her for the worse. Free, for once, of the terrible human being she had become. He. Was. Free!

And as he continued through the night, southbound on the dark interstate, he threw his head back and began to laugh like a man gone mad; howling with hysterics as he began to sing along with the song's chorus, feeling more alive than he had in a long, long time: *"Lunatic Fringe. . . I know you're out there! . . ."*

A staggering panic overwhelmed Billy as he pulled up the driveway, hit with an overwhelming feeling that he missed the pod's hatching while disposing of Diane's stuff. Sweating, shaking, and struggling to catch his breath as he parked his car and raced inside, he was convinced that the grand metamorphosis had begun without him. However, much to his relief, he bounded down the basement stairs to confirm that his quasi-panic attack was nothing more than an overspill of paranoia that some-times accompanied the comedown from the purple mist.

But thankfully, everything was fine. It was nothing.

Standing before it as he slowly entered the room, he approached the pod with an attraction that felt natural and comfortable. "Very soon," he whispered, reaching out again as he gently laid his hand upon its slick, warm surface. He smiled as he could feel it gently rising and falling like the belly of a sleeping dog beneath his palm. "Very soon."

Making sure that the tape was still rolling so that he wouldn't miss anything, he went upstairs, opened the fridge, and grabbed a can of Strohs that was sitting next to a box of some leftover Pizza Hut. Crack-ing it open as he sucked away a bit of foam that had risen to the top of the can, he noticed an orange sticky note that Buddha left for him on the front of the fridge: *Yo! Went to check out that new Friday the 13th flick with Roger. See ya later tonight. -Buddha.*

"Nice," he whispered to himself while taking a swig of the cold beer, pleasantly surprised that he would have some peace and quiet to himself for a while. Plopping into his usual spot along the couch as he turned on the TV, he finally released a long and tired sigh. The last thing that he wanted to do was dwell too much on the horrific scene that went down in his basement earlier, those images sure to haunt him for years. But for now, it was time to clear his head for a bit with some mindless time in front of the boob tube.

Clicking through the channels a few seconds to see what was on, he finally landed on an AFC West rivalry game between the Denver Broncos and the Kansas City Chiefs on *Monday Night Football*.

"Perfect," he said, guzzling down about a third of his beer and releasing a nice sized belch, doing his best to get comfortable and stop thinking about Diane. But try as he did, it was easier said than done. Watching as John Elway conducted an impressive drive all the way into the end zone late in the second quarter, he struggled to block the grisly images of the pod violently consuming Diane. The sounds of her pleading screams howled through the canyons of his eardrums as he physically shuddered, unable to shake the gruesome visuals dancing about his head. All he wanted to do was turn his brain off and enjoy the game, praying that he could block it all out of his mind and pretend it never happened.

But try as he did, he just couldn't.

He could still see the horrible anguish shining within the centers of those bulging, pleading eyes. He could still picture the ooze spilling from the tips of those wiry, slippery tentacles, slowly pulling the skin from her legs like they were made of moldy paper. He could still hear the echo of her bone chilling screams, sending ripples of goose flesh across the surface of his skin. But worst of all, he could still see her face. Her once beautiful, young face melting and disintegrating before his very eyes into something bone chillingly monstrous; bloody and snarling with that awful skeletal grin before slowly decomposing into that wet, red, pulpy, crumpling mush.

He shuddered, killing what was left of his beer in just a couple large gulps, working on shaking those disturbing images from his soon to be lubricated mind. He couldn't bear for the incident to haunt him any longer, set on numbing the recent memory with a steady flow of brew. He was ready to disengage, anxious to black out what he could with his comforting crutch of alcohol.

But before he got too drunk, Billy made sure to call his boss and let him know that he wouldn't be in tomorrow. Knowing that his boss would get the voicemail at work in the morning, he left him a message saying that he contracted a fever from the infection along his arm, and that the doctor told him to take it easy for the next few days. He still had a good handful of paid sick days left before the end of the year, so he knew that it wouldn't be a problem.

"There," he said, hanging up the cordless phone as he tossed it aside, leaning back into the couch as he made himself comfortable again. "All set."

Alright, Billy boy, you know what you need to do, that little voice inside his head told him, knowing that everything was lined up nicely with a solid alibi in place. *When the pigs come poking around asking questions, you gotta be Robert-fucking-Dinero with an Oscar worthy performance that'll cast away any bit of doubt or suspicion. Cool as a cucumber and smooth as a baby's cheek. That's what you gotta be if you want to ease yourself off that suspect list once the questions start coming about her disappearance. 'Cause if you slip and start acting nervous, they'll be so far up your ass you'll finally know what Richard Simmons feels like, buddy. Besides, you've got nothing to worry about ole Billy boy. No body, no crime. Just remember that if they decide to pull you into some tiny, stuffy interrogation room with a bunch of questions meant to trip you up. You're bulletproof, my man. You're untouchable.*

Staring into the glow of the television while repeatedly telling himself that very thing—*no body, no crime, no body, no crime*—Billy proceeded to get drunk. *Really* drunk. Even after putting down close to a twelve pack, the empties piling up along the top of the kitchen trash can, he decided to fetch the tequila bottle from the back of the freezer to help kick it up a notch. The pain and the guilt began to fade, knowing that a good couple of shots should finally flush it all away.

Spotting the frost covered bottle next to a couple of Stouffer's pizzas along the back of the freezer, he fished it out and loosened up the plastic cap. Taking a nice long swig before wiping his mouth with the back of his hand, he grit his teeth against the inevitable burn, feeling it travel its way to the pit of his belly. "It's going to be alright, Baxton," he kept telling himself, taking another shot from the bottle. "Just gotta get through this, and we're home free."

His head—already woozy from the good nine to ten beers that he polished down—suddenly felt like it was swimming as he capped the tequila back up, sloshing itself back and forth like a goblet of wine. If it wasn't already, his balance was clearly impaired now, shuffling his way down the hallway like a drunk passenger on a cruise ship. Ducking into the bathroom and fumbling with his zipper, he let his buildup of urine-flow free, splashing loudly into the toilet below as he lazily glanced down at his forearm. He grimaced in disgust, noticing that it hadn't gotten any better, that yellowish-green pus saturating and soaking through a large section of the white gauze that covered half the length of his arm.

Wobbling back and forth on his feet while trying to zip up his pants, he took a seat on top of the toilet so that he could remove the old gauze. "Gross," he said in a whispered slur, carefully unraveling and tossing the soaked bandages into the garbage. Patting the area dry with some cotton balls, he then applied some of the ointment that the dermatologist prescribed him before re-dressing it with some fresh bandages. Once satisfied that he applied it tightly enough, he slowly got back to his feet as he met his reflection in the mirror before him. He looked tired. His skin, pale and ashen looking. His sunken, droopy eyes were bloodshot as hell, looking back at him with the glare of a man who was half dead. Billy let out a tired sigh that reeked of exhaustion, knowing that it was time to put his drunk ass to bed.

Stumbling across the hall while bumping into the walls, he ducked into his bedroom and shut the door a little bit harder than intended. Kicking off his shoes and sliding off his jeans, he dropped to his bed like a dead fish, rolling over as he did so while turning off the lamp along the top of his nightstand. He was drunk. But not only that, he was exhausted. Mentally beaten from the come down of the purple mist, and the horrors that he witnessed. He was ready to shut his head off and start fresh tomorrow. And even though deep down he was secretly glad that she was gone, he prayed that the evocative images of the pod eating her alive would eventually subside.

The bedroom was quiet. Dark, yet cool. He could feel his chest rising and falling as he listened to the sound of his own breathing, soft and relaxed. The air steadily moving in and out of his lungs came and went in a smooth, calming rhythm. His eyelids grew heavy, fluttering up and down before eventually closing. Right as he did, he once again heard that seductive voice whispering in his ear; a soft puff of breath tickling at the gentle flesh of his earlobe: *Billyyy* . . .

He stirred momentarily, opening his eyes for a second as they eventually succumbed to the weight of fatigue. He quickly drifted again as he dismissed the comforting whisper; the potential product of his tired mind as it began to venture off into the world of dreams.

It was then that he felt the sensation of something softly touching him. It was gentle and warm, lightly traveling the length of his leg as the inside of his thigh quickly shuddered with a tiny tickle of pleasure. His eyelids quivered, his head leaning back even further into the pillow.

Wet and caressing, he could feel something else now, slippery in its movement as it slid past the underside of his testicles, making its way up and across the inside of his other thigh. A trickling chill traveled the goose bumped flesh of his legs, provoking a subtle tremble that sent thin veins of golden warmth throughout his entire body. His heartbeat increased, the surface of his skin warming to the pleasures of the touch's subtleness. The smell of exotic fruits tickled his nose as the soft sound of a whisper purred in his ear: *Ssshhhh . . .*

As what felt like the seductive contact of hundreds of fingers, mouths, and tongues began to sensually explore the regions of his exposed flesh, his excitement built, hard as stone now as objects of soft warmth in the darkness fluttered in and out of his mouth as well as the grasp of his curious, exploring hands.

While the fog of this encompassing darkness began to slowly dissipate, Billy began to see that there were hundreds of fantastical humanoid creatures entangled all around him, feverishly enthralled in each other with eager excitement and unbridled passion. Billy closed his eyes again as his entire body tingled with a trickling warmth, experiencing untapped depths of pleasure. It was incredible. Immeasurable. Utopian.

But then, something foreign began to travel across the surface of his skin. No longer sensual and warm, it was cold and prickly. He looked down to find something small and black moving across the left side of his chest. It was a beetle. Its outer shell was dark and shiny, its protruding antennae wiggling curiously about as it slowly made its way upward. He then felt the soft tickle of those tiny, thin legs along his skin, glancing down to find another one traveling the length of his calf as it headed toward the back of his knee. Then he spotted another one, then another. Eventually they were everywhere, looking around the foggy darkness at the humanoid creatures as they slowly became covered in tiny, scuttling beetles.

And then, that cool, soft female voice soaked heavily in seduction whispered again; the breath of her voice gently tickling the tip of his ear: *You have been chosen, Billy. You are the key.*

Billy's memory of the end of the evening the following morning was a blank slate. The disturbingly erotic dreams that came to visit him as he slept were as fleeting as a whip of smoke vanishing in the wind. Sunlight began to spill through the blinds. The house was quiet. He looked at his alarm clock to find that it was past nine, and Buddha had already left for work. Billy scratched at his itchy scalp as he smacked his tongue about his dry, sticky mouth. He could imagine that his breath must be hideous, his mouth tasting absolutely rancid. Head pounding and a queasy stomach, he needed to get up and brush his teeth, even take a shower so he can pull himself out of the rough trenches of yet another hangover.

Standing zombie-like before his reflection in the mirror, he could almost see his own fear swimming beneath his bloodshot gaze. Yet as nervous as he was, he knew that he shouldn't be. He had nothing to fear, for the black mirror told him so. The voices from the other world assured him many times over that everything was on the right course. Nothing was going to happen to him. This little pod incident with Diane would eventually go away. Sure, there would be a lot of questions and a lot of fruitless searching initially, but eventually, the search for Diane would lose steam. It was okay, and he needed to let it go. Everything was going according to plan.

"Alright," he sighed, flushing the toilet as he let the seat drop, making a loud smack as he continued to stare into the mirror. "Diane's gone. She's gone for good. Time to take a shower and finally face the music."

Relishing the spray of the hot water coming down on him, he eventually brought his attention back to his arm as he washed himself, running a nearly dissolved bar of Zest soap along the infected area. He scrubbed away a thin layer of yellow, crusty gunk that formed along the surface of his arm, watching as it shed free from his forearm like snake-skin, circling and eventually disappearing down the drain. The infection looked better than it did yesterday, but there was now a subtle yet annoying pain that seemed to pulsate deep beneath the pink bumps that still covered most of his forearm.

"God-damn," he hissed, grimacing as he ran his finger along it. "That shit hurts." He watched as something purplish white seemed to move beneath his skin, sliding back and forth in reaction to the pressure and weight of his pressing fingertip. "What the hell is that?"

After drying off and meticulously smoothing a thin layer of the stuff that the dermatologist prescribed him over the infected area, he wrapped it with some fresh gauze and threw on some dry clothes.

Determined not to waste any time, he headed downstairs to check on the pod, knowing that the camcorder had been recording all night. Popping out the full VHS tape, he labeled it with a Sharpie and cata-loged it away with the rest of their footage. He then turned, curiously gazing in the pod's direction. He raised an intrigued eyebrow, his heart fluttering with a deepened excitement as the pins and needles became too much. His gut was right. Something definitely was different about it now. Something changed. Something was happening.

As he took a few steps closer, he realized just how accurate his intui-tion had been. The breathing sped up significantly since he last checked. No longer rising and falling subtly at a nice and steady rhythm, it was now fluttering up and down with a significantly increased pace. In fact, if he stared at it intently enough, he could even spot the occasional flutter of something physically moving just beneath the surface of its tightly stretched, dark green skin.

Filled with a wondrous fascination, he stepped into the room, slowly walking in its direction as he reached his hand out. His fingers hovered just inches above its rapidly rising and falling flesh as he whispered softly, "It's happening." He could feel his heart beating faster now, suddenly filled with a nervous anticipation as to what was next. "Very soon, now," he whispered. "Very soon."

Satisfied that the video camera had a fresh tape and was recording everything, an abnormally powerful surge of hunger suddenly hit Billy, an audible growl rumbling from the pit of his demanding stomach. He was starving, feeling as though he hadn't eaten in days. His mouth was watering, too. He even felt a little lightheaded and shaky now, knowing that before he did anything else, he needed to eat.

Heading back upstairs, he fired up the Mr. Coffee machine before swinging open the refrigerator door to see what he could scavenge. Bending down and squinting as he scanned its scarce contents, he fished out a carton of eggs and a bag of wheat bread with only a few slices left. All out of butter but able to find a can of Pam in one of the cluttered cabinets, he greased up a skillet and went to town on the eggs. After cracking open the last four into the pan and scrambling them up, he popped a couple slices of bread into the toaster and waited for them to brown.

After taking down four scrambled eggs, three pieces of toast, an apple, and two yogurts that he found hiding beneath some rotting lettuce at the bottom of the crisper, he continued combing the cupboards to see what else he could find. Still having a little bit of room left in the tummy, he boiled up a couple packets of Ramen noodles and sucked those down, as well.

"Holy shit," he said, tossing his empty bowl into the already overflowing pile of dishes in the sink. He ran a hand over his protruding belly while releasing a gurgling belch. "I haven't eaten that much since the last time I got stoned with Buddha!"

After finally taming his wildly ravenous appetite, he started chipping away at the dishes, loading up and running the dishwasher while he went to work on the rest of the kitchen. After filling and taking out several bags of garbage, wiping down the counters, taking out the empties, mopping the kitchen floor, vacuuming the family room, and even cleaning the disgusting bathroom down the hall, Billy's heart was thumping away at a decent pace, sweat oozing from every pore. He stood there for a moment as he surveyed the house, amazed at the progress he had made and what just a little elbow grease could do.

Cracking open a beer as he continued to putz around the house; doing some laundry, watching *The Price Is Right*, and even sneaking in a couple games of Pac-Man, he still felt antsy, waiting nervously for that phone to ring. Sure, the chores had proven to be constructive distractions for his wandering mind, yet he couldn't help feeling incredibly anxious. He kept expecting Diane's sister to call all frantic, asking if he knew where Diane was, going on and on about how she didn't come home last night and how her work called wondering where she was. It was inevitably going to happen. It was just a matter of when.

Yet as much as Billy felt like he was going to jump out of his own skin, that nervous energy continued to work to his advantage, allowing him to proceed with the cleaning as he went over his story in his head, finding himself more productive than he'd been in weeks. But still, as productive and accomplished as he'd been while going to town on the place, he couldn't deny that something was horribly wrong with his arm. Trying to ignore it as he did while continuing to follow the doctor's orders, it continued to fester, itch, and burn uncontrollably beneath the bandages no matter how much he attended to it. Whatever that stuff was that the dermatologist prescribed him wasn't working. In fact, it got worse. By early afternoon the dressing along his forearm was already soaked through again, the infected area throbbing with an unrelenting pain.

Sitting on top of the toilet while slowly unspooling the soiled bandage, he literally winced and gasped softly, unveiling the wound for the first time in several hours exposing that it was worse. *Much* worse. His arm was a mess. Grotesquely raw, the growing surface of soft, pink skin was now covered with areas of wet, bumpy, purplish looking flesh that stretched from the start of his wrist to the beginning of his elbow, throbbing with a burning pain beginning to be impossible to ignore.

"Jesus Christ!" he hissed, slugging down his beer then tossing it angrily to the bathroom floor. Recoiling in disgust at the mere sight of his arm, he gently probed at it again with the tip of his finger, quickly pulling away as it stung with a fiery pain at even the slightest touch. "What the *fuck*?"

Flinging open the medicine cabinet and grabbing the medicated ointment, he frantically unscrewed the top of the tube before applying a thick line of the clear, gooey ointment along the surface of the hideously infected flesh. Satisfied that he applied an ample amount, he rubbed it in evenly before wrapping it again, praying that it would finally make a turn for the better as he headed into the kitchen to fetch the *White Pages*.

Flipping through it to the dog-eared page where he circled the dermatologist's number with a red marker, he picked up the phone and called them up, tapping his foot nervously as he waited for the receptionist to answer.

"Doctor Vargas's office," a nasally sounding woman said as she answered the phone without much enthusiasm. After explaining that he needed to make another appointment as soon as possible, she explained to him they are booked until next Tuesday. Reluctantly agreeing to anything that he could get, she penciled in for an appointment that Tuesday, telling him that they would see him then.

"Gee, thanks!" Bringing the phone crashing down into its cradle with a frustrated huff of anger and wondered if he should head to the ER.

Whoa, whoa, easy there, Billy Boy, that cool, calm, collected voice suddenly spoke from somewhere deep inside his head. *No need to get all mad there, Billy Boy. Keep your cool, my man. Keep your cool. Everything's gonna be just fine. Everything's gonna be A-okay! I know that it hurts now, but your arm will get better. It's just a little infected, that's all. But it will get better, trust me. And not only is your arm going to be alright, but no one's gonna toss you in some stuffy, cramped jail cell, buddy. No way, man. Not gonna happen. Just keep telling yourself—nobody, no crime. 'Cause believe me, Billy Boy, Diane Zajnecki is gone for good. You of all people should know that. You had a front row seat as you saw that thing down there devour her till there was nothing left. Yep, Billy Boy, nothing to worry about in the slightest. Your problems are gone for good. Now why don't you go ahead and do what you do best, okay. Go on over to that fridge over there and grab yourself a cold one. Go on, pal. You deserve it!*

So, without skipping a beat and deciding to heed advice from that little monologue inside his head, Billy did just that. "Nothing to worry about," he said self-assuredly, cracking open a fresh beer and sucking the collecting foam along the top. "Nothing to worry about . . . the pod will be hatching soon."

CHAPTER 25

Buddha got home after hanging out with some buddies later that night to find Billy camped out in front of the pod. He was mumbling to himself incoherently, sitting cross legged as he rocked gently back and forth in succession with the thing's breathing which was now faster than ever. An accumulating pile of empty beer cans lay scattered along the floor next to him as he sipped from a freshly opened one. A couple of Buddha's encyclopedias from a set he reluctantly purchased back in the day lay scattered about the floor. Glossy and colorful pictures of slimy cocoons, furry millipedes, and even a bright green praying mantis splayed across their open pages; a few skinny cats slinking apprehensively around the doorway to the pod's lair.

"Holy shit, dude," Buddha said as he stepped to the edge of the door, a look of complete shock plastered across his face. "You're pretty close to that thing, brother. Aren't you worried that one of those tent—"

"Shhhhhh," Billy hissed, bringing a rigid finger to his pursed lips as he swung his head in Buddha's direction. The intensity of Billy's troubled gaze wasn't quite right, quickly fading into a disarming smile, slowly turning while bringing his attention back to the pod. He grinned slowly, bringing himself back to that meditative state, rocking steadily as he continued to stare at it. "No," Billy finally said, shaking his head back and forth as he began to smile again. "This thing won't hurt me. It understands us now. We're safe around it."

"Umm, are you sure dude?" Buddha asked, noticing that Billy wasn't acting quite right, totally perplexed by his newfound bravery around the pod. In fact, Buddha couldn't believe it. Billy was just sitting there all Zen-like no more than five feet from the thing! He could feel his heartbeat speeding as he watched him, praying that one of those jelly tipped tentacles didn't come whipping out from the top of it before wrapping itself around Billy's head.

Yet oddly enough, the pod did nothing. It just sat there as it always did, breathing up and down with the increased pace of a dog sleeping during an enticing dream.

"Holy shit dude," Buddha said, taking a few steps closer. "The pod's breathing. . . it's getting faster!"

"It is," Billy replied with a tranquil calm. "It's almost time."

"Holy shit, it's happening," Buddha said, his face suddenly beaming as the excitement grew. "It's really happening." His stomach fluttered with nervous anticipation, unable to contain his sudden rush of anxious energy. He was pumped, feeling like a kid on Christmas Eve, suddenly geeked beyond belief. After all this waiting, after all this preparation, it was *finally* time. Whether the world was ready or not, it was time. It was time for the great metamorphosis to begin. Not to mention, they would have video evidence of the entire thing. A documentary of monumental proportions that would shock the world.

And for some strange reason, Buddha's fear started to subside as well. Though initially apprehensive as to what might come hatching out of that interdimensional, monstrous little cocoon, once he tasted the unfiltered bliss and spiritual harmony of the mist, he knew—he couldn't explain why, but he just knew—that something monumental and grand was about to bloom forth from the all-mighty pod. It was something special. Something magical. Something that they sensed was going to change the world as they knew it forever more.

And knowing that he wouldn't miss it for anything, Buddha glanced in the direction of the camcorder, unable to tell if it was running from where he was standing, but assuming that Billy had it under control. Regardless, he wanted to make sure. They couldn't afford to miss a moment of footage at this point.

"Hey Billy, you're taping this, right?"

"Of course," Billy snapped, acting as if offended that he would even ask such a thing. "Paradise is about to spill over into the world as we know it, and you ask if I'm taping it? It shouldn't be a question that I'm taping this, Buddha. Of course, I am."

"Hey, just making sure, man." Buddha rolled his eyes, sliding his hands into his pockets as he glanced around the basement, scratching curiously at his head. "Does Diane know? I wasn't sure if she was here yet or not."

"Not sure," he calmly replied, still smiling and gazing blankly toward the pod as he steadily rocked back and forth. "Haven't seen her yet today."

"Gotcha," Buddha replied, nodding his head nonchalantly. There was no doubt about it, Billy seemed off. Something distant and strange replaced his normally positive and upbeat personality. He wasn't sure if it was the half rack of beers that he already cut into, or if he just fed the pod one of the cats. Either way, the guy was acting weird as hell. Definitely not himself.

As though following something around the room that wasn't there, Billy gazed blankly about the once sealed off room before bringing his attention back to Buddha. He began to smile, his previously stiff and ominous exterior beginning to slide. "Hey man, we should celebrate. You got any weed that we could smoke?"

Buddha looked at him as though he asked the stupidest question in the world. "Dude, do the members of Poison look like a bunch of fags? Hell yeah, I got some weed we could smoke! Stay here, I'll be right back."

Elated and suddenly hopeful that a little herb would help to mellow Billy out and get him back in his usually carefree mood, Buddha bounded upstairs to go grab his stash. Coming back down with that all too familiar wooden cigar box in hand, he popped it open and began stuffing a small metal pipe with some broken up grass as they prepared to puff.

Coughing uncontrollably on a couple good hits, Billy started laughing hysterically. He wheezed and struggled to breath with a raspy roar of laughter, suddenly sounding like Dudley Moore from the movie, *Arthur*. As they passed the pipe back and forth, Billy almost instantly transformed into a new man, dropping the spaced-out serious demeanor for the party guy that Buddha had come to know from so many years back. Continuing to pound back the beers while mixing it hard now with Buddha's grass, they decided to crank some tunes on the boom-box and play some games of Pac-Man; all while checking in on the pod occasionally to make sure that they were there once it hatched.

Buddha smiled, digging the fact that his roommate decided to release whatever tension built up inside of him. Billy looked as happy as could be, focused now as he gobbled one of the blinking pills in the corner of the board before giving chase to the blue ghosts as they raced across the screen. Cranking up, down, left, right, up again, then left again on the sturdy joystick, Buddha sat back and watched Billy zero in on his high score as he puffed away on his second joint.

Watching and waiting for his turn, Buddha couldn't help but notice the bandaging wrapped around Billy's arm. Buddha was no doctor, but it looked like the wound was badly infected. The gauze around his forearm crusted over with blood and puss, all loose and hanging off his arm like a mummy's wrappings from some 1950's horror movie.

"Jesus Christ, Billy, what's going on with your arm? Not to scare ya brother, but seriously, it looks like it's gotten pretty infected. You should get that looked at."

Refusing to pull his eyes from the game for even the briefest of seconds, Billy told him all about the doctor appointment, and how the ointment that they prescribed him didn't seem to be working, and how he called for another appointment but had to wait until next week to get it looked at again. Rambling on excitedly with a slight slur now, Buddha watched the vibrant video game colors reflecting off his sweaty face, that tiny twinkle of madness dancing again within the center of his glossy looking eyes.

After finally making a mistake on a board that Buddha never thought he'd make it to in his condition, Billy's last guy finally succumbed to the speed of the ghosts as they cornered him and took him out. "Fuck," Billy said, softly pounding his fist down along the game's edge, watching as his yellow Pac-Man character slowly dissolved for the final time. *Waw-waw-waw-waw-wabub*. Game over.

He then spun in Buddha's direction; an insane looking smile crested on his face; his beady, bloodshot eyes gleaming with an unfiltered excitement. Billy grit his teeth with glee, looking like a hungry wolf slowly sizing up his prey. He then clapped his hands together, those loose, drooping bandages saturated with congealed, yellow crust swinging beneath his arm. "Say," he said, looking alive again as though struck with the inspiration of some sudden, brilliant idea. "Let's do a shot!"

Deciding to bust out the Cuervo again, Buddha watched as Billy proceeded to get wrecked. Not buzzed. Not drunk. Absolutely and completely *wrecked*. Not wanting to look like a pussy and get called out, Buddha agreed to do the first one with him, knowing damn well that he'd be cutting himself off after that. But of course, the first one was just a start for Billy. Oh yeah, he was just getting warmed up. Doing his best Indiana Jones impersonation, he'd swig down the shot before slowly turning the shot glass upside down before slamming it down on the surface of the pool table, roaring with laughter as he did so. "Ahhhh, getting fucked up, Dr. Jones!"

As Kim Carnes's *Betty Davis Eyes* played over the boombox in the corner, Billy began rambling on with some random facts he learned about insects from the encyclopedias scattered about the floor. "Hey, Buddha," Billy said, drooping his arm over Buddha's shoulder as he tried to rack up the balls for a game of pool. "Hey, did you know that Monarch caterpillars shed their skin four times before they become a chrysalis, growing over 2,700 times their original size?"

"Uh, umm, no. No, I had no idea."

Completely sloppy at this point while totally oblivious to how close he was getting while talking—tiny particles of spittle shooting from his slurring lips—Buddha did his best to back away from him, grabbing a pool stick from the wall as he agreed to break. "Check this one out," Billy slurred, resting against the pool table as he struggled for balance. "Did you know that a cockroach can live for three weeks without its head? Ha! Oh, oh, and get this—insect blood is *yellow*! Yellow, can you believe it? Ain't that some nasty-ass shit?"

"Man," Buddha said, leaning into his shot as he smashed the cue-ball into a racked triangle of colors, sending the balls scattering about the green felt, one of them eventually dropping into a side pocket. "You've really been soaking up some info from those encyclopedias. I think you've gotten more use out of them today than I have the whole time I've owned them. I pretty much only used them to fill out my old bookshelf, occasionally pulling one out when I needed a flat surface to break up some weed." Buddha smiled as he chalked up his stick, walking slowly around the table as he scoped-out his next shot. "Feel free to keep the set in your room if you want. They just take up space for me."

Billy, who was fairly wobbly on his feet at that point, gazed lazily in Buddha's direction with that blank, distant, drunken stare that bordered on complete blackout. His eyes narrowed into a look of pained confusion, appearing as though he momentarily forgot where he was or what the hell was going on around him. *Oh boy*, Buddha thought, moving around the table to set up his next shot. *Here we go again!*

Buddha had seen that look more times than he cared to admit. Billy was nearing that state of complete blackout while he was still awake, usually achieved when he decided to hit the hard stuff after plowing through more beers than the average person could handle. And right now, the guy was well past the point of no return. He was absolutely plastered. Wasted. And considering it was a work night, Buddha sure as hell wasn't in the mood to babysit and deal with a sloppy, blacked out Billy Baxton.

"What's that?" Billy barked, his face contorting into something completely different from the personality he was projecting only a moment ago. It was something aggressive. Something angry. Something distant and disoriented. His jaw hung open in dumb confusion, almost losing his balance as he grabbed again for the billiard table to steady himself. He glared in Buddha's direction with a look of fuming anger, his slack jawed mouth now twisting into an ugly scowl that wasn't him. He was a mess, staring Buddha down as something barely audible croaked forth from the bottom of his throat. "The fuck you say?"

"Uh, um, nothing man. Nothing. I was just saying that if you want, you can use my encyclo—"

"You fuckin' think I'm . . . idiot? Fuck you . . . Gary."

"Gary? No, Billy it's me, Buddha."

The sloshed stare down continued as Billy's tequila induced anger suddenly morphed into a look of bewilderment and confusion. Like a toddler learning to walk for the very first time, Billy slowly stepped forward with a hesitant step before losing his balance and grabbing the edge of the pool table again for support. At that point, he was struggling to open his eyes, desperately trying to aim his glassed over gaze straight ahead as the gears seemed to crank and grind reluctantly inside his foggy head. But clearly it was no use. It was time for inebriated Billy to call it a night.

Mumbling something incomprehensible, he took another step toward Buddha as he finally lost his balance, teetering on his feet momentarily before falling backwards and crashing into a pile of accumulating pizza boxes and Chinese takeout cartons along the wall. Muttering gibberish and cursing under his breath as he struggled to push himself up from the pile of garbage, Buddha came around from the other side of the pool table to help him up.

"Shit, you alright man? Here," he said, giving his roommate a hand as he lazily took it. "Let me help you up and get you to bed, man. You're pretty wrecked." Struggling to get him to his feet and keep him there, he took Billy's arm and tossed it over his shoulder, putting his own arm around Billy's shoulder as he did his best to hold him up. "Okay buddy, here we go!" Cautiously stepping forward with his drunken pal wavering back and forth like a boxer that had gone too many rounds, he did his best to guide him slowly across the basement and to the stairs. "Slow and steady, Billy. Slow and steady."

Focused on merely keeping the guy square on his feet as he came close to falling a few times, Buddha managed to get him up the basement stairs, through the kitchen, down the short hallway, and into his bedroom. Removing Billy's arm from around his neck, he went to ease Billy onto his bed as the guy fell to his mattress like a limp sack of potatoes. He looked up at Buddha through sleepy, bloodshot eyes, his head rolling around on his neck as he mumbled something incomprehensible under his breath. He then rolled over and pulled some blankets over him, mumbling something again as his eyes quickly closed.

"Alright buddy, get some sleep. You'll feel better in the morning." Like a father tucking in a child, he pulled the comforter over Billy and turned off the lamp along his nightstand. By the time he reached the doorway and slowly shut the door behind him, he could already hear the soft rumble of gentle snoring. Billy, to no surprise, was fast asleep.

After putting Billy to bed, Buddha smoked the rest of a tapped out joint sitting in his ashtray before squeezing in a couple games of Frogger on the ColecoVision. After finally getting squashed by a speeding semi after a pretty good run, he decided it was time to turn off the video games and hit the hay. He was beat, likely to be out for the count the moment his head hit the pillow. He couldn't hang like that guy could anymore. No way. Not even close. Except for the occasional Bacardi and Coke, Buddha didn't like to tip 'em back the way Billy did. A true stoner at heart, Buddha always cringed when Billy was all revved up and in rare form, that look in his eyes showcasing that he was well on his way into a heavy blackout.

And wouldn't you know it, right as Buddha's mind began to submerge itself into the world of subconscious rest, there was a loud crashing sound coming from somewhere beyond his bedroom door—BANG! It was substantial, too. Enough to startle him awake, his head jerking upward as he glanced about the darkness. *What the hell was that*? He looked toward the door as he began to hear the steady thump of footsteps moving down the hall: *thump-thump- thump- thump* . . .

Buddha knew that someone was definitely up and moving around. And they weren't being coy about it, either. Probably Billy just getting up to take a piss. He was so drunk; he probably lost his balance and fell into the hall closet. That, or it was Diane letting herself in after another night of cocktails and some toot with the girls.

Rubbing at his tired eyes as he slowly sat up, the footsteps came to a sudden stop before his bedroom door. Whoever was in the hallway paused momentarily, standing quietly for a few seconds without movement. Their feet were blocking the light from the hall that normally crept in beneath the crack along the bottom of the door. Wondering if Billy was so far gone that he mistook Buddha's bedroom for the hallway bathroom, he heard the doorknob suddenly turn as the door swung open. Shielding his eyes against the light pouring in, he could see the dark silhouette of Billy standing there against the backdrop of the illuminated hallway. He looked different, oddly slumped over like an old man as he steadily shuffled into the room. He stood there for a few seconds. Quiet and still, holding something in his hand that looked like a wrench or a hammer.

"The pod needs to eat," Billy said. His voice sounded tired. Raspy and gargled. Buddha ran his hand over his face, squinting against the light. This was the last thing that he wanted to deal with right now. He needed to get Billy and his drunk ass to bed. And this time, for good.

"Right now?"

"Yes," Billy hissed. "Get up."

"Dude, what time is it? You really wanna chase down one of those cats and feed it right now? Look, I know you're off for a few days, but I gotta work tomorrow, man. I gotta sleep."

"It *needs* to eat!"

His voice sounded agitated, laced with a seething anger that wasn't like him. Knowing that he had to get up fairly early for work tomorrow, Buddha was quickly growing annoyed. Pissed, in fact, but the truth was—he didn't know what to say. Billy was wasted, *really* wasted. And who knew what was flying through that boozed up brain of his when he reached that kind of state. He wasn't necessarily an angry drunk, but at this point he was unpredictable. And the last thing Buddha wanted to deal with was an unpredictable drunk standing in his bedroom in the middle of the night barking demands.

"You saw it! You noticed the changes: its breathing, its increased size, the late stages of its metamorphosis. Come on, dude, get up! It's time to feed!"

Was this guy out of his fucking mind or what? Buddha ran his hand through his hair as he shook his head back and forth with frustration.

"Come on, man, I gotta work tomorrow. Go grab one of those ca—"

But before Buddha could finish, Billy took a step forward while quickly swinging the object up above his head. Like the strike of a whip, he swung it downward in a swift, fluid arch. Engulfed in darkness, Buddha couldn't see it coming as it smashed right it into his nose, sending a shattering firework of excruciating pain blasting across his face. Gritting his teeth, he watched their colors dance together against the darkness of his eyelids, feeling his nose crunch sideways, warm blood splashing his lips. Buddha hollered while instinctively bringing his hands to his face, unable to comprehend what the hell was happening. Billy brought the wrench down again, this time connecting with the top of Buddha's skull. There was a quick flash of white across Buddha's field of vision, the wave of a numbingly dull pain ricocheting and spider webbing its way across the top of his head.

Frantically scrambling to get to his feet, Buddha lost his balance. Unsuccessfully grabbing for the nightstand beside his bed as he fell, Billy dealt another blow. A shot of pain like white lightning raced through his arm as the metal wrench came down again. Buddha toppled to the floor as the nightstand, lamp, and glass of water came crashing down with him.

"Damnit!" Buddha hissed, rolling onto his hands and knees as he began to crawl away. He struggled to bring the room into focus as his head hummed like a struck bell, the warm flow of blood running through his hair and trickling down his face. "Billy, what the hell are you doing?"

Billy paused, standing there clenching the wrench in his hand while breathing heavily. He loomed over Buddha who crab-walked and cowered into the corner. "The pod is hungry," Billy hissed. He then swung his body with that quick yet graceful speed that made him a high school baseball standout, bringing the wrench down again with one clean stroke, hitting Buddha perfectly square across the forehead. There was a loud crack as his tensed body went limp, sliding unconsciously against the wall before thumping to the floor with a solid thud.

Billy dropped the wrench as it clanged loudly against the wooden floor. Gradually bending down, he took a deep breath before tightly grabbing Buddha's ankles with both hands. Grunting quietly as he pulled, he began to drag his buddy's limp body across the dusty, wooden floor. "Let's go, Buddha. It's time for the pod to eat!"

CHAPTER 27

Bits of dust, dirt, and cat hair stuck to the corners of Buddha's open mouth as he gradually came to. Though his head was ringing like a struck bell, struggling to bring the world into focus through his pulsating eyes, he quickly realized that Billy was dragging him across the kitchen floor by his feet. Struggling to muster what tiny flame of strength still burned alive inside of him, he fought to lift his head, spotting Billy for a brief second before allowing his head to drop again. The room was a buzzing blur, everything swimming and shifting as though he were looking through a turning kaleidoscope. A whirling of nausea spun about his stomach as he felt like he was going to throw-up, the coppery taste of warm blood filling his mouth.

Fighting with everything he had to lift himself up again, it was no use. His body seemed to fail him when he needed it the most, gravity yanking his head back down as it smacked lazily against the kitchen floor. Though greatly crippled from his injuries, he was still conscious enough to realize where he was going. It was unfathomable, but true. Billy was pulling him toward the basement stairs.

Grabbing onto his ankles tightly as Billy turned the corner and began pulling him down the stairs, he looked back at Buddha with a devious grin. It was a chilling grin. A tooth-filled smile that charmed a great many ladies in his day. Only this wasn't the flirtatious, arrogant smile of some handsome jock with a smooth tongue. This was the terrifying sneer of someone who had clearly lost their mind. His eyes were aflame with the lunacy of a madman, screaming silently with a madness that was chilling to the bone. But Buddha knew that it wasn't Billy looking back at him through those eyes. Something had taken over him. Something malicious. Something evil. Something, if he were to guess, controlling him from somewhere beyond the black mirror.

"It's feeding time, buddy," Billy declared with that twisted, malevolent grin curled along his face. "We're almost there!"

Moaning, groaning, and fighting to break free with what little bit of strength he had left, his efforts were met with too much resistance. He couldn't get up, the back of his head smacking against the edge of the stairs one by one as Billy dragged him down into the basement: *thud-thud-thud-thud* . . .

As his eyes welled with burning tears at the very thought of his unfathomable fate, he kicked his legs with every ounce of energy he possessed, almost choking on a couple of loose teeth inside of his bloody, mangled mouth. He sobbed and begged desperately for Billy to stop, his possessed friend smiling and laughing hysterically the entire time. He sounded like some mad scientist from an old horror movie, his eyes shining with a devious glee that sent waves of goosebumps across the surface of Buddha's flesh.

Screaming and begging for mercy as Billy began to pummel him again with a series of blows from his clenched fist, he then grabbed a piece of rope from a small shelf along the closet wall, applying it tightly around Buddha's ankles. He grappled to wither free somehow, but he just couldn't win. Barely conscious now as his head still hummed, he coughed and choked on the thickness of his own blood; dragged across the closet floor before Billy stopped at the door leading to the pod's lair.

Fading in and out, Buddha could hear the clicking of the disengaging locks along the door; the squeaky whine of its metal hinges as it slowly swung open. He could smell the musty funk of the room, the physical cold from its evil forces sending waves of chills up and down the surface of his skin. He finally knew, without question, that the black mirror was bad news. His gut told him that from the very beginning, but no one would listen. He tried to warn him, but Billy's promise of paradise and fame sold him. Seduced by the effects of the purple mist, and what was to emerge from the other side into their own world. But sadly now, it looked like it was too late. That very room, now set to be the stage of his own impending doom.

"Alrighty now, looky, looky what we got here!" Billy roared with excitement as he dragged Buddha into the cold, dingy lair; a roped-up hog ready for slaughter. Setting him down just a yard or two from the pod, Billy slapped his hands together and began rubbing them back and forth, grinning like a mad fool the entire time. "Looky what we got here. Some good ole pod food! Whatcha say now, huh? Let's eat!"

Buddha laid there along the dusty cement floor, bloody and beaten, moaning dejectedly with an anguished sound of misery that reeked of defeat. That evil, unsettling grin curled its way onto Billy's lips once again as he hauled back and gave Buddha a good, swift kick to the ribs. He curled inward, grunting in reaction to the cheap blow as Billy marched to the edge of the room and slammed the door shut.

"Alright, motherfucker! It's feeding time!"

Flooding with panic as he pathetically crawled across the cold hard floor, he kept the pod in sight from the corner of his eye. It was breathing even faster than it was earlier, the top of its smooth, curved apex steadily flaying open. Billy was clapping and skipping about the room with the spastic energy of a little kid, loudly cheering and egging the thing on, chomping at the bit for the creature to devour him.

"It's feeding time! It's feeding time! Here we go, it's feeding time!"

As he had seen many times now, a viscid, green tentacle wriggled its way from the pod's orifice. It wagged and slithered its way across the floor like a cat's tail, teasingly whipping itself back and forth as it drew closer. Buddha grit his teeth while tapping into every last bit of strength left in the tank, doing his best to get as far away from the thing as possible. *The door*! *If I can just get to the door*! He could hear the pod's raspy, wet breathing behind him, the echoes of Billy's demented laughter bouncing off the walls. His heart thumped rapidly inside his chest with the speed of Alex Van Halen's double bass drum. *Oh my god,* he thought, watching as Billy guarded the only way out. He could hear the tentacle lifting and smacking off the floor as it quickly drew closer, realizing that it was game over. There was no way out. He was toast. *I'm going to die,* he thought, clenching his teeth and he struggled to get up. *Oh my god, here it comes*!

He screamed out; the pain felt like a beaker of acid got dumped over his ankle, the burning accompanied by a tightening grip of improbable strength clamping down. He screamed till his throat was raw, pressure from the tentacle crushing his bones like they were eggshells.

Instinctively reaching for his leg, he looked down to find a tentacle coiled around his calf that had already disintegrated down to the muscle. He watched as that horrible off-white colored slime began oozing forth from the tentacle's tip, quickly eating away at the flesh along the top of his leg like that old 1950's movie, *The Blob*.

His blood curdling screams filled the room as Billy continued to dance and laugh. He hovered over his friend like a one-man cheering section, clamoring for the demon seed from the dimension existing alongside their own. "It's time to eat! It's time to eat! Boy, oh boy, it's time to eat!"

Squirming and struggling against the unbearable pain searing through his leg, he now prayed for a swift death. His throat burned raw against his perilous screams, glancing back to witness the tentacle ripping half of his leg free with the ease of a piece of taffy pulling apart.

Billy laughed with sinister delight as another tentacle came whipping in Buddha's direction. This one snapped up and down the cement floor like a cracking bullwhip, moving with the arching grace of a sea serpent.

Buddha continued dragging himself toward the door, his severed leg leaving a trail of glistening, wet crimson in his wake. Reaching a trembling hand toward Billy who merely stood there watching, Buddha cried and pleaded as the pod struck again. His eyes nearly bulged free from their sockets, watching helplessly as another tentacle wrapped its way around his arm like a steel cable. It flayed the sides of its dark green surface as pads of the white goo engulfed his arm with an uncanny speed. Screaming with the crescendo of a girl, he watched as the creature's appendage ate away his skin with a sickening speed, the glistening muscle beneath it beginning to crumble like a sugar cube in hot water.

And as the excruciating pain couldn't get any worse, he could feel something smacking him over the top of his head. It felt as solid as a baseball bat, crashing over the top of his skull before engulfing his entire head with something slimy and wet. His face felt like it had been doused with gasoline and lit on fire, his head yanked backwards so hard he thought his neck would snap; the whole time those chanting words ringing through his head like a soundtrack to this hellish fate: *It's time to eat! It's time to eat! Boy, oh boy it's time to eat!*

CHAPTER 28

That night Billy dreamt he traveled miles and miles across a very vast and empty desert. He knew not how long he gallivanted, nor the site of his eventual destination. Yet still, he continued to walk. Step by step, followed by the next step, he forged ahead. Though he knew he had to, he could barely endure the excruciating trek. His leg muscles ached as though they were cramping inward on themselves, his feet throbbing with a pressing pain that burrowed its way into the very bones of his feet. The sun's heat beat down relentlessly as a wicked wind blew across the vast, expansive world of dirt. He shielded his eyes against the blowing sand, the grains like tiny shards of glass against his weathered skin and his squinting eyes.

As darkness eventually engulfed the great and boundless desert, he continued forward, battling the fatigue and famine that fought to defeat him, destined to leave him dead in the open wild. Oblivious as to why, he could not quit. His body yearned to carry on as his spirit slowly crippled. It was as though his heart knew something his mind did not, destined to carry onward into this blinded journey that carried no cathartic end.

After traveling for at least another mile or so, his body finally gave out. The last bit of strength that carried his feeble legs evaporated beneath him, dropping him to his very knees right there in the sand. He looked to the sky with his wandering eyes, the clouds overhead steadily parting like drifting ships on the open sea. As they did, he gazed in wondrous intrigue as they began to swirl in a circular motion like a forming typhoon. Spinning and twirling, the swirling clouds increased in speed as the entire sky came alive, possessed by a life beyond that of their natural power. And as the clouds continued to reel outward in a circular motion like some fantastic tornado, a brilliant light of lavender fell from its widening center. It was absolutely magnificent, shining down on him like a spotlight cast from the very heavens above.

It was glorious. Magical. Magnetic to something that was absolutely primal and spiritual within as he strived to draw the light closer; engulfing him with a warmth of bliss that he could bask in for eternity.

The air then began to change, funneling around him as it started to thicken. And then, he watched in astonishment as it took on the consistency of something liquid, encompassing inward on him as it began to solidify with a gradual pace. It was soft, warm, almost wet in its composition; yet providing him with a sense of comfort and protection that was sublime.

His eyes fluttered as he felt that womb of fantastical warmth enveloping his entire body. But where is he? Is he alive? Is he awake? Still dreaming, possibly? Smothered, but comfortable, able to breathe just fine as it came and went in slow, deep breaths. His sunlit bedroom was a watery blur of light. He could feel his heart beating beneath his chest, but he could not locate his limbs, focusing on wiggling them about within this warm, jelly-like coffin.

His last recollection was witnessing the cloud of tiny purple spores spewing forth from the pod, gently fluttering down to earth as they tickled and burrowed their way into the surface of his skin. He choked and coughed as he could feel the tickle of something withering its way into his lungs, once again hearing that soft, seductive whisper as he began to embark on yet another psychedelic trip: *You have been chosen, Billy . . . you are the key. . .*

Pushing his way through the gelatinous membrane that engulfed his entire bed, he quite easily busted through with a soft and wet *pop*. His entire body felt warm, moist, and sticky. He coughed and hacked profusely before spitting up a wad of thick, bloody phlegm. It landed on the wooden floor of his bedroom with a soft *splat*, spotting a couple of teeth resting within the glob of his bloody spit.

Holy shit, he thought. *What the hell is going on with my teeth?* He could tell right away that something felt very strange with his mouth and his entire jaw. Unable to locate his tongue or his teeth, it felt as though the entire inside of his mouth was moving around in various sections, no longer able to move his mouth up and down in the manner that one's jaw normally moved.

And then he looked down, filled with a riveting horror that shook him to his very soul.

Holy Christ, my hands! My arms! What the hell has happened to me? Seized by a sense of terror so powerful it was suffocating, he gazed upon his once normal hands. A shrill scream began to build inside of him as he found a pair of curled, black hooks that felt as hard as wood replaced his hands; covered in patches of long, black hairs protruding like slender spikes along the coarse surface of his newly formed skin.

He spun in the direction of his dresser, quickly locating the mirror to confirm his darkest, deepest horrors. His entire body spasmed violently with repulsion, launching him into a coughing fit that almost caused him to lose the contents of his stomach. He then curled upward and released a scream that was inhuman, glaring again at the mirror and the monster within it glaring back at him.

His large, round eyes were as red as hell fire, their centers glowing and moving with the life of burning flames. His jaw became something resembling a large, black claw. It opened and closed like one of those cootie catchers that kids used to make in school, grotesquely exposing various sections of glistening, purple flesh lined with hundreds of tiny, razor-sharp teeth. His entire head was shaped like an ant's; much like a large, black helmet sprouting two very long, quivering antennae wavering about with a life of their own.

Releasing a rage-filled scream from the top of his lungs that rattled and hissed with the sound of something monstrous, he lunged forward and smashed his club-like hands into the mirror's surface. Broken shards of shattering glass flashed and sparkled in the morning sunlight as they exploded in every direction, splaying and falling to the wood floor in hundreds of tiny fragments. Smears of gooey, yellow blood littered the smashed, spider webbed sections of glass that still clung to its rickety, wooden frame. The mustard-colored blood seeped and dripped in syrupy strings from the cuts along his freakish insect hands as he pounded them again and again against the mirror; quickly demolished beneath the force of his otherworldly strength.

And then, in that moment of absolute horror, that moment of rage, that moment of realization of what he had become as he catapulted into a tornado of destruction throughout the house, granted him clarity. He could see now, clear as day, as though walking through a foggy dream all this time and he finally woke up. His destiny now mapped out before him like a blueprint, he now knew what he was and what this other world had planned for him all along.

You have been chosen, Billy . . . you are the key . . .

Yes. That's it! That's what he is—*the key*; the world beyond the black mirror chose him, using him as a puzzle piece for its ultimate agenda for global colonization. He is the key, and the pod is the seed. And once it hatches, it will force him to mate with this "female" counterpart whose metamorphosis is taking place inside the pod. But eventually, he would plant his seed. Put fire to the wick that would lead to a rapid procreation that would spell the extinction of humanity. Their communion would give birth to thousands, eventually billions and trillions of otherworldly, insect-like creatures that would feast on the flesh of Earth's inhabitants while utilizing it for its natural resources.

It was all so clear now, but much too late.

He began to sob uncontrollably, curling into a fetal position along the kitchen floor. Try as he did to fight it, he still felt helplessly drawn to the pod and the mysterious creature it harbored inside. Even though the intentions of their apocalyptic plan came to him like some clairvoyant prophecy, the hypnotic qualities of the dimension beyond the black mirror made resistance impossible. It was his destiny now. His mission. And no matter how hard he fought against the temptation of its powerful lure, the power of the forces within the black mirror were always stronger.

He screamed and cursed himself for what a fool he'd been. What had been promised and packaged as paradise would be nothing more than the end of times; the extinction of mankind as they would be consumed as food, the creatures from their dimension, roaming and ruling the earth for the next several million years. And he, of all people, would be the one to set it into motion. The key to open the door into their world as they know it.

But total doom and annihilation did not befall upon them yet. There was still time. There was still hope. There was still a chance to un-do everything, a shot in the dark to step up and save the human race. It had to be done, for it was Billy who set the wheels into motion. *The pod*! He rose to his knees as he stared toward the garage past the kitchen window. *I have to destroy it*!

Ducking into the garage, he located the axe that hung along one of the hooks on the wall, picking it up as best he could with his newly formed claw-like hands. "I must destroy it," he said in a voice that sounded garbled and distorted; nothing like his own. "I must destroy the black mirror and the pod!"

Bounding down the basement stairs as he had countless times while taking care of the very thing he now looked to slaughter, he could feel the adrenaline flooding through his newly formed insectile veins. Billy now knew he had gone too far, knew what needed to be done. Though the compulsion to carry forth the black mirror's bidding was incredibly powerful, he fought to resist it. It was the only way out. He had no choice. If he wanted to close off the bridge into their world and save mankind, they would need to be destroyed.

Ducking into the cedar closet, he paused inside the entranceway to the once secret and hidden room, standing there like some humanoid praying mantis on the fringe of the pod's lair. He could hear his own wet, rattled breathing as he stood there ready, the axe hanging in the grip of his massive, hook shaped claws.

"You," he snapped in that gargled, rattling voice, staring at the black mirror hanging along the wall through his red, fiery eyes that were the size of snow globes. "You did this! You did *all* of this!"

Running at the black mirror with an inhuman speed, he raised the axe high, swinging it downward with all his strength as the head of the axe caught the mirror dead center. He watched as it shattered and smashed before him in an explosion of a million sparkling shards of brilliant, raven-black glass. Again and again, he pulled back and heaved the weight of the axe downward, attacking it furiously like a creature possessed till there was nothing left of the great and powerful black mirror.

And then, something very peculiar began to happen.

A sound like billowing wind began to whisper and purr along the base of his feet. He looked down and watched as the countless shards of black glass along the cement floor began to defy the laws of physics, slowly materializing into black smoke, lifting and swirling and taking on a life of its own before ultimately vanishing into the air around him with the sound of a burning whisper. *What the hell?*

Momentarily standing there as he watched in a stunned state of astonishment, he then spun on his heel, glaring at the pod as it pumped up and down with the speed of a thrusting piston. Releasing that harrowing, inhuman scream again as it echoed off the brick walls of a room he should have never discovered, he raised the axe high, holding it there a moment as it began to tremble in his insectile arms. He couldn't move, feeling like the pod and the forces behind it were now taunting him, daring him to bury the head of the axe into its cocoon-like flesh.

Wanting nothing more than to swing the axe downward again and again into the center of the pod, slaying it once and for all along with whatever it was growing and stirring about inside, the forces from the other side seemed to be stopping him. His arms trembled as his entire body began to shake violently. Something more powerful and other-worldly than himself was now controlling him, and there was nothing he could do about it.

"I can't," he cried, his voice deep and distorted. He dropped to his knees as he let the axe slide from the clutches of his alien grip. "Goddamnit, I can't do it!"

But then, plunging into the belly of this hopeless pit of desperation, a lightbulb went off, suddenly providing him with his last option to save the world and mankind as they knew it.

The shotgun! He suddenly remembered his old man's Remington that he kept at the cottage about three hours north of there. *I'll get myself black out drunk, bury the muzzle into my mouth, and say goodnight. I can't go on like this otherwise, and it's my only hope . . .*

Leaving the pod's lair and locking the door behind him, he raced upstairs to his room and pulled a large hoodie over his newly acquired, hulking frame. He wanted to get out of here and get out fast! The pod would be hatching in the next few hours, if not sooner, and he had no choice. Running into the garage and sliding behind the wheel of his Grand Prix, he fired up the engine and hit the button along the garage door opener before reserving it out of there. *Alright, Billy Boy*, he thought as he headed down the driveway, putting the car in drive and punching the gas once he hit the street. *Time to end this thing for good and save the world.*

While driving into the night, Billy soon realized that he had been fast asleep inside that jelly-like cocoon for much longer than he imagined. Twilight had already cast its natural shadow across the world as he finally made it to the freeway without being spotted. He pulled the hoodie over his head as best he could, always looking straight down when he hit a red light to avoid someone noticing his monstrous looking face. His heart pounded like an out of control metronome as he maneuvered the vehicle onto the entrance ramp with his freakish, hook shaped hands. It was hard to believe that within a few hours he'd be taking a mouthful of buckshot for the future of mankind. He just prayed that the pod wouldn't hatch before he was able to carry out his plan. The cottage was just three hours away, and he knew he could make good time now that it was night and rush-hour traffic had long subsided. He had to make it. He had no choice.

But once the pod hatched, whatever it birthed would surely follow him. Billy knew it without question. He couldn't explain how, but he could feel the thing's biological sonar honing in on him. Though Billy now cursed the day that he discovered the room that housed the black mirror and the doorway into their world, there was no denying that there was some strange, telepathic bond between him and the pod. The procreation that would change the world forever was inevitable. And the only way to change the course of history was to destroy the grotesque monster that he had become.

Besides, what is the point of going on living anyway? Billy is now a monster. A freak. An absolute abomination that resembled something from the darkest, most disturbing nightmares. Not to mention, his friends were all dead. He killed them, allowing the black mirror to do its egregious bidding. The historic trio composed of the jock, the burnout, and the homecoming queen were no more. The good times were gone; the apocalypse of the entire world as they knew it now upon them.

Yep, just like John Cougar Mellencamp said, the walls had come a crumblin' down. And in his heart of hearts, he knew what he had to do. But as he gazed out onto the dark interstate that stretched within the illumination of his head beams, something deep and primal began to brew inside this newly formed body of his. He could not ignore it, yanking insatiably at the strings of the infantile instincts running through the helix of his DNA. And as much as he tried to ignore and fight it, it could no longer wait. He was hungry. And this uncontrollable appetite needed to be fed.

A good hour now outside his point of departure, he looked for a rest stop, knowing that they were usually dark, secluded, and scarce of people at night. Most travelers chose to stop at a McDonald's or a gas station along the exits off the freeway; places that were usually a bit safer and well-lit at night. But the well illuminated exits that harbored small clusters of Shell stations, Mobil's, and Wendy's restaurants along the freeway exits just wouldn't do. He needed somewhere dark. Somewhere discrete. Somewhere desolate. Somewhere he wouldn't be detected, able to use the night as his camouflage, a stealthy cloak. There was no question that a cop or some macho, heroic citizen wouldn't react too favorably to the sight of something like what David Hedison became in that old black and white movie, *The Fly*. No, he would have to be much more cunning than that. And there was no more waiting at this point. His beastly urges would have to be satisfied before traveling another two hours. As much as the mere thought of it repulsed him and horrified him to the core, he was starving. Time to eat.

CHAPTER 30

Mike's bladder felt like it was going to burst as he killed what was left of the tallboy, shaking it momentarily before nonchalantly tossing it along the passenger side floor of the Camaro. Flipping on his right turn signal as he barreled down the dark exit ramp, he eventually whipped his car into one of the many empty spots along the interstate rest stop's parking lot. He initially planned on taking a piss at the Burger King or the Mobil station along exit 49 a mile further down the freeway, but that was out of the question now. He had already knocked back a good three or four beers over an hour into his drive, and he knew that if he tried to hold it, he wasn't going to make it.

His little brother, Paul, had been bugging him to come visit him up at his college. Little Paulie, as Mike liked to call him, was now a sophomore up at State and living in his own apartment. And from what Mike had heard, Little Paulie had quickly taken to the campus's social scene while amassing a rather impressive network of friends. And knowing just how much his older brother loved coming up to visit, he called Mike up earlier in the week, raving endlessly about some legendary house party that was about to go down that very weekend.

"You gotta come up, man. You gotta come!" He pleaded over the phone, "I'm telling you, if you're going to head up to visit one of these weekends, *this* is the one. This party is going to rad, man. A total bash!"

Though Mike quickly dismissed the idea of college and continued managing the body shop after graduating high school a couple years back, he wasted no time in experiencing firsthand the "college life" his brother always talked about. While visiting Paulie a handful of times his freshman year while he still lived in the dorms, he quickly immersed himself into the experience while briefly living it to the fullest: the massive keg parties, the freedom, the drugs, the late nights and their endless conversations, not to mention, the cute young girls whose inhibitions were often shed by the lubricant of alcohol. And being that he lucked out and got the weekend off for once, he jumped at the opportunity to get back up there and blow off some steam for a few days.

Throwing the Camaro into park, he crushed his Marlboro out into the car's ashtray, killed the engine, and jumped out. The night was wet and cold as he lifted the collar of his black Members Only jacket over the back of his neck. The amber colored streetlamps overhead sent a rippling reflection across the wet blacktop parking lot as he jogged toward the rest stop, doing his best to avoid the drizzling rain and the possibility that he was going to piss his pants.

The men's room was dead silent aside from the soft hum of the fluorescent lights buzzing overhead. It was strong with the smell of stale piss and that dank, weird odor so commonly found in public bathrooms. Fumbling with his belt and unzipping his fly just in time, he let it flow with the pressure of a garden hose, dropping his head back while releasing a long sigh of relief. "Holy shit," he said while he drained his aching bladder, shaking off a few reluctant drops before zipping himself back up. "That was a close one!"

Flushing the urinal as it whooshed with the sound of a roaring jet engine, he buckled up his stud covered leather belt and headed over to the sink to wash his hands so he could get the hell out of there. He always heard rumors that those places were meeting grounds at night for weirdos and faggots looking to hook up. Even some deranged serial killer lurking in the darkness, waiting for his next victim.

Shit, that would be just my luck, he thought. *Some queer coming in here, trying to hit on me and shit. Fuck that, it's time to hit the road!*

Pressing down on the cylinder-shaped metal button along the top of the sink, he got a good four seconds of water flow that was hot enough to scald his hands. "Damnit!" Instinctively yanking them back, the faucet automatically stopped as its water saving mechanism timed out. Shaking them free of the excess water, he eyed the dirty looking paper towel dispenser, deciding it best to skip it as he patted his hands along his jeans.

Quickly sliding a small plastic comb from the back pocket of his jeans, he winked at his reflection with a cocky smirk, running the comb a few times through his perfectly feathered mane. Satisfied, he then slid it back into his pocket with the natural ease of a medieval knight securing his sword. Playing with the collars of his shirt and jacket a bit, he studied the angle of the dangling gold rope along the top of his chest. Yeah, that was it. He looked rad, but not too flashy. After licking the tips of his fingers and flattening down a few spidery looking eyebrow hairs, he stepped back from the mirror for a second for a better look.

"Alright, bitches," he said to himself with a playful wink, running his fingers gently over the top of his impeccably trimmed mustache. "It's time to meet yours truly—the party god."

Exiting the bathroom and crossing the sidewalk that separated the small building from the rest of the parking lot, he shuddered momentarily, chilled by a sudden gust of wind blowing across the wet parking lot. He put his head down while marching at a quick pace, doing his best to ignore the cold drizzle and get back to his warm car.

The night was turning to shit, but it didn't matter. Not only was this party that Paulie knew about gonna have eight barrels to start out with, but it was at a huge house with a massive basement. Plenty of room for all the drunk college kids that were gonna be there. Yep, no way around it now. Rain or no rain, old Mikey boy was sure as shit getting laid tonight.

Nearing his Camaro as he slid his hand into his pocket to gather his keys, an uneasy feeling came over him as he noticed the faint silhouette of someone approaching from the darkness. Unable to remember seeing any other cars parked along the lot, it startled him pretty bad, finding himself flinching reactively as they emerged suddenly from the inky shadows of secluded darkness. Whoever it was, their face hid beneath the shadowy concealment of a large hoodie. Their hands, suspiciously lunged deep into the sweatshirt's front pockets; their pace quickening as they drew closer to Mike's car.

Holy shit, he thought, watching as the approaching figure was now no more than a good fifteen to twenty feet from him. *I'm about to get robbed*! Mike could feel his heart pounding as he reached for his lock blade, his fingers searching for it as it slid about his jacket pocket. Finally grabbing it, but before he could get the fingers from his other hand on the blade to open it, it was too late. The mysterious stranger lunged at him with underestimated, athletic speed, latching onto his jacket before Mike had a chance to jump backward. The attacker then lifted him right off his feet as though he weighed just a few pounds, the blood suddenly draining from Mike's face as he finally caught a glimpse of his attacker beneath the light of the streetlamps overhead.

It was absolutely hideous, like some otherworldly monster from a Stephen King movie. Staring down at him with a pair of large, fiery-red eyes the size of cantaloupes, some kind of magical magnetism mesmerized him into sudden submission. Its face was black as the night, snarling with the mouth of an insect that moved about with a series of black hooks and strange, wet pinchers. As its rows of mandibles opened and closed like the mechanisms of a machine, what looked like several strands of flesh colored spaghetti began to slink downward from a small opening along the bottom of its face where small flaps of purple, wet flesh exposed themselves.

Mike screamed like a little girl as he flailed about helplessly within the grasp of the creature's vice-like grip. He watched as the fleshy, noodle shaped things hanging from its mouth began to move like sea snakes, slinking up and down in mid-air just inches from his face. The thing hissed at him with a wet, rattling sound as the strings of pink spaghetti shot forward, piercing the skin along the front of his neck with a quick, hot poke. He could feel their pointy ends burying themselves into the flesh along his throat as he began to choke, his entire body suddenly convulsing uncontrollably. An intense burn began to swim through his insides, quickly followed by an overwhelming cramping throughout each and every extremity. He watched as his skin began to turn a flakey gray as it shriveled inward on itself, quickly taking on the texture of brittle, flaking papier-mâché.

Finally siphoned of everything that his body could offer, Billy dropped the shriveled looking corpse to the wet pavement below. Mike's shrunken face looked like one of those mummies that you would find preserved at a historical museum. The features of his once young face were now brittle and bone-like. Taut and skeletal, staring upward with these wide eyes frozen in time and a gaze of absolute terror. The rain began falling harder now as a flash of lightning sent a spectral spasm of light across Billy's monstrous features as the depleted corpse lay along the base of his feet.

Looking away from his prey in guilt laced disgust, he dropped his head back and stared into the darkness of the swirling November sky. He released an inhuman wail that echoed into the darkness, chilling himself to the bone as the rain continued to fall; telepathically ingrained with the sudden knowledge that the pod was finally hatching.

VI: IMAGO

CHAPTER 31

Miles away at that very moment, on the quiet suburban street of Hickory Leaf, a metamorphosis of apocalyptic proportions was about to unfold. It was happening in the very basement of a small, green ranch that sat tucked away amongst the other homes that lined their picture-perfect block. Families having dinner at their kitchen tables or watching *The Wheel of Fortune* in their family rooms were numbly oblivious to the hatching of an inner-dimensional seed right there in the backdrop of their beautiful, suburban sprawl.

As the camcorder's tape continued to roll, the pod's rapid breathing came to a sudden halt. It sat there for a moment, still as a stone before a loud pop sounded from somewhere along the top of its slippery exoskeleton. Shortly after, a small section of its dark green covering began to push outward as though something within tried to poke its way out, falling to the basement floor with the consistency of a piece of shattered eggshell. Then another . . . and another. Soon, a couple of wiry, wiggling antennae began to protrude from a fractured opening along its top. A yellowish-white liquid began to bubble upward along the aperture, seeping and oozing down the sides of its smooth, rounded surface like a pot boiling over. And then, a dome shaped object began to push its way upward through the narrow orifice as sections of the chrysalis's exoskeleton began to shed outward in a bloom of multiple layers. Beneath the widening fissure along its apex was something large and wet, twisting and shimmying slowly as its protruding extensions squirmed and struggled to push itself free from its clear, wet membrane.

Breaking its way through, it began to thrash and shake vigorously, shedding aside its layer of slimy film that acted as some kind of placenta. Eyes like a pair of lemons: large and yellow, shining like lanterns as they gazed about the dimly lit basement, taking in the details of these foreign surroundings. Its face was long and smooth, formed in the shape of a banana or a crescent moon with rounded tips. The nose consisted of two thin slits along an area of taught flesh as tight as a drum. Its unusual looking mouth consisted of a series of blue tentacles, wiggling and squirming about with the movement of a sea anemone. Antennae as long as a couple of bamboo reeds sprouted forth from its long forehead, twitching and wiggling about slowly.

As it stretched out into the space of its newly discovered freedom, it gradually spread a pair of wings as wide and magnificent as the span of a bald eagle's. Yet as grotesquely fantastic as the creature appeared, it possessed the perfectly sculpted body of a beautiful woman; naked and covered in a bright blue skin that appeared reptilian in texture with a series of tiny scales that sparkled and shimmered beneath the room's meager light. Like something that could have traveled from a distant world—lightyears away, or risen from the very bowels of hell below, it was both horrifyingly gruesome yet strangely phantasmagoric at the same time. Unearthly; a specimen that man could only fathom in their wildest dreams.

Releasing a rattling scream that shook the entire house, it shot upward with the force of a launching rocket, smashing through the basement's ceiling straight into the kitchen above. Its head jerked about with the movement of a bird's, studying its surroundings while sniffing curiously at the air. It could smell him. It could feel him. It could sense that he was a good distance away yet still accessible, focused and homing in on his proximity.

"Hey Billy, is everything okay in here?" Leo—the old Italian guy who lived next door—barely finished his sentence as he walked through the front door. His mouth fell open as an unlit cigar fell to the floor, finding himself frozen in a state of bewildered disbelief at the sight of what loomed before him. It was a monster. Some kind of inconceivably bizarre creature that you might find inside the deep realm of some kind of Salvador Dalian, feverish dream. "Holy shit," he was able to muster, the power drill that Billy lent him falling from his trembling hands.

The creature slinked its way closer as Leo stood frozen, sniffing at the air all around him with its flat looking nose as a system of small tentacles along its mouth wiggled and squirmed just a few feet from his face. It then released another inhuman scream that was almost deafening; shaking the dishes along the shelves and nearly shattering the windows within the confines of their brittle frames; the walls trembling in the wake of its alien-like howling. Bending its human looking legs as it gradually crouched downward, a low, gurgling sound revved from somewhere deep within its throat as its antenna began to wriggle about wildly. Its massive wingspan like that of some prehistoric beast sprang outward again, sending several dishes and glasses along the counter space smashing to the kitchen floor. It then shot its legs upward while jumping into the air, smashing through the kitchen window with the speed of a bullet as though its frame and glass were made of paper.

Leo stepped out onto the porch as he watched the creature shoot into the air, its massive wingspan gracefully carrying it into the sky as it began to shrink in size against the backdrop of a brilliant autumn moon. "Sweet mother Mary in heaven," he whispered, watching with his head dropped back as the fantastical winged beast had already put a good distance behind it, vanishing into the dark sky as though the night itself consumed the monster whole. "What in the hell was that?"

CHAPTER 32

It had stopped raining by the time Billy arrived at the cottage. Even though the closest neighbor was well out of sight, he pulled the car as far up the long, dirt driveway as he could before dropping it into park and killing the engine. He took a deep breath, glancing up at the rearview mirror before quickly looking away, still horribly frightened by the grotesqueness of the monster staring back at him.

There was a stillness to the night that was almost eerie and unsettling. The world smelled like pine needles and wet cedar as he got out of the car, the soft sound of raindrops falling along the tree's leaves whispering all around him. Glancing about the property, he noticed that everything looked the same as it always did—the wooden cigar shop Indian Chief standing guard beside the doorway along the porch. The sound of the wooden wind chimes clinking gently in the wind. Even the faint smell of the lake out back wafting through the cold Fall air; a reminiscent scent that immediately teleported him back to his childhood.

Gathering the key hidden in its usual spot beneath a cement frog sitting along the edge of the porch, he managed to maneuver it with his claw shaped hands and let himself in. Greeted by the familiar smell of knotty pine and moth balls, he shut the door behind him as best he could and walked inside. He turned on a few lights as he moved about the cottage, thinking about what he was about to do to save the fate of mankind, knowing that it was his only choice.

How did this all happen? He thought, throwing open a set of small wooden doors to reveal his old man's liquor cabinet. Struggling at first, he was quickly becoming more accustomed to his newly formed hands, carefully grabbing a bottle of whiskey sitting near the back. *How had I been so blind to the magnitude of the dark forces beyond the black mirror? How did I allow it all to slowly take over our lives like that? How had I not known the moment I looked into the mirror's infinite darkness that it was bad news? Buddha was right all along. I should have destroyed that thing before the pod ever had a chance to spill forth from the other side. Good God, what have I done!*

Then again, in the grand scheme of things, what would that have really accomplished?

Even if they had, Billy was fairly certain the mirror would have magically found its way back to them. He was pretty sure that no matter how they chose to destroy it, they would walk into the basement the very next day to find it hanging there on the wall in its usual spot. But what was the use of wondering about all that now? None of it mattered anymore. It was too late. Hindsight was always twenty-twenty, and that chance of altering his horrific fate had long sailed. The only way to stop it now was to engage in the ultimate sacrifice. And sadly, he had to do what he had to do. The world and the future of the human race depended on him.

Slugging back the burning whiskey as he took a seat along an old wooden rocker, he eased back and stared at the dark lake beyond the bay window, enjoying the motion of the squeaky chair as his life began to flash before his eyes. It was all so clear as though it were just yesterday: Catching bluegill at the end of the dock with his old fishing pole as a kid, calling for his old man to grab a rag since he was too afraid to grab it with his bare hand. Walking to the corner store to get a soda and a comic book with his older brother, Brent, occasionally stopping to pick up a stone along the dirt road before sending it skipping across the lake's waters. Lighting fireworks off the end of the dock with his cousin Ryan on the fourth of July; watching them launch into the dark sky before fizzling out and dropping back to Earth. Shooting his first deer while hunting up north with his Uncle Dave, feeling that glowing sense of pride while they took pictures of him holding it up by its rack of antlers.

Losing his virginity in the backseat of his mom's old car, still able to recall what song was playing on the radio. The day that he bought his first Trans Am, a car that he had always dreamed of owning ever since he was a little kid. Even the events of recent memory, like watching the pod devour his buddy and his onetime girlfriend; shuddering at the vividness of those grizzly images, still able to hear the echo of their horrible, pleading screams while met with a horrific demise that neither of them deserved.

He shivered momentarily, snapping himself back to reality as he realized that there was no more time for procrastinating down memory lane. The past was in the past, and there was no going back. He had to let it go. This wasn't his fault. The forces from the dimension beyond their own were enough to seduce any man, forcing them into a spiraling obsession while using them as a pawn to inherit and take over the Earth. Besides, he could telepathically sense that whatever hatched from the pod was now on its way. He knew what he had to do. It was now or never.

He took another long swig of the whiskey before he went to stand, his legs momentarily wobbling beneath him before finally finding his balance. Not only did the alcohol work, but it worked a little too well, affecting his new body even more than anticipated. The room was a bit of a blur, focusing and working to balance himself just fine as he steadily crossed the length of the room. Slowly maneuvering his way toward an old, wooden desk sitting in the corner of the room beneath the mounted head of a six point that his brother Brent had taken down years ago, he slowly slid open the top drawer and peered inside. There it was—the tiny brass key to his dad's gun closet, right where he always kept it. Scooping it up, he did his best to slide it into the sweatshirt's pocket as he hunkered toward the basement stairs, ready to retrieve his dad's shotgun, head out back, and finish this thing once and for all.

Clicking on the basement light, he stared down the length of the narrow stairway leading into the dimly lit basement. Grabbing onto the makeshift handrail that he helped his dad install years ago, he began his gradual descent down the stairs. He took each step as slowly and steady as he could, his insectile legs wobbling horribly beneath him. After making it about halfway down, his large black claw of a hand slipped from the handrail at the very same time that he lost his balance again. He was unable to recover in time as he went tumbling down the basement stairs. It all felt so dream-like as he fell forward, slamming the front of his head against one of the wooden stairs followed by his shoulder, rolling again and again till he finally hit the cement floor along the base of the stairs.

His head throbbed and his shoulder ached, but he was okay. This new body of his was pretty resilient, that was for sure. But even so, he could tell that it wasn't tough enough to endure a shotgun blast to the mouth. At least he didn't think so. And if that was his plan to save the world, he knew that he had to step up the pace and get moving.

Slowly pushing himself to a sitting position along the dusty cold floor, a sharp pain shot through his elbow with the force of an electric current. He could feel something wet trickling along the front of his face, watching as it dripped and splattered into a small, yellow puddle forming along the cement floor.

And then, he could hear it.

A scream that was neither animal nor man, wailing powerfully in the distance. It sent a wave of chills traveling across the surface of his newly formed flesh, quickly realizing that it was getting closer. He could sense it coming. Not far beyond the walls of the cottage, the echo of its bellows rumbling softly like the sound of a thunderstorm in the summer night.

Scrambling to get up and get to the gun safe, he grabbed onto the end of the wooden railing and slowly pulled himself to his feet. As the yellow insect blood trickled into his eyes, he wiped it free with the back of his long, black arm, stumbling in the direction of the gun safe toward the back of the basement. Using both of his claw-like hands to the best of his ability, he carefully withdrew the key and steadied it slowly, gently sliding it into the tiny slot along the front of the safe as he began to twist it to the right. After sliding free from his grasp a couple of times, he kept at it with every bit of focus he possessed, eventually hearing the soft clicking of the lock finally disengaging, watching as its door gently popped open.

Bingo!

Grabbing the Remington 12 gauge from the safe, he hunkered with the weapon tucked beneath his arm, waddling his way back toward the basement stairs. Grasping tightly onto the handrail with one claw and the shotgun with the other, he carefully pulled himself up the stairs one painfully grueling step at a time.

He would do this down by the water, allowing himself one final view of the spot he loved most as a young boy. The spot where they would roast marshmallows over the campfire and chase fireflies. The spot where they would fish off the end of the dock or watch shooting stars on those clear summer nights. The spot where he would allow himself one more view of it all before taking a plunge into the deep, dark abyss of the great unknown.

Reaching the top of the stairs, he heard that blood curdling cry again roaring in the distance. Only this time, it was much, much closer. Making sure there was a shell in the chamber, he opened the door leading to the deck out back, spotting something soaring over the horizon well past the other side of the lake. It was beautiful and horrific at the same time, gliding through the air with an angelic grace, an oddly magnificent creature from the ominous world existing just beyond the cosmic fabric of their own. Its massive wingspan—like that of a dragon from some fantasy tale of long ago—flapping in the wind with the snap of a whipping sail, gradually drawing closer with an uncanny speed.

Making his way down the deck's wooden stairs as they creaked beneath his weight, he headed toward the fire pit down by the water, eventually easing himself into one of the outdoor chairs sitting along its circumference. Taking a deep breath, he placed the shoulder stock of the shotgun against the damp earth as he pointed the barrel's end upward. As his own fiery red eyes gazed upon the beautiful monstrosity that soared through the sky in his direction, he slid the end of the barrel past the sharp mandibles protruding from his face and into the opening of his maxilla-like mouth. The metal was cold and hard. Its metallic tang kissed the inside of his mouth as he rested the tip of his black claw along the weapon's trigger.

Do it! That voice inside of his head now told him. *Come on, Billy, you can do it*!

Yet as determined as he was to get this over with as he began to apply enough pressure along the base of the trigger, he abruptly found himself entranced by the magnificence of this monstrously gorgeous specimen from the world beyond their own as it quickly closed in. It eyed him like a barn owl spotting a mouse scurrying along a field, taking a quick nosedive from where it flew. Snapping its wings even further outward now as it caught a puff of air, it began to hover downward toward the edge of the water. It was gorgeous, abhorrent, repulsive, elegant, frightening, yet grandiose all at the same time. He couldn't explain it if he tried, but it had him. It controlled him. And try as he did to fight this compulsion to lay down and surrender, it was no use. Whatever power this creature possessed, it simply shadowed that of his own freewill.

Glaring down at him with those igneous yellow eyes, they shined like a couple of torches in the black of the country night. Its body was long and slender, voluptuous and feminine like some beautiful alien from another world. Its mouth looked like the underside of a squid—a grouping of slippery, blue tentacles slithering about as a pair of huge antennae moved around along the base of its bean shaped head.

Placed in the grip of something more powerful than his own will, his furry claws released their grasp along the gun, watching with horror as it fell to the wet grass with a soft thud. *Oh no*, he thought, staring helplessly at the shotgun lying along the ground. He felt like a cobra that had fallen under the spell of a charmer, a puppet at the end of its master's strings. He knew not why, but he was suddenly powerless against this alluring monster, watching helplessly as the thing drew even closer now.

You have been chosen, Billy . . . you are the key . . .

Those whispered words like a passing wind, granting him a momentary vision of the future in which he was essential in creating. The sound of people laughing and relishing in the joy of their lives replaced by terrible screams of incredible anguish and suffering; the procreation of their species spanning the globe quickly like an insatiable cancer that the world cannot eradicate.

He could almost hear the sound of Stevie Nicks's voice singing in the wind with those familiar lyrics that he couldn't shake, talking about a magical encounter that was once in a lifetime; long ago, far away:

If I live to seeeee, the seven wonders, I'll make a path to the rainbow's end. . .

And so, he did. He reached the rainbow's end. It was all over. Yet that promised paradise at the end of the rainbow turned out to be the spark that would ignite the extinction of mankind. He was powerless. Hopeless. Nothing more than a slave of its cogent clutches, destined to serve his unchosen purpose in utilizing their world for its food and resources. It looked upward, roaring with the power of an angry lion into the dark November sky, its ear-piercing scream cracking the silence of the placid night. Flapping its massive wings as it hovered ten feet above him, it swooped downward as it steadily mounted him. He shuddered with the cold premonition of a countless army of flesh-eating insects taking over the world; that cool, seductive voice whispering in his ear one last time:

You have been chosen, Billy. . . you are the key . . .

A Note to the Reader

Thank you for taking the time to read this book. If you will, kindly leave a review for the book as this gives the author kudos or feedback for improvement. Both are very important to an author.

Warmly,
Lily Gianna Woodmansee
Executive Editor for Cactus Moon Publications, LLC

About the Author

An insatiable fan of horror and crime thrillers (as well as the occasional rock biography), Matthew Pongratz is an avid writer and reader of tales that dive in and explore the darker side of human nature. While taking a break from his current projects, he also enjoys hiking, Pickleball, working on his jump shot in the driveway, cooking, reading, and going for walks with his dog, Buddy. He currently resides in Michigan with his wife and their daughter, and his first novel is set to be released by Cactus Moon Publications later this year.

If you liked this book, you may like:

Warren Worth believes he is more highly evolved than many of his human counterparts. He experiences an epiphany that states natural selection must be accelerated in the modern world, ridding the earth of lesser evolved humans.

Lanny Pape is looking to "be seen". To stand out instead of being the meek and forgettable person he sees in the mirror every day. He becomes obsessed with the serial killer responsible for the recent unsolved deaths in and around Atlanta, Georgia. After following the case closely, he has a hunch he may know the identity of the killer—Warren Worth. Worth tends bar at a local pub where Lanny approaches him with an unusual proposal.

Then Lanny's sister comes back into his life, and he learns the true meaning of three is a crowd.

Made in the USA
Monee, IL
23 May 2024

58843869R10166